I0551915

To read more stories by Dakota Caldwell
please visit
www.leadpyramidpublishing.com

Apocolyps

Squad II

Dakota Caldwell

Dakota Caldwell
5125 W. 75th St
Prairie Village, KS 66802
www.leadpyramidpublishing.com

cover design copyright © 2019: Alexiss Eastman-Edmonds

Printed in the United States of America

ISBN: 978-1-947155-09-1

First printing, 2019

Acknowledgements

To my wife, Jordan, who has yet to give up on my writing. To my daughter Willow, who brings me more inspiration than anyone else. To my son Fletcher, who we wait for eagerly to join us in just a few short months.
To Alexiss Eastman-Edmonds, for once again helping visualize my characters and truly bring them to life!
And, as always, to my Lord and Savior Jesus Christ. May his light always stand against the monsters in our own lives.

CHAPTER 0

General Herford sighed as the helicopter slowly coasted through the sky. In reality, he knew that the machine was traveling at several hundred miles per hour, but it certainly *felt* like he was crawling.

Stretching out below him, as far as he could see, was nothing but sand. Endless, extraordinary sand. If the helicopter was to crash, he knew that their bodies would likely never be found. And, if that were to happen, it was a price he was willing to pay.

"Coming up on the blast zone." The pilot shouted back. "Are you sure you want to do this?"

"Quite sure." Herford nodded, though he knew the pilot couldn't see him. "I just need to see things for myself."

The pilot, well-trained, gave no answer. The machine began to slow, and Herford leaned forward, gazing down on the ground that they were heading toward.

Though they were certainly still in the desert, the sand dunes that should have been there were gone, replaced by a shining sheet of glass. The only blemish in the glistening expanse was the blast crater itself, a hole several hundred feet across. The edges of the crater were ringed with toothpicks, spindly walls that had somehow survived the force of a nuclear bomb.

The helicopter sat down only a hundred feet from the rim of the crater, and Herford slowly stepped down onto the fused sand. He felt the soft heat through his lead boots, reminding him that even with a protective, military-grade hazmat suit, he had only minutes before the background radiation ate through and began to affect his body.

Slowly, he glanced back and forth. There had once been a town where he was standing, now nearly completely erased from the face of the world. The only question was: Why? Why nuke such a small, innocuous town? If Herford hadn't received a cryptic message from a certain insane doctor only moments before the explosion, he might have written the detonation off as a tragic misfire.

Not wanting to waste time, Herford moved towards the crater itself. He stepped up to the edge, gazing across the expanse. It was exactly as he might expect a crater to look, with blackened soil and fused glass. No indication of what may or may not have been happening. No clues for him to follow.

Herford shook his head. It had likely just been a mistake. Dr. Incacheck was a lot of things, with 'insane' being first and foremost on the list. He turned around and started walking back towards the helicopter. He didn't have much time left. If it truly *was* important, Incacheck would either send him more information, or he would go back in a few weeks once the radiation had died down a bit.

He was nearly to the helicopter when he heard a loud crack behind him. Curious, he turned to see a withered arm thrusting up through the glass. Broken chunks of the fused sand lay scattered next to the arm, leaving no doubt about what had just happened. As Herford watched, a second arm smashed up through the nuclear glass, making the hole larger. Painfully slowly, the hands reached down and gripped the ledge of the hole, pulling a creature up and out of the ground.

Slowly, Herford took a deep breath. He didn't know what he was facing now, but he was quite certain that it was nothing good. Slowly, he maneuvered his bulky hazmat-covered gloves to grab hold of a large pistol that hung at his side. If he was going to go down, he was going to die fighting.

CHAPTER 1

"You know, it's been years since I've actually been to one of these in person." Aaron settled down into the plastic seat, trying to ignore the stickiness of spilled soda, leftover from games gone by. "We've just always watched them in the control room, you know?"

"Yeah." Frank muttered as he dropped into the seat next to Aaron. "I was the one who suggested it in the first place. My back gets so messed up from walking up and down these stairs."

"You didn't have to come." Aaron shrugged. "I was perfectly fine coming by myself."

"Well, without Jasper here, someone has to watch your back." Frank held up his hands. "None of the security cameras really point at the crowds, so unless the kisscam pans your way, there would be no one to keep an eye out for suspicious activity."

"Well, I'm glad you're on the ball." Aaron chuckled. "Oh, sounds like they're starting!"

He looked down across the bowl-shaped stadium, which, as per usual, was packed with thousands of adoring fans. Down on the field, charging across the diamond-shaped track, was a line of crimson. The opposing team, the Centaurs, had just taken the field.

"And now, your Kansas City Monarchs!" The announcer's voice shook the stands, and Aaron grinned. Idly, he turned to Frank and crossed his arms.

"Do you remember the team from the days before the name change?"

"That was a bit before my day." Frank shook his head. "I can remember the uproar it caused, though. People were rioting in the streets."

"That would have been something to see." Aaron sighed and turned back to the stadium. One by one, the Monarchs ran out across the dirt, waving their hands for the crowd to cheer. Aaron held his tongue through it all. He was waiting for…

"Lloyd Bergil!" The announcer's voice sounded even more excited than before, and Aaron leapt to his feet to applaud. No longer a rookie, the boy was starting his second season stronger than ever, hitting multiple home runs without the need for the squad's assistance.

The baseball player jogged across the field, pumping his fists, and entered the dugout. Aaron sat back down as they got ready for the first inning.

"So, what's the play here?" Frank leaned forward. "Did we do something to the baseballs? I'm assuming neither of us are going to try and snipe like Jasper."

"None of the above." Aaron shrugged. "We're just here to watch the game."

"You really *are* getting out more." Frank chuckled. "You mind me asking-"

Aaron held up a finger as the first Monarch's hitter stepped up to bat. Three strikes later, he was walking back to the dugout, and Aaron turned back to Frank. "Yeah?"

"I was just wondering what changed?" Frank frowned. "You used to never want to leave the office. Now, this is the third time this month that you've actually gone out and done something."

"I guess getting attacked by zombies will do something to you." Aaron shrugged. "Besides, I'm not the only one. Jasper and Harold have gone off on their own little excursions half a dozen times since D.C., and Bertha has kept the office spick and span like you wouldn't believe. Shoot, the other day, she called into work sick! I'm pretty sure she just did it to stalk Garmund, since he was off meeting with Herford at the time, *but...*"

"The whole team has changed, haven't they?" Frank shrugged. "You know, there's something that-"

Aaron held up a finger while the next batter got up to hit. After two strikes, he managed to land a grounder between the second and third basemen. It wasn't much, but it allowed him to get to first.

As the play ended, Aaron turned back to Frank. "Yeah?"

Frank shook his head. "Nothing really. Just thinking it might be time for you to meet a girl."

"A girl." Aaron chuckled. "Me? I don't think so."

"You saved the world." Frank held up a finger. "That's something."

"That's something that we've been forbidden from talking about." Aaron nodded back. "Remember? Kind of a big deal? At least it was to Birch."

"Birch can shove it." Frank grumbled. "Your romantic life shouldn't have to suffer just because he's a dimwit. In any event, you have more going for you that that!"

"Name one thing." Aaron crossed his arms. "What do I have going for me? I'm overweight, I spend all my free time-"

A crack sounded through the stadium. Aaron spun to see the ball arcing high into the sky, only to come down in the left fielder's glove. He sighed, shook his head, and went back to the conversation.

"See? What girl is going to want this?"

Frank shrugged. "You'd be surprised. I was like you, once, back in my prime. All I cared about were the latest episodes of the television show I loved to watch. I think you would have liked it, actually. It was this post-apocalyptic-"

"I've about had enough apocalyptic events for now." Aaron chuckled. "In fact, I would be just fine if we never faced down one of those world-ending events again."

CHAPTER 2

"Man, I wish we could face down another world-ending event." Jasper muttered as they stalked through the jungle. "It might get me away from all these bugs, you know?"

"Believe me, I hear you." Harold swatted a mosquito away from his arm. "You'd think that since I don't bleed, they wouldn't be as attracted to me, you know?"

"You would think." Jasper muttered. "Of course, you'd also think that you would be dead, but…"

"Let's not harp on the details." Harold chuckled. "I'm perfectly happy not being a rotting corpse. I'm not planning on rocking the boat anytime soon."

"We're trying to track down the pieces of the philosopher's stone." Jasper held up a hand. "I'd say that that's rocking the boat quite a bit."

"You're probably right." Harold shrugged. "Speaking of which, we should be getting close. I think."

Harold frowned as he stepped around another tree. They were stumbling through the jungle in southern Mexico, near some old Mayan ruins. It had been a nightmare trying to get past all the guards at the airport who were doing their absolute best to keep tourists from doing exactly what the duo was now trying to do. After a few tries, though, they had managed to bribe one of the guards and slip out a side door.

Harold closed his eyes and tried to focus. In the instant he grabbed the shard back in Washington D.C., he had been connected with each and every other shard on the planet. Some of them had been on display in famous museums. Others were buried deep in personal collections, locked away in church strongboxes, or even worshiped by different cults.

There were a few, though, that were left completely unguarded. Assuming that these would be the easiest to find, Jasper and Harold had set out to start gathering up as many of the pieces as they could. The only problem was that it appeared that someone *else* was also traveling around, trying to find the pieces. Time and time again, they had arrived at a shard's location, only to find it missing.

"You think this one will be here?" Jasper spoke up as they started climbing what Harold desperately hoped was the side of a mountain. "Or do you think we're too late?"

"Honestly, I couldn't tell you." Harold shrugged. "I tried connecting with the shard again, back in the base, but without all the energy from the zombies pouring through it, I didn't get so much as a flicker. I can tell you that it *was* here, but it's anyone's guess whether or not it still is."

"Well, with how much I made the government pay for that plane ticket, I sincerely hope it is. The paperwork when we get back is going to *suck*." Jasper muttered. "Not to mention that facing all these bugs isn't exactly fantastic. The shard we went after in New Mexico was much more pleasant."

"Believe me, I know." Harold swatted a particularly large bug that seemed to be trying to fly into his mouth. Something caught his eye, and he grinned. "I think we're here."

He stepped across the side of the incline and bent down to where a small stone protruded from the soil. It was cut into a perfect rectangle, and he nodded. Without another word, he started upward, climbing as fast as he could.

"Hey!" Jasper called out as Harold pressed upward. "Some of us still have lungs to contend with!"

"Not my problem!" Harold called back. "I left all that behind me!"

"I'm your ticket out of here!"

Harold sighed and slowed down while Jasper caught up. Once he was there, they continued walking upwards. The carved stones peeking out of the hillside became more and more numerous, and Harold grinned. Almost there.

They finally reached the top of the slope. A small Mayan pyramid graced the summit, a tiered edifice that still appeared quite intact despite the countless years of weathering. Stairs led up the side, which Jasper quickly mounted. Harold followed, moving a bit slower. He was quite certain that the shard was in the pyramid, but something seemed off. He couldn't tell what it was, and after a moment, he shrugged it away.

A few moments later, they were standing at the top of the pyramid. Harold bent down, frowning in thought. There should have been an entrance, a hole, *something.* That was what Harold had seen, at least. After a short examination, he stood back up.

"There should be a hole in the top of this thing. The shard is in a vase, in the middle of a large room just below us."

"At least we can be fairly sure that no one else has been here yet." Jasper shrugged. "Oh, well. Shall we bore through?"

Harold thought for a moment, then nodded. "Bore away. Just be careful not to harm the shard."

"Oh, I won't." Jasper knelt down onto the stone. "You know, you might want to learn this trick, too. It's good for escaping from places."

"Okay." Harold knelt down next to Jasper. "Another alchemical technique?"

"Only the best." Jasper adjusted his beanie. "Do you remember what I've been teaching you?"

Harold nodded slowly. "The premise of the stone is that everything is made from the same composite elements. We just change the substance of those elements on a microscopic level, which results in a fundamental change on the macroscopic level."

"Exactly." Jasper held up a hand. "The early alchemists tried to classify four basic elements, which were in turn composed of four basic Principals. The elements, of course, being fire, earth, water, and air, and the Principals being *hot, cold, dry,* and *moist.* Now, what's important to remember is that they weren't exactly *wrong*. It's just a bit more complicated than that."

Jasper ran his finger over the stone, frowning as he did so. "Basalt, I believe. We need several leaves, they have a small amount of organic acid that we can use here."

Harold nodded, ran down the pyramid, and started grabbing several leaves off the nearby trees. After a moment, he finished, and ran back up to where Jasper waited.

"Perfect." Jasper nodded, took the leaves, and started rubbing them against the rock. "All matter *is* composed of the same material. All molecules are composed of atoms of varying sizes and properties. All atoms are composed of protons, neutrons, and electrons, which in turn are composed of quarks. If you want to delve into theory, these quarks are then composed of smaller and smaller materials, eventually coming down to strings. This, my friend, is the fundamental truth of alchemy."

Harold frowned. "I know you've explained this before, but it still doesn't make any sense."

"Watch and learn." Jasper finished rubbing the leaves onto the stone, took a deep breath, and blew on the green rubs. Instantly, the concoction crackled and burst into a pink flame. Harold's eyes narrowed as the flame began to burn through the rock, creating a hole about three feet across.

"You see, when it comes down to it, these strings define how the world works. They serve as the strong and weak nuclear forces, holding the protons to the neutrons, keeping the electrons moving in a circle around them. They serve as the force of magnetism, they serve as the force of gravity." Jasper's eyes twinkled. "They serve as the force known as light, they serve as fire. Heat, kinetic energy, it's all the same. Matter, energy, there's really no difference. It's all the same substance, just structured in different ways."

"Which is why you can do things like make fire out of leaves." Harold frowned. "How did you get it to ignite like that?"

"A technique known as slipping." Jasper shrugged. "It's how all alchemical compounds are created, by causing the strings to 'slip' and realign elsewhere. It's quite fascinating, really."

"You're telling me." Harold grinned as the flame finished burning through the roof of the pyramid. He glanced down, following the single shaft of light to a floor about ten feet below him. "Alright, I think we're good. I'll go first."

"Why you?" Jasper frowned.

"Because if there are any poison darts or suffocation traps, I stand a substantially better chance of survival than you do." Harold shrugged. "It's as simple as that."

"You know, I suddenly find myself just fine with standing watch up here." Jasper waved his hand. "Have fun."

Harold nodded and jumped into the pit. He landed on the floor, paused, and took a look around. Glyphs stood out on the wall, most of which seemed to depict some sort of vengeful god wreaking havoc on the local village.

The important part sat on the far wall. Set in an alcove, ripe for the picking, was a small vase. Hardly daring to breathe, Harold walked over to the alcove, picked the vase up, and looked inside. Something rattled as he did so, and a grin split his face. Slowly, he flipped the vase over, holding out his hand.

A small shard, almost exactly the same size as the first shard, dropped into his hand. He could feel power pulsing from below the surface, and he grinned. This was the real deal. Slowly, he walked back to the center of the room, where he held it into the light.

This one had a slightly different symbol. Rather than a drawn bow, it had an image of a circle inscribed with an X. Curious. After a few moments of pondering it, he held up his hand.

"Alright, ready to come up now!"

"You may want to stay down there." Jasper's voice sounded more than slightly quaky. "In fact, if that room has any exits, you might just want to leave. Run. Quickly."

Harold glanced around, looking for any sort of exit. Unfortunately, the room was sealed tightly. He backed up against the wall as a shadow covered the small hole. His hand wrapped around the shard tightly, and he felt the sharp edge break skin.

A blast of light echoed through the room, and fire erupted over the entire ceiling. It burned pink, just like Jasper's fire, and consumed the entire roof in a matter of moments. A few specks of dust dribbled down, and Harold fought to keep from screaming.

Standing on the edge of the new crater was a man who could only be described as intense. A long, dark green robe flowed off his shoulders and hung down behind him onto the jungle floor. Straps ran over and around his shoulders and torso, fixing a large, golden pendant in the middle of his chest. Whatever it was, it glowed brightly with an internal energy that made Harold cringe.

The man's face was another story entirely. Sharp eyes looked down over a hooked nose, and a thin mouth graced a crisply-trimmed beard. There was something about the face, something familiar.

"Give me the shard, boy." The man's voice almost seemed to echo in the trees, and Harold winced. "You don't know what kind of power you're dealing with."

Harold glared up at the man. "You're the one who's been taking the shards before we get there."

"You're very astute." The man shrugged. "I assumed that you would beat me to at least one or two. I had no idea that we would have the good fortune to meet, finally. Now, the shard."

Harold clenched it ever-tighter in his fist. "You'll have to take it from my cold, dead body."

"That can be arranged." The man held out his hands. Lightning pulsed from his pendant, lashed up and down his arms, and erupted outward. The energy poured through Harold's body, arcing back and forth between a hundred nerve endings. For a brief instant, his heart restarted, and he gave a mighty hack as his lungs tried to dislodge the blood he had inhaled while inside the zombie plant.

The lightning let up a moment later, and the man frowned.

"What kind of alchemy is this?"

"You're the one who just threw lightning at me." Harold shrugged. "I'm not sure that you should be the one asking that question."

With a rush, the man jumped down into the pit and started stalking towards Harold. Harold clenched his fists, ready to do anything he needed to do to keep the shard safe. The man raised his hand, bent down, and placed his palm against the rock. Instantly, the floor liquified, and Harold sank in the newly-formed muck.

Through it all, the man stayed on top of the liquid, simply watching as Harold sank. Before he could vanish, the man pulled his hand up, leaving Harold about waist-deep in solid basalt. Without any ability to run away, Harold simply thrashed as the man walked over, grabbed his wrist, and started prying at his fingers.

Harold held on for his life, glad that he couldn't feel the pain as the man peeled back his fingernails and broke away his extremities. The man grew more and more frustrated as he went, and Harold glared back. If he was going to make an enemy, he was going to make it worth it.

"I could just liquify your bones and be done with it." The man snapped. "That would be easier, I suspect."

"I think I would survive." Harold muttered. "You're not getting this thing."

"Got it." The man breathed a sigh of relief as he snapped Harold's last finger and took the shard from his palm. "I think this makes us even, don't you?"

With that, the man reached up and snapped his pendant open. Harold's eyes opened wide as he peered into what looked like an infinite abyss, an open hole far larger on the inside. Dozens of shards floated in the darkness, emitting a soft light. He dropped the latest shard into his collection, snapped the pendant shut, nodded, and turned to leave. His cape swirled through Harold's face, and Harold snapped at it.

"You even going to tell us who you are?" Harold called out as the man reached the edge of the pit. "It won't hurt anything!"

"Oh, I rather think it could." The man raised his hands, light pulsed, and stairs formed out of the rock. "Good day. I rather hope we don't meet again."

The man climbed up the stairs and vanished into the woods, and Harold sighed. "Jasper? Jasper!"

"I'm still here." Jasper appeared at the top of the crater and sighed. "He must have knocked me out or something. Wow, that was weird."

"Weirder than me being stuck in solid rock?" Harold slammed his palm on the basalt. Idly, he glanced at the hand that had once held the shard. The fingers had already healed, a nice side effect of being a zombie. "Come on, get me out of here."

Jasper nodded, jumped down into the pit, and walked over. He knelt down next to Harold, and Harold sighed.

"Any idea who that guy was?"

"Not a clue." Jasper shrugged. "I've heard of alchemists being able to transform things without rituals, but they're few and far between."

Harold frowned in concentration. "Do you know how that would be done?"

Jasper raised an eyebrow. "You want to learn?"

"If there's a chance we could go up against him again, I don't think he's going to let me sit there and mix chemicals before attacking him." Harold shrugged. "If I can learn, I'd like to."

Jasper sighed, then nodded. "I'll give you my family's book on verbal spells once we get back." He shook his head. "All I do know is that I would very much not want that guy getting his hands on all the shards. A fully-formed philosopher's stone would make him a god."

"I agree with you there." Harold took a deep breath. "Any idea what we're going to tell the team?"

"Oh, I do at that." Jasper nodded. "Not a damn thing."

CHAPTER 3

"You feel that?" Jeremy felt something rap on his forehead, drawing him up out of a rather wonderful nap. "You know what that is?"

"It's your finger." Jeremy groaned and opened his eyes to see his roommate, Brad, standing over him. "And not even a clean finger, either. I saw you picking your nose right before I fell asleep. Get that thing away from me!"

"You're too uptight, you know that?" Brad shook his head, jumped off his bed, and walked to the window. "That, my friend, is the feeling of freedom."

"No, that's the feeling of boredom." Jeremy sighed and swung his legs over the side of the bed. "Oh, I'm ready for classes to get started."

Brad just laughed. "You're the *only* student here with that mentality. Don't worry, I'll loosen you up."

"No, you won't." Jeremy shook his head. "I can't wait to get to work. More serious study, more serious-"

"Two best friends, roommates as college starts. Just think of all the trouble we'll get in!"

Jeremy frowned. "What kind of trouble are we talking about? The kind that leaves us laughing at someone's expense, or the kind that leaves us crawling out of the twisted and smoking wreckage of someone's vehicle?"

"I was hoping for the vehicle, but I could settle for pretty much anything." Brad shrugged. "I've got a few ideas already from talking with the upperclassmen. There's actually a series of tunnels that runs underneath this entire campus. It might be worth a visit, later on tonight."

"We'll see." Jeremy chuckled. "I don't want to stay up too late tonight."

"Why?" Brad raised an eyebrow. "It's Saturday night. Classes don't start until Tuesday. Plenty of time to sleep in if we get caught up in things."

"Vanessa is coming in tomorrow." Jeremy let a grin spread across his face. "She'll be on the other side of campus, but she'll be here."

"You keep telling yourself that." Brad walked back to Jeremy, grabbed his shoulder, and hauled him to the window. "What do you see out there?"

Jeremy took a deep breath as he gazed out across the Pennsylvania college. Buried deep within Pittsburg, the massive, ornate, eighteenth-century architecture rose high into the sky. The dorms were sitting on a slight rise, overlooking the expanse. Trees, tall and mighty, rose between the buildings, refusing to give up their place in the landscape. On the far side of campus, behind the massive clock tower that rose to block his view, a small sliver of white stone could be seen, the walls of the dormitory that his longtime girlfriend would be staying in.

"I see promise." Jeremy turned to Brad. "I see a fresh start, away from my family, away from the life I've always known. I get to train as an engineer, get ready to learn how the whole world works, while Vanessa is learning how to run the largest business in the world. The moment we're out of here, we move out to conquer the world, side by side."

"You're the most wordy engineer I've ever met." Brad laughed. "Say hello to Vanessa for me when you two meet up. It's been a few months since I've seen her."

Jeremy sighed. "She's just as beautiful as ever."

"I'm going to have to take your word on that one." Brad shook his head. "Well, I'm running to the store for food. Care to tag along?"

"Not at the moment." Jeremy shook his head. "I'm going to try and get this room organized first. It's pretty much an absolute disaster."

Brad glanced around, apparently noticing the piles of boxes and clothes for the first time. "If you feel like it, you can unpack my stuff, too. Just don't look too closely at the magazines."

"I sincerely doubt that I'm going to be feeling that well." Jeremy shrugged. "But I'll make sure that all your stuff is waiting for you when you get back!"

"You're just full of heart." Brad shook his head. "Back in a bit!"

"Don't get in a wreck." Jeremy waved as his roommate walked to the door. "I don't want to miss meeting with Vanessa because I have to go to a funeral."

Brad just snickered and swept out of the room. Jeremy chuckled and started opening boxes. He hadn't brought much to college, mainly just the necessities. A few boxes of clothes, his laptop computer, a handful of charging cords. After about fifteen minutes of unpacking, he smiled and flopped down on his bed with his computer. He wasn't about to touch Brad's boxes, and besides, he had more important things to do.

It took him a matter of moments to log onto the internet and power up his game engines. At that moment, he was ranked in the top five percent of players in the world in a game known as *Empire*. It was a MMO, set in a post-apocalyptic society where humans and aliens mixed freely. He was playing as a human character, and was currently part of a rebel group trying to take down the overlord who was trying to impose his will on the world.

The interesting thing about the game was that, once the creators built the world, they simply left it open. Players could build fortresses, form alliances, build kingdoms, and tear them down, all at their own will. None of the current factions had been around when the game had first launched. In fact, when it had first launched, Jeremy had been part of the ruling family. Now, it was all he could do to stay one step ahead of enemy assault squads. Hopefully, with their newest attack, all that would change.

The hours slipped away as he started his trek. He spent the time moving towards the capitol, trying to stay in the shadows and out of patrol groups. He had the best weapons he could afford, good armor, and the will to succeed. All he needed to do was…

"I'm back!" Brad burst into the room. "Thanks for… Oh."

"Sorry." Jeremy shrugged. "I got sidetracked."

"Well, get un-sidetracked." Brad grinned. "I found something fun to do."

"Give me a second." Jeremy frowned in concentration as he started looking for a good spot to log off. After a few minutes of searching, he found a hollowed-out log. It wasn't much, but it was something. A few clicks of his mouse later, the avatar had crawled inside. He logged off, and the character went to sleep, dormant until the next time he logged on. Hopefully, he was far enough away from everything that his sleeping avatar wouldn't be found. "Done."

"You're way too obsessed with that game." Brad shook his head. "I like to live in the real world."

"And that's why you spend all your time looking through magazines?" Jeremy raised an eyebrow. "We both have our vices. Mine just happens to bring me international fame or derision, depending on current company."

"Well, right now, it's derision." Brad shrugged. "Are you ready yet?"

"For what?" Jeremy scowled. "You'd better have something good."

"Oh, I do." Brad set several bags on the bed and pulled out a handful of ingredients. "Look familiar?"

Jeremy's eyes scanned over the eggs, chemicals, and paint. "You're making a stink bomb?"

Brad grinned. "Why not?"

Jeremy held up his hands. "Because that's *such* a high school thing."

"So?" Brad shrugged. "We're barely out of high school. Besides, it'll wear off quickly enough. Just give the early church crowd a bit of a bite."

Jeremy fell back onto the bed. "You just love seeing people roil in agony, don't you?"

"I enjoy seeing people holding their noses and groaning loudly." Brad shrugged. "So, you game? I found a way into the tunnel systems. We can plant it in the center of campus without ever being seen by a security camera."

Jeremy sighed deeply. "Alright, fine. Just this once, though. If I smell like eggs when I see Vanessa tomorrow, I'm killing you."

"Fair enough." Brad swept his arms out. "We need to head down to the basement. Let's move!"

Jeremy stepped out into the hallway, feeling an odd sense of foreboding fall over him. Everyone in the building seemed to look his way, their questioning eyes wandering over the bags that he was carrying. Who was he kidding? A small Pennsylvania high school was one thing, a college was something entirely different.

As they reached the stairwell at the end of the hallway, Brad clicked the door open, swept inside in one smooth motion, and grinned as the door shut.

"We're home free, now."

"And you say *I'm* the poetic one." Jeremy shook his head. "Lead on, then."

Brad grinned and raced down the stairs, two at a time. They reached the basement in a matter of moments, took a deep breath, and opened the door into the area.

Jeremy raised his eyebrows at the sight. He wasn't sure what he had been expecting, but a massive party room hadn't been it. Brad just walked straight on in, past the pool table, the foosball table, between the arcade games.

"What kind of dorm has this kind of stuff in its basement?" Jeremy hissed. "This is so weird."

"The kind of dorm that knows that college students are going to fill that machine with more quarters than it ever saw at the arcade." Brad chuckled. "You should have realized that."

Jeremy shrugged. "Never been around arcades much."

"You've just never been around *towns* much." Brad shook his head. "Ahh, this is going to be fun."

On the far side of the party room, several more doors led to another stairway, a laundry room, and a number of study rooms, soundproof boxes that could be used for preparing for important tests. Brad walked to the third study room, grinned, and swung the door open.

Jeremy stepped inside. The door was windowless, thankfully giving them total privacy. He set the bag of materials down on the single table that the room held, took a deep breath, and sat down in a wheeled chair that looked entirely too dangerous to be around college students.

"Well, what now, grandmaster?"

"Now, we open the door." Brad chuckled. "Watch and learn."

Brad bent down in the corner of the room. Jeremy watched in fascination as he peeled up the carpet to reveal a small trap door in the concrete floor.

"Apparently it used to be common for parties to extend into the sewers." Brad shrugged. "They put carpet over it after several incidents, but the students made sure to leave it accessible. Ready for this?"

"I'd be lying if I said yes." Jeremy shook his head. "After you, I suppose."

Brad grinned, pulled the door open, and slid inside. Jeremy took a long breath, picked up the bag, and hung it down into the opening. It was taken from him a moment later, and he glanced down into the hole. Rungs hung to the side of a wall leading into the depths, meaning at least that he didn't have to jump. Slowly, feeling as if a death sentence had been planted on him, he put his foot on the first rung.

At that point, an odd confidence flowed through his veins, and he began to climb down faster. His head passed the floor, and he reached up to flip the door shut. Hopefully, the carpet would flop back over the trap door, too.

The moment his feet hit the floor, Brad flipped a flashlight on. The tunnel extended in two directions, stretching as far as the light would reach. The walls formed a perfect box, no curves, no arches. Just a simple tunnel.

Brad gestured to Jeremy's left, and they took off. For some reason, Jeremy felt an unusual urge to remain quiet, as if speaking would ruin the whole event. Brad seemed to feel the same way, as neither of them so much as breathed.

It didn't take long before they came to a T in the tunnel. To the left, stairs led deeper into the earth. In the other direction, the tunnel began to curve back in the same direction they had just came from.

"Going right will take us to the other dorms." Brad whispered. "We need to go down."

"Why down?" Jeremy frowned. "I thought we were heading onto campus?"

"The campus is on a hill." Brad shrugged. "The tunnels can't just run in one direction without going up or down."

"That's true." Jeremy shrugged and stepped onto the stairs. As he did so, a slight scuffle rose in his ears. It wasn't much, but... "Did you hear something?"

"Only your breathing." Brad chuckled. "I swear, you're sucking in more air than an overheating laptop."

Jeremy turned to stare at his friend. "*Great* comparison. Seriously, that's the best you could come up with?"

Brad chuckled. "Hey, I think-"

Another scuffle sounded, this one much louder. Brad froze, and Jeremy held his breath.

"So I'm not crazy."

"You actually heard something." Brad shrugged. "I don't know if that makes you-"

A blast of air blew Jeremy's hair on end, and a black profile erupted from the darkness. Before Jeremy had a chance to react, needles sank into his neck, and he felt warm liquid splash down on his chest. His mouth opened wide to scream, but nothing emerged. The light vanished as Brad made a hasty retreat, and his world went dark.

CHAPTER 4

Aaron took a deep breath as Jasper and Harold walked into the office. "What's up? Your new excursion not go so well?"

"Not quite as we planned." Harold shrugged. "It was something, though. Learned a few things."

"That's good, I suppose." Aaron scratched his head. Every bit of him was dying to ask what they had been doing, where they had been, what kind of new weapons that they had cooked up. At least, he assumed they were building some sort of new weapon. That was the only thing they could be doing, right?

"Yeah, I guess." Jasper shrugged. "I'm going to get back to work on the disintegrator now. We could use it if we run into any more events."

"Events?" Aaron chuckled. "Like another zombie apocalypse?"

"That would qualify." Jasper shrugged. "I had an idea to run by you, if you wanted."

"Shoot." Aaron leaned back in his chair. "A good one, I presume?"

"I think it is." Jasper shrugged. "Basically, I was thinking about having Garmund research varying undead mythologies from across the globe. Zombies were relatively easy to kill, you know? Even the big ones, you just shoot in the head. Vampires, you use wood. Werewolves, use silver. What if there are more legends out there? Larger, nastier, undead monsters? It might not hurt to have an arsenal on hand to fight that sort of thing."

Aaron raised an eyebrow. "You think we'll have more of these events to face? I was kind of hoping that the zombies were a one-and-done thing."

Jasper shrugged. "Just a hunch. In any event, it can't *hurt.*"

"That's true, I suppose." Aaron held up his hands. "Alright, go for it. Let's see what he can dredge up."

"I'm assuming you're talking about me." Garmund poked his head in the door. "I'm always the one doing the dredging."

"You're so good at it, too." Aaron paused. "Jasper was thinking about-"

"Can it wait a moment?" Garmund frowned. "I came in here for a reason."

Aaron chuckled and glanced around at his office. "Do we need to move somewhere else? This place is getting awfully crowded."

Garmund sighed and nodded. "It might not hurt. Have everyone meet in the conference room."

Aaron nodded, reached over, and pressed the alert button. A blaring alarm shook the facility, and he grinned. "I love this new toy."

Garmund cocked an eyebrow. "You do realize that it alerts the central military command every time you push it, right?"

Aaron's eyes shot open, and he smacked a second button next to the first, canceling the alert. The alarms went silent as Bertha and Frank's heads appeared in the doorway.

"What's happening?" Frank seemed peeved at the interruption.

Aaron waved his hands. "Everyone out! Bertha, get the conference room cleaned up. Everyone else, meet there in five minutes."

Everyone filed out of his room, and Aaron took a deep breath. He desperately hoped that there wasn't another world-ending event happening. He was still riding the adrenalin from the last one, and he was in no hurry to repeat it. Not to mention the fact that if another one happened so soon, it would mean that there was probably something causing the events, which meant more work as they tried to dig up what was doing all the causing.

A few minutes passed, and Aaron stood up and walked into the conference room. Everyone else was already there, looking up at him expectantly. He sat down at the head of the table and waved to Garmund. "Take it away."

Garmund nodded. "So, as I'm sure you all know by now, I'm a pretty avid player of the game *Empire*."

Bertha batted her eyes at him. "It's hard not to know. I even created a character just so I could be with you in your world."

"You also accidentally signed up for a rival guild and kept getting killed when you tried to get to me." Garmund glanced at her uncomfortably. "I almost got kicked out because of the security risk. *Anyway,* at the moment, my avatar is one of the leaders of the ruling society. One of our scouts recently reported that a rebellion was forming under the avatar XM1932. We beefed up our security, got ready for any impending attack.

"To make a long story short, the attack never came. XM1932 just vanished. We sent out patrols, and found the avatar sleeping in a hollow log about five miles outside the kingdom. Naturally, we brought him back and locked him up, stripped of all his weapons. He's just a prisoner now."

Aaron held up a hand. "This is a bad thing why? First off, it's a video game. Secondly, it seems to be helping your cause."

"I know." Garmund sighed. "I just thought it was really weird that we had been able to take him so easily, so I hacked into the game servers to check on the sleep clock for XM1932. The character had been sleeping for three days when we found him last night."

Aaron cocked an eyebrow, waiting for the explanation. Garmund glanced around at everyone, let his head drop, and continued.

"In the game, your avatar sleeps when you're not logged in. It prevents people from disconnecting in the middle of combat to prevent gear from falling into enemy hands. That means that he hasn't logged in for almost three days. For a normal person, that's fairly normal, but XM1932 was one of the top players in the game, *and* on the cusp of regaining lost glory. That kind of player doesn't just *forget* to log in."

Aaron held up his hands. "What did you find out about him?"

"Not much." Garmund shrugged. "I hacked the servers to find his real name, and came up with Jeremy Morgan. He's registered as a college student at a university in Pittsburg, Pennsylvania, but after hacking into the university system, I found an email from a dorm monitor that he had gone missing. Roommate won't talk about what happened, you know the drill. I then expanded my search, and found that almost twenty kids have gone missing at the same university in the last two weeks. Something is happening there, something big."

"Does it involve the world ending?" Aaron held up his hands.

"I don't know." Garmund shrugged. "If the missing kids were turning into zombies, they would just spill out and eat everyone. If there was something more intelligent doing the killing, though, it's possible."

"Why does everyone keep *assuming* that we're going to be fighting more undead monsters?" Aaron threw up his hands. "The zombies were Dr. Incacheck's ordeal."

Harold snapped his fingers, and Aaron turned to look at him. "Yes?"

"Nothing." Harold shook his head. "Just put something together in my head."

"Alright, then." Aaron shrugged. "Anyway, the zombies were a creation of Dr. Incacheck. Why would there be more to it? Why would anything else materialize?"

"The Pandora Principal." Frank crossed his arms. "Pandora opened the box. One thing came out, and before you know it, the world is full of monsters. Thousands of wars were with swords, bows, and eventually muskets. One war breaks out with machineguns, and before you know it, wars are being fought from behind computer screens. We fight zombies once-"

"And before you know it, the world is full of monsters." Aaron sighed. "I get where you're coming from, but-"

"There's no buts about it." Frank climbed to his feet. "At least take the team and head that way. I'll stay here and watch the news, keep in contact on the headsets. It can't hurt anything."

Aaron nodded and sighed. "Has General Herford gotten back to you with the jet requisition form?"

"Not yet." Garmund shook his head. "Birch is doing everything he can to stop us from getting access to anything more sophisticated than a bicycle. I've been hacking every system he has access to to try and slow him down, but he's good."

A buzzer at the end of the table lit up, and Aaron groaned. "What *now?*"

Frank's eyes went wide. "Isn't that the alarm that Garmund installed?"

Aaron frowned at Garmund. "Is it? I wasn't told about any other alarms."

"That's because I just got it installed last week." Garmund held up his hands. "Come on! You've had me upgrading this base every time we get a circuit board in the mail from Herford. I can't be expected to tell you *every* minor upgrade I make."

"Right." Bertha nodded. "My Garmund-"

"I'm not *your* Garmund."

"Hold on!" Aaron held up his hand. "What does that alarm *do?*"

A soft hiss sounded behind him, and the door to the conference room swung open. Inspector Birch swept into the room, a smug look on his face. Aaron groaned and glanced over at Garmund.

"It warns us when he steps into the building, doesn't it?" Aaron did his best to ignore their nemesis.

"Yep." Garmund's voice was quiet.

"And you didn't think to make the doors *lock* when he walks into the building?"

"You *do* realize I can hear you?" Birch walked up next to Aaron and pulled an empty chair away from the table, slowly sitting down next to him. "Well, I suppose that might be a stretch. You people aren't the most intelligent, are you?"

"We beat your dad in D.C.." Aaron shrugged. "I'd call that an accomplishment."

"And I've been beating your uncle ever since then." Birch taunted. "You don't even know in what ways."

Aaron crossed his arms. He had no idea what Birch was talking about, but there was no real reason to get into those details. "Is there a reason you're here?"

"Of course." Birch flashed a small grin. "I'm actually here for the same reason I was last time. To inform you that, if you don't start doing your job, you're going to be shut down."

Aaron snorted. "And us saving D.C. wasn't doing our job?"

"Oh, it most certainly was." Birch nodded and snickered. "However, the world has nearly ended twice since that time. Both times, you've stayed safe and snug in your little hideout back here in Kansas City. Now, that's a thirty-three percent success rate, which has you back on the chopping block."

"What?" Aaron leapt to his feet. "What are you talking about?" He glanced at Garmund. "What's he talking about?"

"I don't know, but I'll find out." Garmund ran from the room. Bertha glanced at him, evidently torn between following and tormenting Garmund and getting the juicy details from Birch. After a moment, she ran after Garmund, allowing the door to bang shut behind them.

Aaron took a deep breath and turned to Birch. "Start talking. Now."

"Oh, I *enjoy* this." Birch stood up as well, frowning down at Aaron. "Please note that the only reason I'm telling you any of this is because I'm required to do so by law. Given a choice, I would happily see your group flounder and perish for good."

"Noted." Aaron growled. "Talk."

Birch held his pose for several seconds longer. When he began speaking again, it was with a continuously smug grin. "Since D.C., as I stated, two more world-ending events have been triggered. In both cases, it was *my* father's squad that managed to take them down and prevent the apocalypse."

"Good to know the world is in such safe hands." Aaron snarled and stood up, matching Birch pose-for-pose. He was almost certain that Birch was lying, of course. If the world had nearly ended, *why* hadn't the Squad been told about it? "So what's the deal now?"

"The deal is simple." Birch crossed his arms. "We believe that yet another world-ending event is on the horizon. My father's team is already en route. Based on your previous two failures, if you fail one more time, the Armageddon Response Force will replace the Apocalypse Squad as the official disaster force of the United States Military."

"So we have to stop the Apocalypse before they do. Easy enough." Aaron balled his fists. "Where is it?"

"That much, you'll have to figure out on your own." Birch turned to leave, and then paused. "Oh, and one final thing."

"Spit it out." Aaron growled.

"I notice that you depend on your hacker a great deal." Birch grinned. "You should get as much use out of him as possible, because you aren't going to have him around much longer."

"What are you talking about?" Aaron grabbed Birch's collar and slammed him up against a nearby wall. "Don't you *dare* threaten one of my team."

"I'm not threatening. Simply informing you that it won't be long before my father has Garmund on his own team." Birch shrugged. "You can make sense of it however you please. Now, please remove your hands from my shirt before I report you for threatening *me*."

Aaron let go of the inspector, rage boiling in his blood. "My uncle will stop this."

Birch laughed. "Your *uncle* is out of the picture, at least for a time. He's been sent overseas on urgent matters." Birch's face grew deadly serious, and he leaned forward. "You won't be able to rely on dear old Herford for help."

With that, Birch spun and swept out the door. Aaron glared after him, desperately wishing that the man would just drop dead. Or something. After several seconds of loathing Birch's existence, Aaron slowly turned back to face the remainder of the room. Jasper, Harold, and Frank all stared at him, eyes wide. Frank's face was a mask of anger, and Aaron slammed his fist into the desk.

"Last time we got this news, we drove across an entire state and fought a town of zombies to prevent the loss of our jobs." Aaron took a deep breath. "We all need to get to the control room and see what Garmund has pulled up. I don't care if we have to drive across the entire world this time. We beat Birch once." Aaron forced a pained, determined smile. "And we'll do it again."

CHAPTER 5

"What are we looking at?" Aaron walked through the doors of the control room, to where Garmund and Bertha were hunched over a computer screen. "Anything fantastic?"

"Not in the slightest." Garmund shook his head. "I'm working on hacking into the government servers, but they've beefed up the security quite a bit since the last time I was here."

Garmund reached over and pressed a button, causing the floor-to-ceiling monitors of the control room to light up with streams of code. Garmund continued to type, while Bertha slowly stood up, eyes flicking back and forth as she took in the streams of numbers. Aaron's head started to hurt, while Jasper and Harold slowly stepped through the door into the larger portion of the room.

The control room was set up for a far larger operation than the Squad currently had going for them. A smaller room, just inside the doors, consisted of a series of computer terminals that sat just below a number of two-way mirrors. On the other side of the glass, between the smaller room and the wall-covering screens, were dozens of monitoring stations. The computer terminals could theoretically connect with any computer system on the planet, allowing a small team of people to issue commands to group troops anywhere in the world. To top it off, the mirrors were completely soundproof, allowing the commander in charge to express his frustration at how poorly things were going without damaging the morale of the workers in the control room itself. Now, though, it just meant that they couldn't hear what Jasper and Harold were talking about while Garmund continued to work.

"Well, you're the best." Aaron sighed and sat down next to Garmund. "You'll get it."

"I hope so." Garmund shook his head. "That's just low. Not telling us what's happening and still holding us responsible."

"That's not the worst thing they're doing." Aaron hung his head. "In theory, aren't we all supposed to be untouchable? General Herford made sure we were safe, right?"

"Right." Garmund didn't look up from his typing. "Why do you ask?"

Aaron winced. "After you left, Birch… Birch is insinuating that General Birch is going to try and take you away from us."

Garmund paused, while Bertha's head snapped around like a top.

"He can't do that!" Bertha shrieked.

Garmund just lowered his hands down into his lap. Aaron frowned and crossed his arms.

"We'll get through this." Aaron did his best to reassure the hacker. "If you have any idea what to do, what angle Birch is taking, we can fight him."

"No." Garmund shook his head and slowly turned to look at Aaron. "No, you can't."

"Why?" Aaron held up his hands. "We've fought him before!"

"If Inspector Birch told you that General Birch was taking me, it's because he's confident." Garmund just stared down at the keyboard. "He told you about the possibility of losing our jobs because he's required to by law. He told you about *me* because he wanted to gloat."

"Herford has protection on us!" Aaron protested. "We can fight it!"

"No!" Garmund swore and slammed his fist into the metal next to the computer. "No. I thought I had hidden it, but if he found it…" His voice trailed off, and he took a deep breath. "When I hacked into the Pentagon all that time ago and stole those files, I played around with my own official file. I didn't do anything major, but I *did* flip around a few things about my childhood. I think I changed the hospital room that I was born in or something. Now, *if* Birch managed to find my original files, some sort of hard copy that existed before I hacked the pentagon, it would mean that Herford promoted and is protecting someone who doesn't technically exist."

Aaron felt his world spin. "So how do we fix it?"

"We can't!" Garmund spun and held up his hands. "If I hack my files a second time, I'll be court-marshalled for good. I won't get a third chance. The only way we could get past it would be to steal whatever file Birch managed to get his hands on, which is probably impossible. He's certainly duplicated it, locked several copies away in vaults-"

"So we get the files back." Aaron shrugged. "We fought off a herd of zombies, we can break into a few vaults."

"Not with the fate of the world at hand." Garmund swore again and slowly sat back up. "You've only got me for a few more days, which means that I need to help you as much as possible in the time that I have." He slammed his hands onto the keyboard, sending code flashing across the screen. Slowly, steadily, he began pecking at the keyboard forcefully. "Our only hope of keeping our jobs and staying out of jail lies in preventing the next Apocalypse. To do that, you need to know what you're up against. And I'm going to find that for you."

With a soft whir, Garmund's fingers danced across the keys. Code began to flow faster and faster, and Garmund's face grew more determined. Aaron just sighed and sat there in silence. Bertha's eyes never left Garmund's face.

They remained in silence until the massive screens lit up with images. Half the screens showed a peaceful village in what appeared to be Europe, while the other half showed a desert with dozens of pyramids. Text appeared on Garmund's screen while half the videos began to play.

"Looks like these are the two events." Garmund's voice was hollow. "The ones on the left are from Norway. A bunch of plants pulled up roots and started attacking the populace. The Armageddon Response Force, or ARF as they're called here, responded and eliminated the threat."

The images on the screens began to move. Several trees near the edge of the village lurched upward and smashed into the town, tearing through stone walls. Screams rose on the feed, and Aaron winced.

A small dot appeared in the sky over the village. A plane. Aaron held his breath as it streaked over the screaming people and dropped a single package. It fell towards the village, and Aaron frowned. Were all the members of the Armageddon Response Force parachuting together? Was it a machine of some kind? Was...

With a blinding flash, the object fell onto the village and exploded. Most of the cameras cut out, and were replaced by other cameras from much farther away. Nuclear fire belched into the sky, forming a small mushroom cloud. Aaron felt something hit him in the gut, and Garmund switched over to the pyramids.

"The ones on the right are from Egypt. Several archeologists investigating an ancient tomb reported hearing thumps from within the sarcophaguses. Upon opening one, a mummy came out and possessed the leader of the expedition. From there, the ancient ruler moved to a nearby town and proceeded to resurrect a legion of undead to enslave the local populace. The last report from inside the town was that the mummy was preparing to reach out and gather more of the ancient rulers, preparing an army to overwhelm the entire world."

Once again, the images started moving. Once again, a plane simply flashed overhead, dropping a nuclear bomb on the population. Fire belched across the sand, and once again, Aaron felt like someone hit him right in the chest.

"He bombed two civilian populations." Aaron shook his head. "He blew up two towns!"

"To be fair, we leveled Lambspoint." Frank's voice was quiet, in shock.

"At least we *tried* to save people!" Aaron roared at the monitors. "And we did! We saved people! Not many, but more than would have been lost if we had just nuked the place!"

"If he already nuked two cities, what's to stop him from doing it again?" Bertha glanced at Aaron. "We know that there's another event going down. What if Birch only warned us a minute or two before he dropped another bomb? There could be more people already lying in cinders right now."

"I'm in his system now." Garmund's voice was still deathly quiet. "Hang on. Let me try something."

His fingers moved so fast that Aaron couldn't follow them. The screens changed, lighting up with images of beautiful, limestone buildings. Garmund hit a few more keys and nodded.

"You remember what I said about the disappearances at the college?" Garmund glanced back at Aaron. "This is the college. Looks like it's all over Birch's servers, too."

"Is he going to drop a nuke on the United States?" Aaron's jaw dropped. "He wouldn't!"

"No, he wouldn't." Garmund muttered in a sarcastic voice. "He values American lives more than that. Specifically, he values American lives that exist in heavily-watched areas of the country. Notice how no one has heard of the last two towns just vanishing from the map? That's not going to happen if he blows up something in an area as dense as Pennsylvania."

"In that case, we need to get moving." Aaron sighed. "Since we don't have a jet and can't really take our weapons through public airport terminals, we're going to have to drive. How quickly can we get there?"

Garmund changed the rhythm of his typing. A map appeared on the screen, a projection of the United States bisected by a curving blue line.

"Eighteen hours if you follow the speed limit." Garmund struck another key, and the line vanished. "Less than that if you speed."

"Then we'll just have to speed." Aaron reached up and rapped on the glass, drawing Harold and Jasper's attention. They climbed to their feet and started making their way back, and Aaron took a deep breath. The moment they were all in the same room, he crossed his arms.

"This isn't anything like last time." He nodded to Jasper. "Load up the van with as many weapons as you can get. Bertha, Harold, help him. Garmund, grab whatever tech equipment that you'll need."

Garmund nodded, climbed to his feet, and slowly walked out of the room. Bertha followed him with her eyes. A single tear dripped down her face before her resolve solidified and she marched out as well. Jasper and Harold were a bit slower, a bit less morose, but even they seemed horrified by the turn of events.

For a long moment, Aaron just stood there. He puffed out his cheeks and closed his eyes. A hand came down on his shoulder, and he slowly opened his eyes again.

"It's going to be okay." Frank looked up at him, a soft smile of compassion on his face. "We'll beat this."

"Maybe." Aaron shook his head. "While we head out, get set up in the surveillance room."

Frank's eyes opened slightly. "You don't want me along?"

"Like I said, this isn't like last time." Aaron shook his head. "I want someone keeping an eye on the news at *all* times. Our command center can tap into whatever surveillance feeds are around us or any drones we take along. Without Garmund's help in the field-"

"You need better eyes." Frank nodded slowly. "We may not lose Garmund yet."

"But we might." Aaron ran his hand through his hair and slowly walked out of the room. "I need to think. Just keep an eye out for any other world-ending events. If we're losing the battle in Pennsylvania and can get to another location faster than Birch, it might just save us."

"If you plan for a failure, that's all you'll receive."

"Then give me another plan." Aaron held up his hands. "Anything?"

Frank simply looked at the ground and slowly shook his head. Aaron nodded firmly, turned around, and walked into his office. With a dull thud, he fell into his chair and closed his eyes, trying to think.

All they knew was that they were going to a college in Pennsylvania. That was it. No leads on Incacheck, no leads on what they might be facing once they got there. No idea how to keep hold of Garmund, or if Birch's threat was even valid.

He was still sitting there when a knock sounded on the door frame. Slowly, he brought his head up as

Garmund appeared in the doorway. Aaron gestured to the spare chair, and Garmund sank into it, a look of horror on his face.

"I'm toast."

Aaron shook his head, trying to remain positive. "You're the best hacker I know."

"That's the issue." Garmund shrugged mindlessly. "None of my techniques are legal or even suggested by the black market. Birch is trying to trap me. If I do *anything* and they see me, they'll nail me to a wall."

Aaron closed his eyes for a brief moment. It made sense. If Birch could keep a close eye on the hacker, he could have him thrown away the moment that anything went south. "Just make sure to keep your head down."

Garmund nodded and flashed a pained smile. "I guess… I mean, on one hand, I can supply you with information about their activities."

"Nope." Aaron shook his head. "If you're right, and it *is* a trap, he'll probably have your computer access points tapped, and he'll certainly be watching you. Do *anything* to help us, and he'll court-marshal and execute you quicker than you can blink."

"What do you want me to do, then?" Garmund scowled. "Help them?"

Aaron closed his eyes for several seconds before nodding. "That's exactly what you're going to do. I mean, muck things up for them if you can, but not in any way that could be considered illegal or tie back to us. We'll work on finding a way to bring you back to our squad in the meantime. Birch is operating on a technicality, one that should be easily overturned once we figure things out." He clapped Garmund on the shoulder. "You're not slipping away from us that easily. Besides, we don't know for *sure* that's what he's doing."

"Oh, we know. There's nothing else it could be, and believe me, I'm going to be working on a way out as well." Garmund sighed. "At least we have some time before Birch gets his hands on me."

"That's true." Aaron let out a long breath. "Well, shall we roll out? Jasper and Harold should have the van loaded by now."

Garmund nodded and flashed a determined, if pained, smile. "Let's move. It's a long drive."

"Perfect." Aaron took a deep breath and pushed himself up. "Let's go figure out what we're dealing with."

CHAPTER 6

Jeremy's eyes snapped open as he tried to refocus. Everything seemed blurry. The last thing he remembered was being bitten. What was that all about, anyway? Slowly, as more of his consciousness seemed to return, he sat up and took a deep breath.

He was still in the tunnels, that much was for certain, though in a different part. The walls here rose far higher, forming a room almost twenty feet high and fifty feet across in every direction. There were six total exits, leading away in various directions. After a moment, as he looked around at the ceiling, he frowned in confusion. There was no source of illumination, no lights, no sunlight, and yet he could see almost perfectly. Weird.

Slowly, he took a step and tripped over something. He stumbled a few steps, turned, and glanced down. His jaw dropped at the sight of a body lying on the floor, unconscious. It was a young girl, probably a freshman like himself. She sported what looked like a bite mark on her neck, and her skin was pasty white. Jeremy's eyes widened, and he knelt down next to her.

After a moment, he put his hands on her wrist, feeling for a pulse. It took him only a moment to notice that she didn't have one, though that fact was overshadowed by the fact that his hands were as pasty white as hers. He jumped to his feet and backed against a nearby wall, chest heaving. The action caused his clothes to flutter in the air, allowing him to see that he had apparently been dressed in a black suit with a leather cape. Why would anyone do that to him?

Desperately, he glanced around the room, trying to figure out what was happening. Which was when he finally noticed all the *other* bodies. Almost thirty people were scattered across the room, all in the same unconscious state. He took a deep breath and started to pace. Something was happening. What was it?

"Ahh, you're awake." A tall, bald man swept into the room. He was wearing an entirely black outfit, complete with sweeping black cape. "Finally. At least I had one success."

Jeremy frowned. "What do you mean? What success?"

The man turned and spread his arms. "I'm kind of new to this whole thing. You can feed on pretty much anyone, but there's *such* a delicate balance between killing the person, turning them, and letting them walk away free as a witness. You have to suck *just* the right amount of blood or it doesn't work. Everyone else just keeps dying."

Jeremy held up his hand. "Slow down. What the hell did you do to me?"

"Hell. That would be the operative word, wouldn't it be?" The man shrugged and swept across the room, stepping across bodies like they were simple toys. "You're a vampire now. Removing your blood allowed a demon to possess your system, giving you a number of, well, quite amazing perks."

Jeremy cocked an eyebrow. "A vampire? You're serious?"

The man shrugged. "Don't I look serious? Look at my teeth."

He opened his mouth wide, revealing canine teeth that were far sharper and longer than any teeth had the right to be. The rest of his teeth were sharpened to a point as well, a mouthful of needles.

"I'd tell you to go look in a mirror, but you know how vampires are. Oh, I'd also suggest not stepping outside during the day. I got a nasty burn the first time I tried it."

Jeremy crossed his arms. "I don't believe any of this. I think you cut me, and now you're trying to trick me."

"I had the same thoughts when I first turned." The man held up a finger. "Well, my first thought was how much of a miracle it was. I thought I was dead. Honestly, I can't really tell you how or why I came back to life. If this is, indeed, life."

"You're insane." Jeremy waved his hand. "Let's say you *are* a vampire. You kind of suck at your job."

"Yes, well…" The man shrugged. "Now that you're here, you can be my advisor. My sidekick as we rise to the head of the underground Empire."

"I'm amending my last statement. You're insane."
Jeremy shook his head. "Look, I'm going to go find my
girlfriend, then I'm going to go find my roommate. In that
order, just to alleviate confusion."

"Like I said, just don't step outside. Or into a
church. That would also be bad, now that I think about it."
The man shrugged. "Oh, I also suggest not feeding the first
time you get the urge. It'll probably be in public, and you'll
get attacked before you finish your meal. Trust me, *that*
sucks."

"I'll keep it in mind." Jeremy shook his head, ready
to get out of there. "Which way to the dorms on the lower
side of campus?"

"That way." The man pointed towards a hallway to
his right. "Just remember-"

"I got it." Jeremy waved his hands. "I'll take it as I
see it. I probably won't be back."

"Oh, I think you will be." The man chuckled. "Oh,
I suppose you want to know my name?"

"Nope, pretty sure that I don't."

"It's Gruen." The man smiled, completely ignoring
Jeremy's declaration. "Principal Gruen." Jeremy cocked an
eyebrow, and the man shook his head. "Just Gruen."

Jeremy just shook his head and took off into the
tunnels. Whatever Gruen had done to increase the lighting
without making it obvious, he had done it throughout all
the tunnels. There was no source of light, yet he could see
perfectly clearly. He wound his way through the area, going
down stairs, grinning at the sight of a growing level of
graffiti on the walls. He was obviously getting closer, that
much was certain.

After a short time, he came to an intersection of four tunnels. Three of them branched away, all of them curving, which meant that this was probably the part where the dorm tunnels connected. Belatedly, he realized that he didn't know which tunnel to go down.

After a few moments of trying to figure out which direction to go, he noticed that the walls had the names of dorms written on them. If he was right, Vanessa lived in the Garfield dorm. Without hesitation, he ran down the tunnel, a feeling of anticipation burning in his chest. He was going to see her again! At that point, he had no idea how long he had been out for. She was worried for him, certainly?

After a short distance, he reached the ladder that led upward, into the building. Hoping that it came up in a study room like the last one, he climbed up and pushed the trap door open as quickly as he could.

The moment it was open, a mop came crashing down on his head. He muttered a curse and tossed it out of his way, climbing higher to reveal a small cleaning closet. Once he finally got his footing on the rather slippery floor, he clicked the door shut, took a deep breath, and opened the door.

Instantly, a trio of girls swiveled in his direction. He stepped out of the closet and into a small study area, an alcove in a larger hallway. One of them chuckled at his disheveled self.

"Coming to visit a girlfriend?"

He nodded slowly. "Yeah. Vanessa?"

"I know three girls with that name." She shrugged. "You know, it's an all-girls dorm, but it's one o'clock in the afternoon. People usually don't start slipping in through the tunnels until after visiting hours close at six."

"I got lost." Jeremy muttered. "I think she said she was on the third floor. You know one that lives there?"

"There are names on the doors." The girl frowned. "Are you okay? You look pale. Like really, really pale."

"I'm alright." Jeremy shrugged. "I just… I need to get moving."

Without another word, he turned and stormed down the hallway. He had thought he was getting better, but he was just so disoriented. It was like the world was spinning, back and forth, and he couldn't stop it.

The moment he was in the stairway, he started upward as quickly as he could. Interestingly enough, he found that he wasn't exhausted, or even winded, by the trip. He stumbled onto the third floor as quickly as he could, growing more and more confused by the moment.

Several girls walked out of their rooms, glancing back and forth as he walked past. They all seemed to be eyeing him curiously, and he didn't think it was because of his typical suspicious self. Their eyes held some sort of concern, a terror almost. Something inside him almost seemed to relish in it, and he grimaced. That was the last thing he needed right now, enjoying terrorizing a populace. Gruen would have a ball with that.

He had made it almost all the way to the other side of the building when he noticed Vanessa's name on the door. A smile split his face, and he knocked on the door as quickly as he could. Thoughts began to course through his head. What if she wasn't here? What if…

The door clicked open, and a muffled gasp echoed through the air. It swung wide open to reveal Vanessa standing there, eyes wide. She took a step back, hand over her mouth.

"You're alive!"

"I don't plan on cashing in my chips just yet." He chuckled. "What's happening?"

"The bigger question is where you've been." She scowled at him. "You just vanished. Brad muttered something about getting lost in the tunnel system, but I know you're smart enough to avoid that place." Jeremy glance up at the ceiling, and her gaze turned horrified. "You didn't! You can get expelled for that!"

He shrugged. "It won't happen again, believe me."

She didn't seem reassured by his promise. "I hope not. Come on, what happened? Well, we can't talk out here. Come on in!"

He smiled and followed her into the dorm room. The scent of candles and flowers filled his nose, and he smiled. She sat down on the bed, and he sat down next to her. She leaned against his side, putting her arms around him.

"So, what happened down there?"

"Honestly, I'm not sure." Jeremy shrugged. "We were attacked by something. Bit me something nasty."

Vanessa looked up at his neck, her eyes going wide. "Ouch! That looks like it *hurts*."

"You're telling me." Jeremy let out a breath. "Anyway, it bites me, I pass out, and the next thing I know I'm waking up in the middle of the tunnel system."

"And you came straight here?" Vanessa frowned. "Straight from waking up?"

"Uh, huh." Jeremy thought it best to leave out the part about Gruen, at least for a time. "Straight here. I don't know how long I've been out, but-"

"It's been three days." Vanessa shook. "We were so worried about you. Oh, Brad's going to be so glad to see you! He's been blaming himself for the whole thing."

"As he should." Jeremy muttered. "I never would have gone down into those tunnels if he hadn't drug me. I'd be…" A thought struck him, and he slapped his forehead. "Blast. *Empire*. I've been logged off for four days."

"Well, while you're swooning over your game, I'm just excited that you're here." Vanessa smiled. "I've had these blinds drawn all day because I couldn't stand the light, but now, I'm kind of sick of being in the dark."

Jeremy squinted. "What do you mean? This feels like midday."

Vanessa barked a laugh. "What do you mean? I can barely see you, it's so dark. Just a moment."

She reached over to the window and turned a knob. The blinds twisted to the side, and with a blast, a force like a million atom bombs rained down on Jeremy's skin. It felt like he was burning up, as if his skin was peeling away. Desperate, he jumped off the bed and slid to the wall, away from the sunlight.

"Oh, I'm so sorry!" Vanessa threw the blinds back shut. "Here, let me turn on the light."

She reached behind him, flicking a switch. Jeremy frowned. As near as he could tell, nothing had happened. Vanessa's face changed drastically, and he shrugged. Apparently something *had* happened.

"Your…" Vanessa stammered. "Your skin."

"I know." Jeremy glanced down at it. "It's annoyingly pale."

"That must be why the sun hurt you so much." Vanessa shrugged. "Four days in the pitch black, you just… Got a lot paler."

"What?" Jeremy frowned. "What's wrong?"

"You." Vanessa took a step back. "You got bit, you have pale skin, you hate sunlight, you're wearing a cape…"

"Oh, don't you start, too." Jeremy threw his hands up. "I'm not a vampire!"

"You had someone else tell you that?" Vanessa frowned. "Who?"

Jeremy waved his hand. "A guy in the tunnel. Big pointy teeth, black cape. Pale skin, told me he bit me and turned me into a vampire."

"And you didn't believe him?"

Jeremy held up his hands. "Why should I?"

Vanessa walked over to her jewelry box, flipped it open, and drew out a necklace. As she walked back towards him, an odd sense of curiosity grew in his mind. What was she…

With a flash, she held the jewel up into his face. He had a split second to glimpse a cross before a physical blast of energy hit him in the chest and propelled him back into the door. His head cracked against the wood, and he grimaced. Vanessa dropped the cross in shock, and he groaned.

"Oh…" She stammered. "You're actually a vampire."

"Great." He forced himself off the wall. "Just what I wanted to start out my freshman year of college."

"There's no way you can stay in college now." Vanessa crossed her arms and started pacing. "You'd have to use the tunnels to get from building to building, and that's just not going to be feasible in the middle of the day. Not to mention the fact that this *is* a Catholic university. There are crucifixes at the front of every classroom."

"Great." Jeremy started pacing back and forth. "What do I do now? What do we do now?"

"We?" Vanessa raised an eyebrow. "You think there's a *we* in this?"

"Isn't there?" Jeremy held up his hands. "I may be different, but I'm still the same person!"

"Are you, though?" Vanessa stepped closer. "How do I know?"

Jeremy took a deep breath. "The love I have for you bears no bounds. If I were to lose you…"

"Alright, you convinced me." Vanessa held up her hand. Jeremy frowned, slightly confused. All he had been trying to do was express the depths of his love for her. Was he really *that* poetic? "Look, I'm just going to need some time to process this."

"I think we both are." Jeremy shook his head. "Just… Thanks for not running away. Whatever happened, I hate it just as much as you do. I'm going to start looking for a cure, I promise."

"I'll help, in any way I can." Vanessa nodded. "And hey, it might be cool to have a vampire for a boyfriend." She turned her head sideways and laid it on his chest, coming close to him in an embrace. "Hey. My boyfriend is a *vampire*. Let's see how the other girls stand up to that, huh?"

Jeremy only chuckled. Maybe, just maybe, being a vampire wouldn't be so bad after all.

CHAPTER 7

"Welcome to our fair university!" Dean Hartfield wrung Aaron's hand. "We're so glad to have you here."

Aaron raised an eyebrow. "I would have thought our arrival would be… Unpleasant."

"I mean, I'm in no way saying that I enjoy being the center of a potentially world-ending event." Dean Hartfield shrugged. "As long as it's happening, though, I'm happy that the best in the business are here to help stop it."

Aaron held out his hands. "Well, we're certainly going to do our best. Do you mind if we release security drones to help us keep an eye on things?"

"By all means." Dean Hartfield waved his hand. "Do whatever you need to do. Interrogate students. Just end this, whatever it is. We've lost twenty students in the last week alone, and that's simply unacceptable."

"We'll get right on it." Aaron tried not to think about those lives, so full of hope, snuffed out by *something* mysterious and unknown. "The first thing we need to do is pinpoint exactly what we're dealing with. Can you tell me anything about the disappearances?"

Dean Hartfield shook his head. "There's been no correlation of age, gender, interest, or anything else we can discern. We do believe that the disappearances have been taking place at night. I know that's probably pretty standard, but that's what I have."

"Thank you." Aaron nodded. "If there's anything else you can tell us, don't hesitate to let us know."

"Of course." Dean Hartfield smiled and nodded towards the door. "We don't have much in the way of lodging, I'm afraid. There's an old frat house, if you'd like to take it. It's right on the edge of campus, easy access to everything. It was forcibly vacated after an incident with hazing, so there aren't any structural issues or anything. Should be just what you guys need."

"We'll take it." Aaron nodded. "Thanks."

"Then it's settled." Dean Hartfield took a deep breath. "Delta Sigma Kappa. The key should be under the front matt. Well, let me know as you learn things. I'm most interested to know just what kind of apocalypse we're dealing with." He leaned forward and lowered his voice. "Though if you could manage to stop it *before* it gets as big as the one in D.C., that would be great. Our donors aren't going to appreciate having to pay for a giant hole in the ground."

Aaron smiled thinly. "We'll do our best."

Dean Hartfield smiled, nodded, and stood up straight. Assuming that was a cue to leave, Aaron stalked from the office and through the massive, ornate halls of the administration building. He had to admit, the design was quite impressive. The entry hallway was large and arched, complete with pillars and gold veneer.

The rest of the team waited on the front steps. Jasper and Harold both snapped upward the moment that Aaron reappeared, questions in their eyes. Aaron smiled, crossed his arms, and flashed a grin.

"Boys, we're in business. Garmund, I need you to find Delta Sigma Kappa. That's where we're staying while we're here. Everyone else... Well, hang tight. We really can't do much until he finds the location."

"On it." Garmund nodded, turned, and started pulling things up on his cell phone. A few moments later, he nodded and gestured towards the south. "Looks like it's only a few blocks that way. Take a couple minutes to get there, no more."

"Perfect." Aaron grinned. "Shall we?"

Without another word, they piled into the van, popped a U-turn, nearly taking the mirror off a campus vehicle, and took off across the campus.

It didn't take long to get to their destination. As they pulled up, a collective gasp rose from the vehicle. Solid limestone walls rose high into the sky, at least three stories. The roof was ringed with a metal fence, and parapets graced the corners. Monstrous Greek letters stood out on the walls, and Aaron grinned.

At least, of course, until Bertha drove straight past it and into the driveway of the frat next door. Aaron frowned, finally getting around to reading the letters carved into the limestone. Omega Alpha Sigma. So they weren't going to be staying in a castle. Slowly, he turned his attention to the house they had just pulled into.

The giant Greek letters on the side of the building left no question that it was, indeed, Delta Sigma Kappa. That said, it had to be the smallest frat house that Aaron had ever seen. Brown, peeling siding graced the single-story rise, while the rest seemed to be little more than a few bedrooms with a garage.

Aaron walked up to the front door, bent down, and began fishing around under the front mat. It took a matter of moments to find the key and unlock the door. Slowly, he took a deep breath.

Small didn't even begin to describe it. He was quite certain that, were he to hold his arms straight out, they would touch the opposite walls of the living room. Worse, the living room transitioned directly into the kitchenette, allowing anyone trying to relax a perfect view of whatever culinary disaster they would be forced to consume later.

A single doorway led out of the living room/kitchen combo. Aaron stepped through, having to turn sideways as he did so, and found himself in a narrow hallway. A door at the end of the hallway hung open, leading into the garage, while three more doors opened to two separate bedrooms and a bathroom.

Harold pushed past Aaron and glanced around, chuckling. "Man, I thought *my* town was small."

"It's certainly not ideal." Aaron muttered. "We can make it work, though. Let's see… Bertha gets one of the rooms, obviously. Harold, Jasper, you guys can take the other room."

"Roomies!" Jasper stuck his hand around the corner, nearly taking out Aaron's eye, which Harold happily high-fived. "We can stay up late talking!"

"You keep the rest of us awake, and I'm using your own weapons against you." Aaron muttered. "I'll take the living room. At least it has a couch. Garmund, you can get set up in the garage."

"What happens when they take me away?" Garmund shook his head. "What-"

"They're going to have to fight to get you away." Aaron muttered and slid to the side to allow Garmund passage. "Just get your stuff set up. If possible, I'd like you to get us a working system that we can keep utilizing even after-" His voice trailed off as he realized how the statement sounded out loud.

"After I'm gone?" Garmund shook his head. "Don't I feel loved."

"We want you around." Aaron clapped him on the shoulder. "Believe that. Now get stuff working, we need to be operational as soon as possible." He turned to walk back out to the car, then stopped and shook his head. "Oh, and find out what kind of frat lived in this place to begin with. I'm *so* confused."

"On it." Garmund vanished into the garage, and Aaron sighed deeply. Without another word, he walked out to the van as Jasper was starting to unload some of his weapons. Aaron held out his hands, and Jasper happily loaded him up with as much as he could carry.

After he deposited the load somewhat awkwardly in the bedroom, he walked back out to the van for the next load. He drew to a stop, though, as something caught his eye. In the monstrous castle-esque frat house next door, he was quite certain that he saw the curtains move in one of the upper windows.

After a few moments, he blinked it away. It was probably nothing, just some insects buzzing around. Or even just the frat that happened to live there. As he walked back into the house, he met Garmund coming out of the garage. Aaron held up his hands questioningly, and Garmund nodded.

"The system is all set up, and I have the information you wanted. It looks like the frat consisted of two brothers who wanted to impress several sorority girls. They moved into a house next to a real frat, did what they needed to do to get certified with the campus, and began staking their territory. The problem came when they tried to expand their ranks."

Aaron frowned. "The dean said it was a hazing issue. Anything we need to know about?"

Garmund shrugged. "Depends. How do you feel about living in a house someone died in?"

Aaron grimaced. A house haunted by the ghost of someone who had died in a hazing incident didn't exactly sit well with him. "Not great, to be honest. What happened? Did they try to make him chug vodka or something?"

Garmund laughed. "Nope! Their hazing was actually pretty mild. It involved eating cinnamon in the nude. Anyway, they were getting ready to officially initiate the guy when an escaped convict burst into the house and tried to hole up here while engaging in a shootout with police. He didn't fare so well. The city paid for the repairs afterwards, but the brothers weren't super keen about staying at that point."

"Interesting." Aaron frowned. "Very interesting."

"That's what I thought." Garmund shrugged. "Incidentally, the frat next door *was* shut down because one of their initiates died in a hazing incident. Man, I'm glad I don't have to live in that house."

A knock sounded on the front door, and Aaron waved Garmund away. "No sense in anyone knowing you're here. Stay in the garage until they leave."

Garmund nodded, and Aaron walked up to the front door. Slowly, he turned the knob and swung the wooden edifice inward.

Standing on the other side was the stuff of nightmares. General Birch, in all his military clothing, stood outside, a deep glare etched onto his brow.

"Can I help you?" Aaron crossed his arms. Their time had just dropped from very little to almost none at all. "I didn't realize you were in town."

"No, you didn't." Birch muttered. "Perhaps that's how covert operations should work, wouldn't you think?"

Aaron cocked an eyebrow. "Can I help you?"

"No, I don't think so." Birch shrugged. "I just wanted to come say hello to our new neighbors."

Aaron's head dropped. "You got the castle, didn't you?"

"Of course we did!" Birch chuckled. "We got in last night, long before you could have even known we were making our move. As always, you're one step behind."

Aaron scratched his head. "You know, I seem to remember a time where you were hiding behind a bunch of barricades while we did all the hard work. Looks like you're still trying to play catch up."

"Oh, I wouldn't say that at all." Birch put his hands behind his back in a strict military posture. "Alright, here's the deal. You stay out of our way, and we don't shoot you when we start wiping the monsters off the face of this campus."

"Here's a better idea." Aaron held up a finger. "You stay out of our way, and fewer civilians die as a result."

"I make sure the populace as a whole survives." Birch growled. "If it had been up to me, I would have blown that Kansas town off the face of the planet. Sure, you lose a few people there, but then it stops the disease from being taken to, oh, the Capitol?"

"We still don't know how any of this works." Aaron bit out. "How any of these monsters form."

"And you're an expert on the monsters?" Birch chuckled. "Despite the fact that you've never seen one other than your zombies?"

"You'll pay for what you've done." Aaron muttered. "I'll see to it."

"Yes, well, we'll see about that." Birch shrugged. "Now, is Garmund around?"

"He actually didn't come with us." Aaron shrugged. "You'll have to try again next apocalypse."

"Cute." Birch muttered. "We have security footage of him buying a bag of chips at a gas station in West Virginia. I know he's in there."

"He's out getting groceries."

"Your only van is sitting in the driveway."

Aaron crossed his arms. "You have to have a warrant to enter."

Birch leaned forward. "I'm not a vampire, I don't need to ask permission before I enter a building. Besides, I have requisition orders for him right here. That works just as well as a warrant, especially since you're technically under my command. A military operation, even if unsanctioned, gives me the right to set foot there."

"Oh, can it." Aaron crossed his arms. "Look, we have our team ready to roll. Let us do our job, stay out of our way, and-"

"You have no right to threaten me." Birch grinned. "In fact, I believe that I could court-martial you for doing just that."

Aaron froze, waiting for the heel to drop. Birch just stared him down, and Aaron set his feet.

"You can do whatever you want to us, but I promise you, my team and I are going to do everything in our power to prevent your force from killing a single innocent student on this campus. We're faster and we're more dedicated than any of your squad is."

Birch cocked an eyebrow and grinned. "This is going to be *so* much more interesting than a court-martial. Alright, we'll do things your way. The first thing that either of us is going to be doing is looking for exactly what's causing the student disappearances. First person to locate the source gets... Hmm. What is it that I want of yours, anyway?"

Aaron crossed his arms. "You want Garmund."

"Oh, I already have him." Birch held up the requisition forms. "I'm not leaving this porch without him. No, I'm trying to make things more interesting. Winner gets to raid the other's armory? I know we have weapons and high-powered explosives that you can't possibly have access to, and I know that you have a particular genius who happens to love custom crafting. I'd say that makes even odds."

Aaron was getting more and more frustrated with the situation. "Deal."

"Good." Birch held out the papers. "Now bring me Garmund or I have my people storm the house and take him by force. I can do it, you know."

"None of that needed." Garmund appeared in the doorway, a resigned look on his face. "No need for anyone to get hurt on my account. I'm here, Birch."

"Excellent." Birch clapped his hands. "You will address me as Commander Birch from this point onward. Welcome to the Armageddon Response Force."

Garmund paused. "Do you mind if I have a moment alone with my friends? I don't think you're going to allow house calls once I've moved in."

"At least you're perceptive." Birch waved his hand. "Have your goodbyes. I'm waiting outside."

Aaron shook his head and slammed the door in Birch's face. He turned to Garmund, who grimaced.

"Agreeing to the trade was a bad idea. He already has surveillance sweeping the area. They have dozens of cameras in place, he'll find anything quicker than you can."

"Did you launch our security?" Aaron ignored the outburst.

Garmund nodded. "Yes, of course. I'm trying to cover the ground as fast as possible, but-"

"Don't pay any attention to the areas the ARF already has covered." Aaron paused. "Does this university have a tunnel system?"

"Yeah, it does." Garmund nodded. "How did you know?"

Aaron shrugged. "Student disappearances. They go into the tunnels to make out, and get nabbed by whatever's down there. Pretty much all universities have something similar, and I'd be willing to bet it's not something that the ARF is going to patrol anytime soon."

Garmund nodded. "I'll program the drones to fly down there right now."

"I wish you had that much time." Aaron dipped his head. "Frank can control the drones from Kansas, right?"

Garmund nodded. "He's been training on them. There shouldn't be any problems."

"Good." Aaron flashed a thin grin. "In that case, I think we're good."

"No!" Bertha came flying out of the hallway, pushed past Aaron, and threw her arms around the hacker. "You can't go!"

Garmund swallowed, then slowly reached up to give Bertha a quick hug. She held on for several more seconds before slowly stepping back. Jasper and Harold crowded into the room as much as they could, and, for several long seconds, they just stood there.

"Be safe." Aaron found it hard to speak, as if a hand had latched around his throat. "Remember-"

"I've got it." Garmund's voice was thick as well. "Look, I know what you said. And believe me, I'm going to try to play along, I don't have any desire to wind up executed. Just know that I'm willing to provide you information here and there. I'm sure we can work something out. I'm not ready to leave you guys."

Aaron took a deep breath. "I don't think we're ready for it either."

Garmund nodded, took a deep breath, and held out his hand. Aaron shook it tightly, then pulled Garmund into a hug. Garmund pulled away after a few moments, then turned to Jasper and Harold. Both of them shook his hand, and he flashed a sad grin. A tear slid down the side of his face, and, as Birch started rapping on the door yet again, he turned and walked out of the home. The door slammed shut behind him… And that was that.

"I never thought I'd be sad to see him gone." Jasper's voice trembled. "We're getting him back, right?"

"We're getting him back." Bertha's voice was firm, even as she swept out of the room wiping tears off her face. "We'll find him."

"We'll find a way." Aaron nodded firmly and sighed. "We need Frank out here. I at least need to call him."

"Why didn't you just bring him along to begin with?" Harold frowned.

"I thought he would be more helpful back in the main control room." Aaron shrugged and shook his head. "He could view the overall campus security, he could keep an eye on news reports. Now, I'm starting to rethink it."

"Actually, I think I *am* more needed back here." Frank's voice echoed through the air. Aaron spun, finally stopping to see one of the security drones hovering in midair. Remembering how explosive they could be, he took a step back as the drone inched its way forward. "Garmund left me with a whole bunch of instructions on how to handle things. I don't think I would be able to do everything from that garage."

Aaron shook his head. "You're afraid of the ARF."

"I'm afraid that I'm going to put a bullet through Birch." Frank muttered. "He sullies that uniform with his presence. I hate him."

"Good to know." Aaron crossed his arms. "Alright, you're in charge of the drones?"

"I have them in perfect attunement." Frank's voice sounded quite pleased. "Sending them into the tunnels now."

"Good." Aaron took a deep breath. "Keep up the good work. Yell at us when you find something."

"On it."

"And…" Aaron ran his hand through his hair. "You might start working up some of that good old advice you're so good at."

The drone gave a nearly imperceptible dip, a nod of acknowledgement, before buzzing back to the garage. Harold followed the drone, a curious look on his face. Slowly, Aaron turned to Jasper and crossed his arms. "So, did you hear the deal between us?"

Jasper nodded and reached up, adjusting the beanie on his head. "He's getting the raw end of that deal. Most of my weapons are useless unless Harold or I are there to make them function, and he's got some *sweet* weaponry over there. You know what I could do with a nuclear blaster?"

"No, nor do I want to." Aaron shook his head. "Good. I just wanted to know that things were under control." After a moment, he cocked his head. "You *or* Harold, huh? You're really taking him under your wing."

"He's got talent." Jasper shrugged. "What can I say? The kid was born into it."

"I'm glad you're passing off your unique skill set." Aaron shook his head. "No telling what would happen if we couldn't make weapons that could level a town."

"We might need weapons like that before this is over." Jasper puffed out his cheeks and glanced pointedly at the castle-esque frat house. "Believe me, I've got just the stuff. I also just got my modification bench set up, which means that anything we need to put together, I can make it happen."

Aaron raised an eyebrow. "What happens when we face down werewolves? Got any silver for bullets?"

Jasper paused. "Not at this moment, but I can work something up quick enough."

"Hold off until we know exactly what we're facing." Aaron walked up to the front window. Garmund and Birch were long gone. "Based on the pattern of attacks, I'd say that we're dealing with *something* intelligent."

"Not mindless like the zombies?" Jasper frowned. "What makes you think that?"

Aaron shrugged. "It's sticking to the shadows. If it was mindless, some part of it would be pushing out, you know? A glimpse here, a shadow there. Instead… Nothing. Just the vanishings, which no one can yet explain."

"I think I can explain the disappearances." Frank's voice echoed through the room. "Head to Garmund's monitor in the garage, I'm going to try and pull up the feed."

Aaron grinned as they stepped through the door. "Anything interesting?"

"Oh, yeah." Frank chuckled. "This, you're going to have to see to believe."

CHAPTER 8

Smiling, Jeremy stepped out of Vanessa's room. She had offered to let him stay the night, but from what he had heard, random dorm checks after dark were occasional problems for romantic endeavors. He didn't want to get her in trouble, not so early in the semester. Besides, he had some things he needed to figure out first.

Slowly, he walked to the stairwell and began walking down the steps. For a brief moment, he thought about stepping outside. The sun was almost down, soon, it would be completely dusk. After a moment, though, he shook his head and kept walking. It would still be at least twenty minutes before the shadows extended far enough to give him complete mobility, and besides, he wanted to track down Gruen. Now that he was convinced that he was a vampire, he had some things to figure out.

It didn't take him long to reach the basement level. He was walking up to the broom closet when he heard something. It was like a whimper, barely audible, but for some reason it stuck in his mind. Slowly, he turned around to see a girl sitting in a study alcove, sobbing. She looked up at him, despair written all over her face.

"Anything I can do?" Jeremy paused. It typically wasn't in his nature to help random strangers out, but... Well, something was different about him now. It felt like he was being called to her, as if something in him was pulling them together.

"No, I don't think so." The girl took a deep, shuddering breath. "I just got dumped, is all. Nothing major."

"I'm sorry to hear that." Jeremy shook his head. "If it's any consolation, I think he missed out on a big prize, letting you go."

"You don't know me." The girl barked a laugh. "How can you say that?"

"Just a hunch." Jeremy walked over and sat down next to her. She flinched, and he shook his head. "Don't worry. I'm not here to try and pick you up, hurt you, anything like that. I just want to help. Tell me to get lost, and I'm gone."

The girl sighed. "I appreciate it. I really do. I think I want left alone, if that's okay."

"As I said, I'm gone." Jeremy stood up. "Good luck. I know you'll be okay."

She nodded and flicked her head, sending her hair flying back behind her head. In that instant, her neck was exposed, and something inside Jeremy awoke.

In an instant, the image of that neck filled his mind, like a vice that just kept squeezing harder. It was so smooth, so toned. He could see the veins building just below the surface the skin, filled with a warm liquid that just seemed… Oh, so good.

Jeremy shook his head and turned away. He was dating Vanessa, if he was going to bite anyone, it would be her. Besides, he wasn't about to go drinking someone else's blood. That was disgusting, wasn't it?

"Are you okay?" The girl's voice tantalized him. "Can I do anything for *you*?"

Jeremy's breath came in deeper gasps. His stomach growled, and the image of her neck filled his mind yet again. Desperately, he focused his gaze on the wall, trying to keep his attention on something, anything, else. He knew he needed to walk away, but…

"Hey." She stepped in front of him. Her neck was *right there*, full and pulsing with blood, open for the taking. When she spoke, her vocal cords rippled under the skin, pushing the muscles back and forth. "What's wrong?"

"You are." Jeremy's body snapped, and he bent forward. He could feel fangs slide out of his mouth, reaching across space. The girl didn't even have a chance to scream before he bit into the side of her neck.

Instantly, the fangs punched into her veins, slicing her jugular. Blood filled his mouth, a sweet, tangy liquid that he was certain hadn't tasted this good before he was a vampire. It was like eating the richest cut of prime rib on the planet, it was like sipping nectar from the cup of Olympus. He had to have more, his body was uncontrollable as he sucked every last drop of blood from her body.

After a short time, he didn't know how long, his stomach began to revolt. He had drank too much, far too fast. Slowly, he took a step back, feeling the blood dripping down his chin. Even though his stomach hurt, it was still an incredible feeling, that much power and life.

A dull thud echoed in his ears, and he glanced down. The girl lay on the ground, very much dead. A feeling of revulsion shot through him, and he backed away as quickly as he could. He… What had he just done? He had *killed* someone!

Suddenly, being a vampire didn't seem quite so interesting.

The image of the girl filled his mind again, memories of feeding on her, the feelings that it had brought up in him. With everything he had in him, he tried to force the images to go away. He hadn't done that! He couldn't have done that!

Footsteps sounded in a nearby hallway, and Jeremy raced for the broom closet. He threw the door open, grabbed for the trap door, and dove down into the darkness. Here, at least, no one would see him for his crimes.

A scream pierced his ears, a verbal reminder of what he had just done. Desperate to get away, he tore off into the tunnels, his feet pounding on the hard ground. He heard the trap door wrench open, and he gasped loudly. He didn't want to be caught, not like this! This wasn't him, he wasn't a murderer. He couldn't be!

A light flashed behind him, and he dove forward, desperately trying to put on speed. Something changed inside him, and he found himself flashing forward, zipping through the air with a velocity that he had no idea he could achieve. It seemed off, but he couldn't stop to think about it. He needed to keep running, to escape!

With a fury, he flashed through the tunnels, back to the central room. As he tore in, Gruen turned to look at him. Jeremy slowed to a stop, feeling his body become heavy and drop to the ground again. He landed next to a dead body, but paid it no mind. Slowly, he looked up at Gruen, desperation flooding his mind.

"Well, you mastered transformation." Gruen chuckled. "I suppose I should congratulate you. Still think you're not a vampire?"

"What the *hell* am I?" Jeremy's voice fought against him, words just didn't want to form. "I just…"

"You fed for the first time." Gruen shrugged. "I felt the same way. You get a little disoriented, but the power it gives you-"

"No, I don't feel any power." Jeremy slammed his fist into the ground, cracking the concrete. "I feel awful. I killed that girl!"

"And now you understand why it's so hard to hit that sweet spot where you can turn them." Gruen shrugged. "You have to stop yourself in the middle of all that. It's hard to keep your senses in the middle of a good meal."

"You're sick, you know that?" Jeremy gasped. "I hope you die a long and painful death."

"According to lore, we can really only die if we get staked through the heart with wood." Gruen shrugged. "I'm not in any particular hurry to try it out."

"Maybe you should be." Jeremy exhaled, trying to expel all memories of the girl. "We have to turn ourselves in."

"Why would we do that?" Gruen laughed. "We have all this power! We can rule the world!"

"Or we can let the rest of the world live in peace." Jeremy held up his hands. "I can't be a part of this! I can't just go around killing, and I can't subject *anyone* else to this torture!"

"I'm sure your mind will change with time." Gruen crossed his arms behind his back and started pacing.

"Never." Jeremy snarled. "I just can't sit by and watch while-"

A low buzzing noise interrupted their conversation. Jeremy glanced upwards to see a small drone flit into the room and start flashing around. A blinking red light seemed to focus on their position, and Jeremy growled. He was *not* going to take the heat for Gruen's killings.

"Oh, blast." Gruen muttered. "Keep your head down. I don't know what will happen here."

Without another word, Gruen leapt into the air. As he did so, his cape spread outward, catching the wind and pulling him upward. His face seemed to change, fur exploded outward, a snout formed, white teeth gleamed. In an instant, he had transformed into a bat, about a foot across.

Bat-Gruen slammed into the drone at full speed. The resulting explosion transformed the entire room into a raging inferno. The walls shook under the blast, and Jeremy was thrown backwards. He slammed into the far wall, mere moments before several shards of metal from the drone were propelled through his chest.

With that, the room fell silent. Small pings echoed through the air as bits and pieces of stone dislodged from the ceiling and dropped to the ground. Jeremy pulled himself away from the wall, glad that most of the metal seemed to have imbedded itself in the concrete behind him rather than sticking in his muscle. He could feel the wounds on his chest healing, and he took a deep breath. Good. He was still alive.

Bat-Gruen fluttered over beside him and transformed back into a human. He glanced at Jeremy, an odd look on his face.

"You seem startled."

Jeremy shrugged. "I didn't know we could turn into bats. Does that make us were-creatures?"

"No, it makes us vampires." Gruen shook his head. "Were-creatures are something else entirely, I believe. Besides, you were in bat form when you came in here."

Jeremy frowned. So *that* must have been why he was traveling so fast. "That was a *drone*! Someone is watching us!"

"So?" Gruen held up his hands. "It's not like they're going to come in swinging with stakes and crosses. By the time anyone realizes what we are, our reign will be complete."

"Yeah, well, I'd rather not take the chance." Jeremy stalked from the room. "I'm going to go turn myself in. I'm done living like this."

"I think you'll be back." Gruen's voice called behind him, taunting him. "Just you wait."

Jeremy was quite certain that he would not, indeed, be back, except for some unlikely coincidence or desperation. Without another glance back, he headed off into the night. He had work to do.

CHAPTER 9

"So, where does that leave us?" Aaron paused. "A bat attacked the camera. I hardly think that qualifies as noteworthy, except that we now probably have to pay to fix the tunnel system."

"I'd hold off on paying it, and just start keeping notes." Frank's voice came through the speaker. "You'll probably destroy a whole lot more before this is said and done."

"Your vote of confidence in our skills is overwhelming." Aaron muttered. "Does anyone know where his off switch is?"

"I'd say this is worth checking out." Harold frowned as he plopped onto the couch. "When the first few zombies his Lambspoint, they were just shambling corpses that couldn't escape from a seatbelt. A few hours later, they were two-story high monstrosities that could knock down a building. That bat was larger than it had any right to be. We may as well take a look."

"You're right." Aaron let out a breath. "Anyone up for the challenge?"

Jasper paused, then raised his hand. "I'll go. Harold can come, too."

Aaron turned to Bertha and cocked an eyebrow. "Any desire to tag along?"

"Not on your life." Bertha put her hands up and plopped down on a chair. "I'm not moving from this seat unless my life or Garmund's life depends on it."

"The kitchenette needs cleaned." Aaron waved his hand. "You can do that while they're out scouting. And your life *does* depend on it, because I'm giving you to Birch myself if you don't make yourself useful."

"Fine. I'm on it." Bertha stood up and wandered over to the small kitchen.

Aaron turned back to Jasper. "Anything you guys need before heading out?"

"I think we've got everything." Jasper chuckled. "I just need to grab my new gun, and we'll be good."

"New gun?" Aaron raised his eyebrows. "Anything good?"

"Nothing like anything you've seen before." Jasper grinned.

"That is, unless you've seen a standard taser before." Harold raised his hand. "Granted, this has a few more volts running through it, but..."

Jasper turned to glare. "It also doesn't shoot wires. Pure gas-fed electricity, there."

"You just *love* gas-fed weapons." Aaron turned and walked out of the room. "Let me know when you know something."

"On it."

Aaron smiled as his team headed out the door. One way or another, they were going to come out on top. They were going to stop the apocalypse, they were going to get Garmund back, and they were going to do it before the ARF knew what had happened. The thought filled him with pride, and he sank onto a chair in the garage. Things were looking up.

CHAPTER 10

"This looks awful." Harold muttered as he jumped down into the tunnel system. "It's dark. Things could jump out at us."

"You're a zombie." Jasper muttered as he jumped in after Harold. "You could get your head sliced off, and you'd just have a bit of inconvenience until you either grew a new body or got your head reattached."

"Not helping." Harold muttered. "You have no idea how awful dismemberment sounds. I mean, you're talking about getting sliced into pieces and *surviving*. I'd have to lay there, scattered across the ground, while you finished killing whatever it was that just took me apart."

"All you have to do is kill what's trying to kill you, and you're fine." Jasper chuckled. "That's not on me."

Jasper slid the cover back over the top of the tunnels, and he started walking. "The camera was this way.

From what we saw, it looks like the explosion was in a larger room at the center of campus."

"It wouldn't surprise me." Harold shrugged. "I visited a friend of mine at a college in Wyoming. They had a similar tunnel system, and it had a big room at the center. The mechanics at the college always claimed it was for an unbuilt plumbing system, but everyone there pretty much assumed it was built for the sake of throwing parties. That's what we used it for, anyway."

"Good to know you had your priorities lined up."

"Hey." Harold held up a finger. "I was only there once."

"And yet you mention parties. Plural." Jasper shrugged. "What were you doing? One crowd clears out, another files in?"

"Pretty much." Harold chuckled. "You should have seen it. It was-"

"Shh." Jasper held up a finger. Harold froze, not wanting any part of something trying to eat him. "Do you hear that?"

"It's either a leaky pipe or some drunk emptying his bladder."

"Not the dripping noise." Jasper growled. "Never mind. Come on, let's…"

A cloak billowed in front of them, coming out of the dark like a cloud of smoke. Jasper raised his taser and flicked on the light, illuminating the entire tunnel system.

In front of them, a man stood, tall and proud. His dark black eyes seemed entirely unphased by the light, and his pale skin stood out as a stark contrast to his long, dark robes. Something about his face seemed familiar, but Harold struggled to place it. It was like he knew the man.

"What are you doing in my lair?" The man crossed his arms and tried to project his voice. Instantly, Harold recognized the individual. He was several shades paler and quite a bit thinner, but there was no mistaking that air of false authority.

"Principal Gruen?" Harold frowned. "I thought…"

"Wait." Jasper held up his hand. "This is the guy who ran the school back in the zombie apocalypse, isn't it?"

"He's the one." Harold shrugged. "I didn't expect to see you here."

"I'll say." Jasper muttered. 'We thought you died. Some of us *hoped* you died."

"The comedy club is in town, I see." Principal Gruen muttered. "In any event, I am no longer Principal. I have moved on to grander things."

"Shakespeare imitator being another thing you failed at." Jasper chuckled. "Imagine that."

"I'll have you know that I am now Overlord Gruen." The man smiled, revealing a row of fanged teeth.

"You should stick with just Gruen." Harold shrugged. "I take it you're a vampire?"

Gruen glanced down at his robes. "I'm glad my terrifying demeanor comes through."

"Do we look terrified?" Jasper took a deep breath. "Anyone here mind if I fry him?"

"Go for it." Harold waved his hand. "Twenty to one he's the cause of the vanishings, which means that he's not himself anymore. Besides, he was never a great Principal anyway."

Gruen chuckled and took a step towards the duo. "I'm afraid that vampires can only be killed with a stake to the heart. Your weapons mean-"

Jasper fired a bolt of electricity into the vampire. Lightning arced up and down his body, crackling and sizzling. Gruen froze, then collapsed to the ground, twitching and convulsing. Jasper readjusted his aim, chuckling as he watched the vampire writhe.

"This was almost too easy."

"The real problem is what happens when the other vampires he's created decide to start acting up." Harold frowned. "Given their relatively few weaknesses and actual intelligence, they could do some real damage."

"I had the same thought." Jasper frowned in thought as the electricity continued to sizzle and zap. "It's also looking like this thing actually won't kill them. This much electricity would have put a normal person under in a matter of moments."

"He was never normal, even before the apocalypses started." Harold shrugged. "Keep zapping him. I'll check ahead to see what else might be around."

Jasper nodded, and Harold stepped around the convulsing body. He touched his wrist, arming a powerful flashlight strapped to him like a watch. Moving quickly, he made his way through the tunnels. Or, at least, he *tried* to make his way through the tunnels.

Almost instantly, he came to a fork in the path. Three more tunnels branched away, each presumably leading to a different area. Harold closed his eyes and took a deep breath, trying to think. He *could* just start exploring each one, *or…*

Or, he could try out one of Jasper's verbal spells.
Harold had spent almost every single night since the
incident at the temple pouring over the ancient texts, trying
to glean knowledge from them. There was a simple
technique that formed the basis for nearly all other verbal
alchemist spells, a spell that worked marvelously like
echolocation.

Slowly, Harold took a deep breath, then slowly let
it out. Air rushed between his lips, and he closed his eyes.
As he exhaled, he began to cause the air molecules to
vibrate, creating a resonating sound wave. A brief moment
passed, and an image appeared in his mind. He couldn't see
far down each tunnel, but he now had a mental map of a
significant portion of the nearby tunnels. Which, naturally,
allowed him to see that the far left tunnel would lead him to
the massive room at the center of campus.

It took him a matter of minutes before he reached
the center of the system. Slowly, he stepped into the room
and took a deep breath. After a few moments of
observation, there was only one thing he could conclude.
Gruen *sucked* at his job. Whatever had brought him back,
presumably one of the shards, it had chose the wrong
person. Dead bodies lay scattered across the floor, propped
up on pillows and blankets. None of them were moving,
though, and many of them were starting to show signs of
decay. Of the bodies, none of them appeared to be turning.

Behind him, a yelp sounded in the air. Harold
turned and held up his light. If Jasper was in trouble, he
needed to…

Something flickered in the air, and a bat flashed
past Harold's ear. There was a sickening splashing noise as
Gruen reformed in his vampire body, and hands clapped

down on Harold's arms, pinning them to his side. For the moment, Harold decided to play along with it.

"You know what your weakness is?" Gruen's voice purred in his ear. "You're too quick to leave your friends."

Fangs sank into Harold's neck. Though he felt them enter, he didn't feel an ounce of pain, and slowly turned his head to face the Principal. He could feel Gruen's lips on his neck, sucking for blood that wasn't going to appear.

"Actually, I'd be willing to bet that my weakness is getting shot in the head." Harold shrugged, broke out of Gruen's grasp, twisted around, and threw the man into a wall. Gruen gasped, dazed, and Harold continued. "You know, I would start listing *your* weaknesses, but I really don't have that much time."

"You don't know me." Gruen stood back up, fire in his eyes. "I'll destroy you."

Harold walked over, put a hand on Gruen's chest, and slammed him back into the wall. "Here's how we're going to play this. I want to know how you came back to life after that plant tried to destroy the school and we blew it up. I know you died there, because you're technically undead now. What brought you back?"

Gruen shook his head. "I don't know, and I'm not going to tempt the fates."

"Where did you wake up?" Harold held up his free hand. "That's another good place to start."

"I woke up…" Gruen frowned. "Why should I tell you this?"

"Several reasons." Harold paused, let go of Gruen's shirt, then leaned back and slammed a fist into his ribs. Gruen collapsed, and Harold knelt down. "First off, I want to end this apocalypse before the ARF decides to torch the place. Secondly, I know you were brought back by a shard of energy. I've been hopping around the world trying to find those shards, but someone keeps beating me to them. Some of them were taken by the likes of you, but others were taken by a man that makes all of us together look like easy pickings. Now, I'm willing to do pretty much anything to get my hands on that shard before he does, which means you need to start talking, and fast."

"A shard." Gruen paused. "About an inch long, made of stone, had a symbol carved in it?"

"That's the one." Harold nodded. "Where is it?"

"I dunno." Gruen shrugged. "I woke up with it in my hand. I figured it was just some random piece of debris I happened to grab on my trip through the nether regions, so I pitched it in the river I woke up by."

Harold slumped and slammed his head into the wall. Gruen frowned.

"I thought your weakness was heads."

"My weakness is an uncontrollable desire to beat the crap out of people who annoy me." Harold growled. "I'm sure you know how that feels."

"Well, now that I've answered your questions, I feel that you should answer some of mine." Gruen grinned slyly. "How many people do you have with you?"

"Enough to take down the likes of you." Harold shook his head. "Where's Jasper when I need him? I need some wood."

"Hey!" Gruen jumped up, breaking through Harold's grasp. In an instant, he had transformed into a bat and vanished into the darkness.

Harold stood there for a number of long moments before Jasper appeared. He looked out of breath, and chuckled as he stood there.

"Sorry about that. He managed to get away, and I turned down the wrong corner trying to chase him. He hurt you?"

"Not so you'd know." Harold signed and ran a hand through his hair. "The guy had the shard in his possession and threw it into a river."

"Do we know which one?" Jasper frowned. "We could start going through the nearby streams."

"He probably didn't travel very far from when he woke up." Harold frowned in thought. "I just don't see him as really being the planning and scheming type. We should be able to rewire one of the drones to search for the shard. Give it a pre-programed route, we can find it quick enough."

"How do you plan on doing the programming?" Jasper raised his eyebrows.

"I'll just have…" Harold's voice trailed off as he remembered that Garmund had been transferred. "Blast. I don't know. Alright, maybe we just start swimming the creeks. I'll figure something out. It gives us a starting point, at least."

Jasper nodded. "Can you do that thing like you did with the first chip?"

"The thing where I know where each and every one is?" Harold shook his head. "You know as well as I do that that only happened once, right as I died. If they've been moved since that point, I'm useless." Jasper cocked an eyebrow, and Harold hastened to correct himself. "I'm useless in *that* regard."

"Uh, huh." Jasper shook his head. "Well, vampires. At least we know that wood can kill them. Gruen was helpful enough there."

"What are you thinking?" Harold crossed his arms. "Crossbows?"

"Actually, I was thinking about wooden bullets." Jasper shrugged. "You get a real hard wood, something like an oak or a hedge, and we'll be in business. No point in leaving it to chance."

"Can we use alchemy to turn metal into wood?" Harold grinned. "That's got to be complicated."

"Extraordinarily." Jasper nodded. "You have to turn a finely-ordered metal crystal structure into a random, fibrous structure. The ritual to do something like that will take forever."

"Is there anything we could to do expedite it?" Harold bounced on the balls of his feet. "Come on, this sounds fun."

"Actually, I think there is." Jasper reached into his back pocket. Harold grinned in anticipation as Jasper pulled out a small knife.

"Awesome." Harold took the knife and admired its blade. "Do we have to slice someone's wrists? Cut up a mountain flower?"

"Nope." Jasper shook his head. "As I said, the ritual would take forever. As a substitute, we're going to do something just a bit different. Have you ever done much whittling?"

"Of course." Harold nodded. "I… Wait. We're carving all these bullets, aren't we?"

"We'll start as soon as we get home." Jasper grinned. "Get ready, young apprentice. Sometime, doing things well just takes a finer touch."

CHAPTER 11

Jeremy flashed through the air, looking for a safe place to land. His wings ached, but thus far, he hadn't been able to find a location that wasn't well-lit. Finally, ahead of him, a flat-topped building rose into the air, above the pesky streetlights that seemed so prevalent around the campus. Jeremy landed on the roof of a building and allowed himself to transform back into a human. In an instant, his skin started burning, and he leapt off the roof, transforming back into a bat. Idly, he noticed that the name on the side of the building read "St. Mary's Chapel." So much for taking a break.

Jeremy just shook his head and took off across campus. If he was right, a number of frat houses had been abandoned years before during a number of unrelated events. One of them would surely make a suitable lair until he could find a better location than the tunnels.

It took him a matter of minutes to get to the location. Lights brimmed from two of the old frat houses, and he swerved away from those. Across the street, though, another house stood abandoned. Without a second glance, Jeremy closed his wings and dropped down into the chimney, flashing out of the fireplace and transforming back into a human in an instant.

A muffled gasp sounded, and he glanced to his left to see two students making out. He opened his mouth and flashed his fangs, and they exploded out the front door as fast as they could. He chuckled, shut the door behind them, and flopped down onto the couch.

The moment he hit the soft cushion, memories came flooding back. Memories of the girl, the innocent individual he had consumed in an instant of passion. If Vanessa found out...

"No." He shook his head. There was no way Vanessa could find out. He... he hadn't meant to do it! It had been a moment of passion, nothing more. He belonged to Vanessa, and no one else.

Even as he thought it, he shook his head. If he couldn't control a moment of desire now, what was to say that he would be able to contain himself down the road? How would he resist the next time a girl walked around flashing her neck? Or literally anyone with blood? A wave of revulsion pulsed through his body, but he knew that it was a very real possibility. He simply didn't know enough about his new physiology to make any sort of a judgement call.

"I have to turn myself in."

It was the same thing he had told Gruen, the same thing that he continuously told himself. He could fly to the nearest police station, turn himself in, and await judgement. But then what would they do? He wasn't alive, not in the traditional sense. They would put a stake through him and be done with it. That was that, there simply weren't any other possibilities. If the police didn't do it, the government would. He was too dangerous to be out and about!

But then, if he was too dangerous to be on his own, where did that leave him? He didn't want to die, but he also didn't want anyone else to die.

Slowly, he began to think through the possibilities. What if... What if someone knew more than he did? He sat up with the thought. He was at a university, and a heavily churched university at that. Surely there was at least one faculty member who specialized in such things!

With that thought, he stood up and started pacing through the house. It was filled with leftover trash from when the home had been abandoned. Several scattered newspapers dated the home as being about four years without residents. That wasn't too old. With luck, there was a campus directory somewhere in the building.

It didn't take long to find the office for the frat. It was a small room, near the entrance, and seemed to have barely been touched when the home was abandoned. After attempting several times to open the jammed door, he finally resorted to kicking the blockade wide open, shattering the wood and sending splinters flying. A few of the slivers of wood stuck in his palm, eliciting a burning pain. He plucked them out as quickly as possible. Slowly, hoping he hadn't just set off any alarms, he stepped into the room.

A large pile of paperwork sat on the desk, untouched since the departure. Behind the desk, dozens of books were strewn about, including phone directories and address maps. After a few moments of searching, Jeremy found what he was looking for: a directory of all the professors on campus.

Quickly, he began flipping through pages, trying to find… What was he looking for? An expert on vampire lore? A history professor who might know if something like this had happened in the past? After several minutes of fruitless searching, he finally found a Professor Inkwood, an expert in supernatural studies and theory. Jeremy shrugged as he looked up the professor's home address. It would have to work.

Nodding in finality, he closed the book, walked to the front door, and slipped out onto the porch. The frats across the street seemed quite lively. In fact, if Jeremy wasn't mistaken, both of them had groups that were about ready to leave. Interesting. He would just have to be careful, then. No use getting caught just because a bunch of college students liked to stay up late partying.

With a rush, he jumped off the porch. His cape spread wide, transforming into a pair of wings that carried him high into the sky. In a mere instant, he was only a foot wide, flashing through the sky like a lightning bolt.

Several long minutes later, he finally found the street that the professor lived on. Finding the house was a little more difficult, as he couldn't remember if it was eight ten or eight oh one. He flashed back and forth between both houses, finally settling on eight ten after a drunk college student stumbled through the door of eight oh one. He doubted that the professor lived with any of his students.

After taking a deep breath, Jeremy flashed up to the front porch and transformed back into a human. Slowly, knowing that if he had made the wrong decision he was as good as dead, he walked up and knocked on the door.

The professor took only a moment to answer. The door cracked open, revealing a wizened man who looked like he could have been a wizard. His ancient eyes narrowed, and he frowned.

"I just gave out the assignment this afternoon. If you're already resorting to tracking me down at home, I'm afraid I'll just have to flunk you."

"You've got it wrong." Jeremy held up his hand. "I'm not a student. Well, not anymore."

The professor glanced at Jeremy's outfit. "Going to the theater?"

"No, I…" Jeremy sighed and glanced at the ground. "I need some help, and I don't know if you can help or not, but I'm rather desperate. Do you know anything about vampires?"

The professor narrowed his eyes. "What do you want to know about vampires?"

"It's hard to explain." Jeremy paused. "I think I might be one."

The professor's eyes snapped wide open. "I have some books in my study."

He turned to walk away, leaving the door wide open. Jeremy grinned and took a step forward. Rather, he *tried* to take a step forward. As soon as his foot hit the edge of the doorframe, a force field seemed to spring up, preventing him from pushing forward. He pushed against it, but to no avail. A moment later, the professor reappeared, a smile on his face.

"Well, that confirms it. You are, indeed, a vampire."

Jeremy let his head fall. "Because I can't enter a house without permission."

"Well, you have my permission to enter." Professor Inkwood nodded. "Please, come to my study. This is fascinating, don't you think?"

"I had some other words for it, come to think of it." Jeremy muttered as the force field dropped. He swept into the house, shut the door behind him, and followed the professor through the house to a small study. Professor Inkwood gestured to a large easy chair as they stepped into the room, and Jeremy happily sat down.

As he did so, he took a deep breath. The room was covered in books. Every wall was filled, floor to ceiling, with bookshelves. The professor started to pace in front of them, though he didn't grab any of the volumes for reference. When he finally spoke, it was with a sense of awe.

"So, you're a vampire. Wow. I've spent my entire life theorizing about creatures like yourself, but never been able to confirm their existence until now. This is incredible! Can you tell me how it feels to be undead?"

"It sucks." Jeremy crossed his arms. "I didn't come to you because I wanted to learn how to kill people better. I want to know how to be changed back."

Professor Inkwood sighed deeply. "I'm not sure that there *is* any way to change you back. By all accounts, you're dead, just not gone yet."

Jeremy's head fell. "You want to tell me how I'm dead and still sitting right here? I still think, I still react, my skin still looks healthy."

"You're also not breathing." Professor Inkwood shrugged. "I don't know if you've eaten anything yet or not, but by all accounts, vampires have to feed to replenish their bloodstream because they simply don't produce blood anymore. Thus, your body is dead."

"That's comforting." Jeremy muttered. "Look, I…"

"Before I can help you, I need to know a few things." Professor Inkwood held up his hand. "How were you turned into a vampire? Can you do the same to others?"

Jeremy shrugged. "I was bit by another vampire. He drained my blood, and some sort of energy took its place, or something. He mentioned a demon, but I really don't feel possessed."

"Yes, that makes sense." The professor smiled. "Have you tried to turn anyone else?"

"No, I frankly haven't." Jeremy put his hands on his knees and stood up. "Look, earlier today, I *ate* a girl. Not because I wanted to, but because she was there and my body literally couldn't stop itself. I don't want to do that again, not in a million lifetimes. What do I do?"

Professor Inkwood sighed deeply. "As far as my understanding of vampires goes, there really isn't a cure. People infected with vampirism often fight it for a time, but when their fast from blood leads them to extreme hunger and insanity, they accept their new dark nature and simply feed on the human race."

Jeremy shook his head. "Great. My destiny *was* to become an engineer and help build the human race. Now I get to eat it."

"There may be a solution, though." The professor held up a hand. "There are reports of some vampires fighting their nature by only preying on the sick and infirm. Now, several of them died as a result of disease picked up from their prey, but it could still be a viable option for you. Go to the hospitals, and only eat those who are dying anyway. Just make sure to avoid any sort of flesh-eating bacteria. Those could get a bit nasty."

"That just makes me even sicker." Jeremy stood up. "There *are* people in hospitals who get better miraculously. I might unknowingly take that away from them."

"It's entirely your call." The professor held up his hands. "I'm simply relaying information."

"Well, you're not fantastic about it." Jeremy growled.

"How am I supposed to be better?" Professor Inkwood threw up his hands. "It's not like many vampires wrote books on the subject! Most of what I have are secondhand accounts passed down from people who may or may not have been telling the truth. Vampires are a rare thing, they're not your run of the mill backwoods creature. Incidents like this only happen every so often, and…"

Something in that statement caught Jeremy's attention. "Incidents like this? You mean vampires suddenly cropping up in a population."

"Exactly." The professor waved his hands. "It happens through history, every two to three hundred years or so. Vampires show up in a people group, the people turn to fight them, there's a big battle, the vampires flee. Happens the same way every time."

"Are there any known triggers?" Jeremy leaned forward. "Has anyone ever discovered what causes the events?"

"No." Professor Inkwood took a deep breath. "I *can* tell you that such events are rarely isolated. Every time this has happened in the past, it has been accompanied by extended pockets of supernatural energy elsewhere across the globe. The last one occurred in the seventeen hundreds. Vampires rose in central Europe, zombies walked among the colonies, chupacabras hunted in Mexico. After a few years of it, it all stopped. Of course, at the time, no one knew that it was all happening simultaneously, it's only been in modern times that we've been able to piece the puzzle together."

Jeremy nodded. "So the last time was in the seventeen hundreds, no cause discovered. What about the time before that?"

"Before that, the events were actually mostly localized to a single continent." Professor Inkwood chuckled. "Ours. Well, North and South America. That time, someone actually *did* claim to find a cause."

"Really?" Jeremy sat forward, then frowned. "Wait. If we knew what it was, you would have told me already."

Professor Inkwood nodded sadly. "Unfortunately, no, we don't. There was a Spanish missionary who came over to our world with Columbus. He traveled the length and breadth of both continents over the course of fifty years, fighting supernatural elements and working to restore order. He documented all his travels, they've since been published widely. In fact, I think there's a movie about his life coming out in…" At Jeremy's look, the professor continued. "Anyway, you should be able to find his writings relatively simply. Jim Paulo. Any bookstore should have them."

"I don't have time to read or money to buy books." Jeremy spat. "I need answers and I need them *now.*"

Professor Inkwood sighed and rubbed his wrinkled jaw. "Well, if you're *desperate*…"

"Please believe me when I say that I am." Jeremy nodded.

"During my studies on Jim Paulo, I've been somewhat limited by the overwhelming blur between fact and fiction." Professor Inkwood frowned. "Fictitious accounts of Paulo's life began circulating as early as fifty years after his death, making it nearly impossible to discern what was real and what wasn't. Thankfully, I had the good fortune of encountering a scholar of particular note working as a curator for the Smithsonian. A man by the name of Lark, he has a position far lower than his knowledge would suggest. It would be a wise decision to pay him a visit."

Jeremy sighed and nodded. Washington D.C. was quite a distance away, but he supposed that it would be worth the flight. "I'll do it as soon as possible. Thank you."

"No problem." The professor sighed. "I'm just sorry I couldn't help more. Look…" He paused, and Jeremy hesitated. "If you need anything else, don't hesitate to let me know. I'd consider it an honor to help the new wave of vampires. Maybe this time, you won't have to be hunted to extinction quite so quickly."

"Well, I'm not exactly keen on turning too many more people." Jeremy shrugged. "I can't say as I really want the vampire population to start accelerating."

"I can understand that feeling." The professor started making his way to the door. "In any event, I wish you luck. Vampires…" The professor paused. "Vampires are superior to humans in nearly every way. Honestly, I look at these people who fought to stop them from taking over, and I just have to wonder why. Why stop something that can make you immortal? Why stop something that could elevate you beyond your wildest dreams?"

"Let me think about that for a moment." Jeremy shook his head. "They kill more people than they turn, that's probably not an incentive to let them live. Oh, not to mention that being a vampire *sucks*. I have to eat people, I can't enter a house without permission, I can't go out during the day, I can't come near a cross, I can't…"

"You can turn into a bat." The professor held up his hands. "You have increased strength, enhanced eyesight in the dark, and are immune to everything except wood."

"Wood." Jeremy reached over and tapped on a bookshelf. "As in the stuff that almost everything is made from? The material that people can literally just snap in half and turn into a decent weapon? That stuff?"

"I didn't say it was perfect." The professor shrugged. "I merely stated that it wasn't so bad. You do have access to a wide range of abilities that humans don't."

By now they had reached the front door. Jeremy nodded, and shook the man's hand. "Thank you for your help."

"It was my pleasure." Professor Inkwood gripped his hand tightly. Jeremy tried to pull away, but found

Inkwood grasping to his hand like a lifeline. "Before you go, could you do me a favor?"

Jeremy frowned, a feeling of unease rising in his stomach. "What's that?"

"Bite me." Professor Inkwood craned his neck to the side, exposing the skin. "Please."

Jeremy shook his head and jumped back, tearing out of the professor's grasp. "What? No!"

"I've helped you!" Professor Inkwood fell to his knees. "I explained all the benefits! Please, take me!"

Jeremy snorted and shook his head. "If you really feel that way, you need help."

"I'll tell the police about you if you don't help me!"

Jeremy just shook his head, turned, and walked out onto the front porch. Professor Inkwood screamed behind him, begging for transformation. Jeremy reached the open air, shook his head, transformed into a bat, and flashed off into the distance. He didn't understand why *anyone* would want that curse placed on them. Best to just leave the professor to his business.

As the stars turned overhead, a single flicker of light illuminated his world. This Lark person, whoever we was, sounded like a far more valuable resource than Inkwood. A trip to D.C., though… How was he going to manage that? He would need to let Vanessa know, of course. Brad could rot in hell for all he cared about, but…

Brad. The image of Brad's face filled his vision. Brad was the reason he was in this mess in the first place. Brad was the reason that he had killed a girl!

It was time he paid his old roommate a visit.

CHAPTER 12

Garmund peered around a corner as Birch reluctantly allowed Aaron into the basement of the frat house.

"What do we have here?" Aaron chuckled as he stepped into the armory. "Man, you guys have some nice stuff!"

Birch growled low in his throat before glancing up at Garmund. Birch had made it explicitly clear that if Aaron showed up at the house and caught so much as a glimpse of the hacker, there would be consequences. A weight settled in Garmund's chest as he slowly turned away.

"Hey, Gar!" A voice sounded behind him, and he turned to see the ARF's pilot jogging up to meet him. "How are you getting settled in?"

"All things considered, not horribly." Garmund shrugged, trying to force a smile to his face. The amenities *were* substantially nicer than what the Squad had access to. He had his own room, complete with enough outlets to power all his equipment. "I don't know. I just…"

"You're not really fitting in." The pilot took a deep breath. "I understand the feeling. When I was first requisitioned by the ARF, I was pretty much in shock. You have all these great soldiers, and then you have me. You know what I'm saying?"

Garmund nodded. If he was right, based on what Inspector Birch had told them, the pilot was originally supposed to join the Squad, and General Birch had stolen him first. If only he could remember the pilot's name…

"I know exactly what you're saying." Garmund sighed, took a deep breath, and continued. "Okay, I'm going to be completely honest. I don't remember your name."

"That's fine!" The pilot grinned. "Rodger. Aviator extraordinaire. Well, aviator, mechanic, really anything with vehicles. You actually met me a few months ago. Well, you hijacked my plane."

"Rodger." Garmund rolled the name around on his tongue. "Oh, right! That *was* you, wasn't it?" After a moment, he frowned. "I'll do my best to remember that. Names aren't my strong suit."

"I feel you." Rodger nodded. "Machines, or computers in your case, are just so much easier to work on than humans. They always react a certain way, and yet each one has its own unique personality that just makes you love them so much more."

"Uh, huh." Garmund nodded, mostly ignoring the talk. "So, what's up? Aaron obviously found something before Birch did, but I'm low enough around here that I don't really know what."

"Join the club." Rodger leaned against the wall. "I just fly people where they need to go. Oh, and build stuff. Birch isn't about to let me pick up a weapon."

Garmund raised an eyebrow. "Then what in the world do you do around here?"

"Read comics, mostly." Rodger shrugged. "I'm reading through an excellent fantasy series right now, if you'd be interested in borrowing any of them. When I'm not doing that, I'm usually trying to trick out the vehicles we drive around. Keeps me busy, you know?"

"Yeah." Garmund nodded, then sighed. "Well, I suppose I should probably go fire up my equipment. Birch is probably going to want us up and running as soon as Aaron gets done gloating about whatever he found."

"Oh, he'll just send out the soldiers." Rodger waved his hand. "We've got two guys monitoring the security feeds. They'll watch the guys' backs while the soldiers do the dirty work. Unless Birch tells you to do something, you'll probably spend most of your time around here being quite bored."

"Great." Garmund shook his head. "This is the worst, you know that? He pulls me away, just to spite Herford, and he doesn't even have the good graces to let me help out on his side. He's wasting my talents, and I frankly just want to do something."

"Hoo, baby!" Aaron stepped out of the weapons room, an RPG cradled in his arms. "This should be fun to play with."

"Play. Yes." Birch muttered as he followed him out. "You managed to find the source. Congratulations. Shall we raise the wager a bit?"

"First one to bring a dead vampire to the other?" Aaron raised an eyebrow.

Birch nodded after a few moments. "If the vampires crumble to dust, you must bring proof of a vampire kill, whatever that may be."

"Deal." Aaron nodded. "We'll be off, then."

With that, Aaron walked out of the house. Garmund turned to leave, but Birch caught up to him.

"Garnumd, my friend!"

"It's Garmund."

"Yes, I'm sorry." Birch put his arm around Garmund's shoulder. "Just how are you feeling today?"

"Like I'm sick of just standing around." Garmund muttered. "What are we up against? Vampires?"

Birch nodded. "It appears that way. I'm sending out my soldiers now to start apprehending the beasts. I want you to do something for me while they're at it."

"Name it." Garmund crossed his arms. He had very little desire to actually do anything for the general, but if he could do *something*...

"In your room, one of the computers you have access to is a real-world simulator." Birch gestured in the general direction of Garmund's quarters. "It can create any location or situation possible on the planet, complete with every known element and compound we've managed to record. You can do whatever you want, however you want. Create any situation you could ever imagine."

Garmund nodded. "You want me to start running scenarios, try to figure out what approach will work best."

"Basically, yes." Birch nodded. "In your room, you'll find a list of explosives and quantities, containing the exact amounts of each that we have access to for this job. I want you to figure out how to place them around campus to result in the maximum possible level of carnage and destruction."

Garmund froze. "You want to kill lots of people?"

"I want to get results." Birch stepped forward, eyes boring into Garmund's. "Washington doesn't care about how many civilians we managed to save, it cares about how many hostiles we managed to kill. If we take out a handful of students, so be it, as long as we manage to take down the threat. See what I'm saying?"

"No." Garmund crossed his arms. "Preservation of human life should be at the top of-"

"Oh, for goodness's sake!" Birch roared. "If we don't stop it here and now, it could overtake the world!"

"*Could!*" Garmund spat back, not caring how it might affect him. He had been ripped from his squad and thrown into a pack of killers. "There's no guarantee! I will *not* use my talents to aid in the murder of innocent civilians. Not on your life."

"Look, you know as well as I do that things aren't right around here." Birch stepped forward. "Apocalypses are popping up across the globe. Someone or something is causing them, one after another. We have to take care of this, and we have to take care of it fast, or we might miss the next one entirely. Do you want that on your conscience?"

"I'd rather have that than the guilt of killing innocents."

"Alright, then, have it your way." Birch waved his hand. "You'll just have to spend your time here locked up in the brig. Soldiers! Arrest this man."

There was a slight pause. Rodger, who hadn't moved during the conversation, held up his hand.

"You sent the soldiers out on patrol. There's no one around to arrest him." Rodger tilted his head to the side in thought. "Give me a gun and I'll consider it, though."

Birch sputtered. "Why, you…"

"And I'm not arresting myself." Garmund crossed his arms. "I'll be in my room, probably playing with the simulator. However, I will not be figuring out how to destroy the campus, I'm going to be trying to figure out a way to stop this problem. Understand?"

"Perfectly." Birch ground out.

Garmund nodded, spun on his heel, and walked towards his room. The moment he was inside, he shut the door and slumped into his computer chair. Idly, he connected to the internet and began pulling things up. A small smile creased his face as he thought about connecting to his hardware in the Squad's house. The only thing that stopped him was the realization that Birch probably had everything in the room monitored.

With nothing else to do, he pulled up the simulator and began fiddling with settings. He had it, he might as well play with it. Maybe he could recreate the ARF house and blow it up. The thought filled him with joy, and he set about building it in the software.

He had only been working for a few minutes when he found his thoughts wandering. His fingers moved across the keyboard of their own accord, and a face took form on the screen. The wild hair, the way her eyes always bored into him. It was an old photo, a mug shot pulled from Birch's archives, but… It was all he had left of the only woman ever to show interest in him. All he wanted to do was get back to his team. One way or another, he was going to find a way to rejoin them.

CHAPTER 13

"You think you can amp this up enough to take down a building?" Aaron frowned as Jasper took the RPG from his hands. "Not that I'm *looking* to take down a building, but…"

"Yeah, I can do that." Jasper frowned, then turned and handed the weapon to Harold. "Actually, I want to see *you* do it."

"Me?" Harold's eye shot wide open. "Why me?"

I think that you're getting good enough that you can handle it." Jasper shrugged. "That and I'm really tired. I think I'm going to go take a nap. I expect it shining and ready by the time I awake."

Harold glanced down at the weapon. "Do you want it sheathed in wood too?"

Aaron raised an eyebrow. "Actually, that sounds wonderful. Do that."

Harold groaned. "I have to learn to keep my mouth shut."

"You'll learn after awhile." Jasper patted him on the shoulder. "Come on, let's get out of here."

They vanished into the hallway, and Aaron scratched his head. "Bertha? You around here?"

"Right here." Bertha's head appeared around the corner. "What's up?"

"I'd like to go out and patrol for a bit." Aaron shrugged. "I think we should have two heads, though. You're coming with me."

"Why not Jasper?"

"He's helping Harold build a weapon."

"Why not Harold?"

"He's building a weapon."

"Why not…"

"Those are the only two options other than you!" Aaron threw his arms up. "Just bite the bullet and let's go, okay? We have to bring back proof of a dead vampire or-"

"Or what?" Bertha raised an eyebrow. For the first time, Aaron noticed just how puffy her eyes really were. "Or Birch gets bragging rights over you? Gets to gloat? Gets to raid our weapons stash? Jasper and Harold are the only ones who know how to work any of that, the moment they take it, it'll turn into nothing more than a hunk of metal."

"I know." Aaron held up his head. "There could be people dying out there right now. We have to get out there and stop it."

"You can't tell me that you actually care about those people." Bertha crossed her arms. "You just don't want to be upshown. It's the same as Lambspoint."

"I do care." Aaron crossed his arms to match Bertha. "You want the truth?"

"Please." Her voice was short.

"I care about our team." Aaron stepped up. "You and Jasper are still on the chopping block, and aren't going to move from it until we find a manage to beat this mess. Garmund may not be here, but if we fail, you know that he'll go down, too."

"I don't care about myself." Bertha glanced down and to the side before looking back up at Aaron and nodding firmly. "I care about Garmund."

"Good." Aaron nodded. "Then let's get out of here. Soon." Aaron gestured towards the front door. "If you don't, I'll put you on sewer detail."

"I'm coming." Bertha grumbled. "What weapons are we taking?"

"Until Jasper manages to craft some wooden bullets, we're using good, old-fashioned stakes." Aaron shrugged and grabbed a long shaft off the couch. "Just like they did in the olden days."

"In the olden days, I think they just died." Bertha shook her head. "If I'm going out there, I want something more substantial than a stake."

"A stake is what you're getting." Aaron snarled and slammed his hand into the wall. He knew it wasn't fair to yell at her, but... Their team was getting picked apart like a carcass on the highway. They *had* to start showing some results, and soon!

Bertha sighed deeply, walked over to the couch, and picked up a sharpened shaft of wood. Aaron nodded, and they stepped out the front door.

From there, they began wandering towards campus. Aaron frowned as he tried to figure out where the vampires would go. Presumably, they would abandon the tunnels, now that they had been exposed there. That meant that they would be hunting in locations heavy with student traffic.

"We need to head for the gas station." Aaron nodded after a moment. "When we fueled up earlier, I saw a sign that said that they were open all night."

"So?" Bertha looked up at the sky. "It's also really well lit, which means that the vampires aren't going to want to attack there for fear of revealing themselves. Not to mention that fact that anyone could just jump in their car and pretty much be safe."

"I'm not talking about people fueling up." Aaron shook his head. "Not even potheads get the munchies like college students hyped up on caffeine at midnight and later. The convenience store at the college I went to was always busy, even at three in the morning, because college students always want their snacks. All we have to do is watch the path between the station and the dorms, and…"

"Civilians!" A voice echoed from behind them. Aaron and Bertha both turned to see two men, both dressed in what appeared to be SWAT armor, running up to them. As they got closer, Aaron noticed the name emblazoned on their chest. ARF.

"So, your master let you off the leash for a bit?" Aaron crossed his arms as both men drew weapons. "Tell me, how angry is he at the loss of his finest weapon?"

"Angry enough." The man in the lead brushed past Aaron without a second glance. "Stay out of our way, okay?"

"I'll stay out of the way of whomever I please." Aaron started walking again, making sure to keep pace with the two horribly out-of-place soldiers. "You know, you have targets painted across your backs, right? The vamps are going to see that and attack you first."

"That's what we're counting on." The second soldier muttered. "They attack us. We kill them. We go about our business. Get the picture?"

"I get that you guys have no idea what you're doing." Aaron muttered. "Is there even an ounce of wood on that costume?"

"Wood? Now you've got to be joking." The soldier muttered. "Look, I've seen some weird stuff on this team, and I'm not going to say that I can explain it all, but I do know that everything, even zombies, will die if you put enough lead through them. Vamps will be no different."

"Care to test that?" A voice echoed out of the darkness. Both soldiers flipped around and stood, back to back, ready to fight. Aaron gripped his stake a little harder, ready to let Bertha really kick some butt.

With a snap, a dark shadow materialized above them. A man, easily recognizable as Gruen, dropped down from the trees and landed on the opposite side of the two soldiers. The first soldier screamed as Gruen bit into his neck, and the second soldier spun. Almost instantly, the second soldier opened fire, putting round after round into the monster.

Aaron took a step forward, but really couldn't do much with the machine gun fire. The second soldier simply didn't seem to realize that all his bullets were doing was annoying the vampire to no end. In the dim lighting, Aaron could see the projectiles simply passing through the man, doing no harm whatsoever.

After a few moments, the first soldier collapsed on the ground. The second soldier continued to pour machine gun fire into the vampire, up until the point that the vamp latched onto his neck.

Finally, as the bullets died down, Aaron lunged forward. With everything he had in him, he jabbed the stake into the back of the vampire. With a sickening thud, the stake simply slammed into the vampire's spinal cord and skipped off, doing no harm whatsoever. Aaron stood there for several more moments, jabbing again and again at the vampire. Bertha just stood there and watched, angrily, as Aaron continued to fail.

"You're going to need a sharper stake." The vampire finally let go of his victim and turned to face Aaron. "The cape's made of leather. You'll…"

"Yeah, I know." Aaron waved his hands. "Can we get onto the part where you start talking about your evil plan, we listen, and then escape and thwart your plan?"

"I'm afraid not." Gruen chuckled. "You'll have to bow to my glory!"

"His plan sucks." Another bat soared down and transformed into a human, identically-clothed, and crossed his arms. "He's basically just trying to turn lots of people into vampires. I think I'm his only success as of this moment."

"Get behind me, boy." Gruen snapped. "What do you think you're doing?"

"I've *killed* people." The boy shook his head. "People need to know about us. I don't want to be like this."

Aaron held up his hand. "Okay, this isn't what I was expecting."

"No." Gruen turned and glared. "It really wasn't."

"No one cares." The boy waved Gruen away. "The name is Jeremy. I'm just trying to stay alive right now. Please, if you would, just help me."

"How can we help?" Aaron frowned. "What can we do?"

"Find a way to turn me back." Jeremy looked down at his hands. "I don't want to be like this. I don't want to be a monster."

Aaron nodded. "Alright, we'll try. I promise."

"Thanks." Jeremy nodded. He glanced at Gruen and shrugged. "For what it's worth, I didn't mean to interrupt. I was just flying over, and figured I would try to stop you as much as possible."

"I'm going to kill you." Gruen growled.

"If I was actually concerned about that possibility, I wouldn't be doing what I was doing." Jeremy shook his head, then turned back to Aaron. "Look, I'll talk to you later. I do have a few things to take care of, but we'll meet back up, I promise. Any questions you have, I'll be happy to answer."

With that, Jeremy transformed back into a bat and flashed away. Gruen was left steaming, eyes burning with passion. Aaron crossed his arms and raised an eyebrow. "Looks like your own creations aren't willing to respect you."

"I'll make them respect me."

"Have you not figured out that no one accepts you as a credible threat?" Aaron shook his head. "You've killed a few people. Okay, you're a murderer. No one thinks you're capable of ending the world."

"Their loss." Gruen shook his head. "I could kill you right now."

"Do that and die." Harold's voice echoed from behind him. Gruen turned to see Harold walking up with a weapon that looked like a pipe strapped to a tank of compressed air. "See this? Do anything and I fire. This going to be a *lot* more powerful than a stake."

"You people are ridiculous." Gruen shook his head and jumped up into the air. A moment later, he was nothing more than a bat, winging away.

Harold lowered the weapon and stepped up to the fallen soldiers. "Did he do this?"

"You'd better know it." Aaron shook his head. "Even if he can't turn them, he can sure do a good bit of damage."

Harold nodded. "So, we have to stop him. Kind of a letdown, all things considered."

"You're telling me." Aaron sighed. "Here I was expecting an epic battle."

One of the soldier on the ground began to stir. He raised up onto his arms, rolling over to glare at the team. Eyes glinted dark, set against a skin that now looked as pale as ice. Harold fired his weapon into the monster's chest. The vampire had a moment to look surprised before it vanished in a cloud of dust. Harold frowned, then fired the weapon into the second soldier. Nothing happened, and Harold shrugged.

"I guess that one didn't turn."

"I guess." Aaron shrugged. "I don't know, I guess I was just expecting some sort of major apocalypse again.

This… This is kind of a letdown. We're pretty much just tracking a serial killer. Next time, just put a stake through him. We can't have him kill anyone else."

"You think we'll see him again?" Harold raised an eyebrow. "If I was him, I would be flying away as fast as I could."

Aaron shook his head. "He's too dedicated to his pride. He'll be back, I'm certain of it."

"Well, if you are." Bertha shook her head and stuck her stake back in her belt. "I'm heading back to the house. I'm tired and want my beauty sleep before things get really crazy."

Aaron raised an eyebrow. "I thought we just determined that there wasn't that much of a threat."

Bertha laughed darkly. In the glint of the streetlights, he could see more tears dripping down her face. "Birch is going to blame you for the death of his squad. That's something I have every intention of missing."

Aaron nodded. "Go. I can't say as I'm particularly looking forward to that, either."

Bertha vanished into the dark, and Harold paused. "Do you mind if I stay out and patrol with you? That guy *is* a killer, and if we can end him right off the bat, we prevent anyone actually competent at the job from rising."

"Works for me." Aaron nodded. He turned and started walking along the path. "Can you tell me something?"

Harold shrugged as he readjusted the weapon. "That depends. What do you want to know?"

Aaron sighed. "I don't know. There's just something about this whole situation that seems off. We have vampires that don't really seem like a threat, and we have a second squad that's trying to break us apart. Do you see anything wrong with this scenario?"

Harold paused. "Maybe we're looking at this wrong."

"What do you mean?" Aaron frowned. "How should we be looking at it?"

"What caused the vampires in the first place?" Harold shrugged. "What caused the zombies? What caused all the stuff that the ARF is going after? Things like that don't just happen on their own, and I don't think that Incacheck is good enough to have caused *all* of it."

Aaron nodded slowly. It was a possibility that had been growing in the back of his mind, a possibility that he really didn't want to accept. "Do you have any theories?"

Harold hesitated. "No. I really don't."

Aaron was quite certain that that was a lie, but he decided not to pursue it any farther. He was getting ready to ask another question when a burst of light lit up the sky. For a brief moment, it looked almost like daytime. Aaron frowned, glancing through the stars for the source of the light.

"What in creation was that?" He frowned. "Anything you recognized?"

"Not one bit." Harold frowned. "I…"

With a roar, pink flames rolled through the sky. They weren't overly bright, but they were certainly there. Harold gasped and gripped the rifle a little tighter. Aaron noticed the movement.

"You recognize *that*?"

"It looks like something Jasper and I ran into on our last trip." Harold took a deep breath as the flames faded. "I think vampires just became the least of our problems."

CHAPTER 14

Jeremy flashed through the sky, intent on reaching his old dorm room as quickly as he could. He had wasted enough time already, and knew that Brad would be furious at him for not showing up as soon as possible. Oh, but how would *that* play out? Jeremy was a vampire because of Brad. He had split concrete with a single punch. Just *think* of what he could do to his old roomie.

After a few minutes, he reached the dorm building. From there, it took him several more minutes before he was able to figure out which room was his. He could have walked there easily had he been inside, but trying to find the same location from the outside was substantially more difficult.

When he finally did manage to locate the dorm room, he grinned as widely as his bat form would allow him. He could see Brad sitting with his back to the window, relaxing on his bed. The only problem was that the window wasn't open. Oh, well. Idly, Jeremy flashed up to the window, flipped upside down, and latched onto the brick just above the opening.

In that moment, as he glanced into the dorm room, his heart lurched. Brad was relaxing on the bed, alright. Right next to him, arm around his torso, was Vanessa. She was sobbing, chest heaving, and Jeremy's gaze narrowed. Of course. Trying not to be noticed, he edged up to the window and listened as closely as he could.

"He… He killed her." Vanessa gasped. "It had to be him. It had to be."

"Shh." Brad held her close. "I'm sure there was something else going on."

"He's a *vampire*!" Vanessa hissed. "A vampire! Do you have any idea what it's like knowing that your boyfriend is a monster?"

Brad hesitated for a moment. "I don't swing that way, so-"

"You know what I mean!"

Brad sighed and nodded. "Yeah. No, I really don't know what that feels like."

"Well, it's awful." Vanessa shook her head. "I just had to play along until he finally left. And then he goes and eats someone in the basement! He didn't even have the decency to bite me!"

Brad's eyebrows lifted. "You *wanted* him to bite you?"

"If he's going to be immortal, the least he could do was take me with him." Vanessa shook her head. "Now… Now I just want him to leave me alone. I never want to see him again."

"Do you really mean that?" Brad ran his hand along her back. "You guys have been dating for a long time."

"Yeah, when he was still human!"

"Look, I have no idea what you're going through." Brad sighed. "I really can't empathize, but I'm going to try. Just know that I'll always be here for you."

"Thanks." Vanessa snuggled up closer to Brad. "Promise you'll protect me if he shows up. I don't want to die."

"I promise." Brad took a deep breath. "I promise."

Jeremy's blood flared inside him. With a rush, he detached from the ledge, flashed up in the air, and made a flying dive at the window. When he was getting close, he transformed back into his human form and crashed through the window at quite a speed. He hit the floor and rolled, coming up near the door.

Brad and Vanessa jumped up at his entrance. Brad held Vanessa close, and Jeremy flashed his fangs.

"I leave you for three hours and you go hook up with him?" Jeremy growled. "I thought you said things were okay between us."

"You might have eaten me if I said I was freaked out by it!" Vanessa took a step back. "I was scared."

"So you went to him?" Jeremy's voice shook with anger. "All we've been through, all we've done, and you take solstice in him?"

"I had to do *something*!"

"You could have talked to me!" Jeremy roared. "All you would have had to do was tell me I wasn't invited into your room, and I couldn't have touched you. We could have had a normal conversation, and I could have explained myself."

"You've done enough explaining." Vanessa shook her head. "I really *was* going to try and give you a chance, but then you went and killed the girl in the basement."

"I didn't mean to!" Jeremy got down on his knees. "It was an accident!"

"You just lost control of your body, got swept up in whatever hormones you possess now?" Vanessa snapped. "Is that what happened?"

Jeremy nodded. "Pretty much, yeah. I hadn't ever experienced it before, and didn't know how to fight it!"

"You've never experienced it before?" Vanessa took a step back. "You didn't have feelings of hunger when you were around me?"

Jeremy held up his hand. "I'm confused."

"You bit *her*, not me!" Vanessa gasped. "You cheated on me!"

"You want me to eat you?"

"Not anymore!" Vanessa shook her head violently. "Not with what you've become. I… If this is the new you, I don't want to be that kind of monster."

Jeremy sighed. "Are we talking about the vampire or the cheating?"

"I don't know!" Vanessa screamed. "Look, I… I don't know!"

Jeremy sighed and forced himself to his feet. "Let me prove myself, okay?"

"How are you going to do that?" Vanessa shook her head. "What could you possibly do to prove yourself to me?"

"I was going to ask you the same thing." Jeremy hung his head. "What can I do? I'm willing to do anything you ask."

Vanessa took a deep breath. "You have to prove to me that you can fight the monster."

"How?"

"I don't want you feeding on anyone." Vanessa nodded. "Come back to me in two weeks. If you haven't eaten anyone, we'll talk."

Jeremy nodded. "How will you know if I'm telling the truth?"

"I'll know." Vanessa snarled. "Don't try to slip out of it."

"Don't worry." Jeremy nodded. "Just… Promise me one thing as well."

"Name it." Vanessa's voice became substantially more shrill.

"Stay away from Brad." Jeremy crossed his arms. "I made a mistake, but I'm not gone. Let me make an effort before you give up on me for him."

Vanessa nodded. "Done."

"Hey!" Brad's voice sounded hurt. "I…"

"I should be going." Vanessa nodded. "You two probably have a lot to talk about."

Jeremy nodded. "See you in two weeks."

"Yeah." Vanessa shook her head and started to walk out of the room.

"Wait." Jeremy held up a hand. "I have an idea. Something you might want to try."

"Okay." Vanessa crossed her arms shortly. "What?"

"Go get one of those body painting things done to your neck." Jeremy shrugged. "I'm pretty sure a painted cross would have the same effect as a solid one. I'm not the only vampire out there, you know."

"I'll keep that in mind." Vanessa turned and vanished out of the room. Jeremy took a deep breath and turned to face Brad.

"You'd better have one hell of an explanation." Brad's gaze was stony. "Otherwise I don't have a single issue with killing you, here and now."

"Well, I can see that we're on good terms." Jeremy shook his head. "When we were attacked in the tunnels, I got bit."

"And it took you three days to get back to me?"

"I was unconscious for those three days!" Jeremy walked over to Brad and grabbed his shirt, causing him to flinch substantially. "When I came to, my first idea was to go see my girlfriend, not the person who talked me into going into a vampire-infested tunnel system. Sorry if that was the wrong thing."

Brad frowned. "Are you-"

"Angry with you?' Jeremy's blood began to boil. "I wasn't, but now that you mention it, let's talk about some things. I wanted nothing to do with that tunnel. I wanted nothing to do with your scheme. If you hadn't talked me into going, I would be sitting on the throne of *Empire* rather than trying to convince my friends that I'm not trying to kill them."

"You're a vampire!"

"And it's your fault!" Jeremy roared. "You talked me into going down there, and now my life is ruined. I might be immortal, and I might be able to turn into a bat, but I can never again see the sunlight. I can never again enter a church, watch Vanessa sparkle with her favorite piece of jewelry, or walk through a crowd of people without wanting to bite them on the neck. Come to think of it, your neck is looking pretty good right about now."

"You promised Vanessa." Brad tried to flinch away. "It was like two seconds ago."

"I'm not going to." Jeremy moved closer, letting his teeth rest mere inches away from Brad's neck. "I just want you to understand the gravity of the situation. You ruined my life, and now you're trying to steal my girl. I literally have nothing else to do for the next two weeks other than watch you two, so if you make a move, I will know, and I will leave your body where no one will find it. Get the picture?"

Brad nodded. "You'll kill me."

"No." Jeremy shook his head. "I'll drain you just enough that you turn, and while you're unconscious, I'll find a construction site and dump you in a pool of wet cement. It sets around you, and you spend the next hundred years, maybe even longer, imprisoned, unable to move so much as a finger, but painfully aware that you're alive and can't die. Get the picture?"

Brad nodded tightly. "Got it."

"Good." Jeremy smiled thinly and stepped back. "Well, now, I-"

A burst of light lit up the night sky like midday, and Jeremy shrank back from the window in pain. It wasn't as extreme pain as the sun itself, but it sure tingled. A moment later, the burst faded, only to be replaced by a pink flame. As the flame burned out, something inside Jeremy began to twinge.

"What was that?" Brad frowned. "Something to do with the vampires?"

"I don't know." Jeremy felt a physical force within his chest, pulling him towards the window. "I think it's something different, something powerful."

"Good powerful or bad powerful?" Brad frowned.

"Bad." Jeremy gasped as the force blossomed into pain. "Shit. I can't hold this much longer. Whatever this is, it's manifesting itself rapidly. I've got to go. Be careful, okay?"

Brad nodded as Jeremy transformed into a bat and flashed out the broken window. The pain eased, but only for a moment. He began winging across campus, feeling it pull him to the south. If he tried to deviate from the pattern in the slightest, pain rose in his chest, tearing him apart. With nothing else to do, he simply followed the pain.

He just wished he knew what was at the other end.

CHAPTER 15

Aaron and Harold tore back across campus, towards the house. Aaron didn't know what Harold had meant, but he assumed that it was nothing good. The boy was certain that the pink fire corresponded to something on his travels, but he wasn't saying much more than that. All he had done was mutter the word *Incacheck* under his breath.

As they reached the house, Harold ducked into his room. Aaron watched him go, then reached up and keyed his earpiece. "Frank?"

"Yeah?" The voice came back muddled and groggy. "What's up?"

"Have there been any sightings of Dr. Incacheck in the Philadelphia area?" Aaron frowned. "Confirmed or otherwise?"

It took a few moments for Frank to respond. "It doesn't look like it. The last confirmed sighting of the good doctor was actually back in Lambspoint. Unconfirmed sightings have been popping up around the globe, but nothing credible. The most recent was in Europe, right in the middle of Germany."

"Interesting." Aaron frowned. "I wonder what he's doing there?"

"We just established that it was *un*confirmed. That said, if he *is* there, he's probably getting ready to unleash a new strain of zombie on the population." Frank yawned loudly. "Why'd you guys have to wake me up in the middle of the night?"

"We haven't gone to bed yet. You'd still be awake if you were out here, too."

"Add that to the list of reasons why I'm staying here." Frank muttered. "Hey, did something weird happen near you?"

"You mean like a giant flash of light?" Aaron chuckled. "That's next on our list of things to ask you."

"Yeah." Frank's voice sounded distracted. "It looks like it was pretty widespread, whatever it was. People are reporting seeing something as far north as Washington. Given the last panic there, things are being stepped up pretty quickly."

"Where was the light localized to?" Aaron tried to focus. If Washington got involved, The ARF was going to go on the move faster than he could blink.

"It looks like the epicenter was south of you." Frank mused. "About ten miles, above a heavily wooded area."

"Anything special about the woods?"

"Not so you'd know." Frank yawned again. "Looks like it's owned by a super rich guy. Billionaire or something. Owns a resort on one of the mountains."

"We need to get there. Now." Aaron nodded. "I need directions on my cell phone by the time we're in the vehicle."

"Any reason why you need to go there now?" Frank slurred. "It may have been something completely unrelated."

"Is the ARF headed that way?" Aaron scratched his head and glanced out the front window. In answer, three military vehicles tore past the house, screeching into the night.

"As fast as they can go." Frank's voice started to sound concerned. "Looks like their official orders from Washington are to kill anything they find there, including any humans."

"Then we need to get there." Aaron nodded. "I want the fastest route possible. Everyone! Up and at 'em!"

Bertha materialized from her bedroom. "I'm driving, aren't I?"

"Standard assignments." Aaron nodded. "Harold, Jasper…"

Jasper stalked into the room, bleary-eyed, holding a number of deadly-looking weapons. "We're here. Wooden bullets, at least on a few of them. Standard ammo on the ones I couldn't figure out yet."

"Then we're ready." Aaron nodded. "Let's move!"

A few moments later, they tore out of the driveway, screeching through the streets. Jasper fell asleep the moment they were in the vehicle, and Bertha seemed not too far from sleep herself. Which made Aaron quite nervous.

Harold leaned forward. "What's the plan when we get there?"

Aaron sighed and shrugged. "Kill anything undead, protect anything that's still alive."

"What if we find that one vampire there?" Harold frowned. "The one that wanted to help?"

"Him…" Aaron shrugged. "Him I'd say that we leave alive. Shoot, he might even fight on our side."

"Let's hope so." Harold nodded. "He seemed nice."

"I would wager a guess that most vampires probably do. That's how they trick you into inviting them into your house." Aaron sighed and shook his head, trying to stay awake. "Wow, I'm tired."

"I understand that." Harold sighed. "Been there before."

"You don't really seem that tired now." Aaron frowned. "Come to think of it, I don't know that I've ever really seen you get tired."

Harold shrugged. "I don't sleep much."

"I guess." Aaron yawned and leaned back in his seat. "Well, *I'm* exhausted. Wake me up when we get there."

The van went careening around a curve, and Aaron's head smacked loudly into the window. He winced and grabbed his head, which was beginning to throb quite powerfully.

"If you don't wake up, I'll just feed you to the vampires." Harold shrugged. "That sound okay?"

"Hey, now." Aaron muttered. As the van continued to careen through the night, he tried to get more comfortable. If he was right, this was going to be a long night, indeed.

CHAPTER 18

"This should be a quick and easy operation." One of the soldiers leaned over and elbowed Garmund in the side. "We just have to give the site a quick once-over, bust a few heads, that sort of thing. It'll be quick and painless. Well, for us."

"Tell that to the two members of your squad who didn't come back." Garmund muttered. "This stuff isn't all power and show."

"Yeah, it really is." The soldier shook his head. "How'd you guys in the Apocalypse Squad manage to stop the zombies, anyway? You just want to edge around the issues, always try to do things the hard way. Sometimes, you just have to charge in and take some losses."

"We value life."

"We value results." The soldier shook his head. "You want to know the reason I haven't told you my name?"

"You don't want your death to be personal to anyone." Garmund shook his head. "Barbaric, if you ask me."

"You're actually right on the money." The soldier laughed. "If we die, no one cares. That's why we're part of this operation. No family, no friends. Just battle and enemies, death and destruction. Get the idea?"

"I have a pretty good idea that you guys are insane." Garmund couldn't believe what he was hearing. "Well, my name is Garmund. If I die, I want to be remembered."

"More like *when* you die." The soldier shook his head. "Why are you even along, anyway? I thought you were the computer genius?"

"Your boss took away my toys." Garmund shrugged. "He had this great particle simulator, so I started playing around with what would happen if all the weapons in the house simultaneously detonated. Spoiler: it's not pretty. He decided that I was too much of a liability to let run around, so he stuck me here."

"Probably so you'll die and be out of the equation." The soldier laughed. "Perfect!"

"I royally hate you people." Garmund shook his head. "I don't even get a gun."

"Hope you know how to use your fists." The soldier chuckled. "Now why don't you-"

"We're here!" The call came back from the front. "Deploy in ten!"

Garmund took a deep breath. He was more than ready to be done with it all. With a screech, the vehicles slammed to a stop. The doors flew open, and Garmund leapt from the vehicle. Whatever was happening, he felt powerless to stop anything. All he hoped was that he could see his friends before he died.

CHAPTER 17

Jeremy's beating wings flapped harder and harder as he got closer to the call. Idly, he became aware that other bats were also flying along the same path. Great. Gruen had actually managed to create a few more. Granted, he should have suspected that a *few* of the other victims would survive, but it was a bit disconcerting all the same.

Before long, the city gave way to trees as he neared a small mountain. It was easy enough to see the monstrous house sitting on the side of the massive construct, and Jeremy knew instantly that that was where he was heading.

The force drew him to the upper landing on the mansion. As he came down, he transformed back into a human. Gruen was next, standing next to him on the balcony. Two more individuals appeared, just behind them. A quick glance revealed two girls, both of whom looked glazed and stunned. Gruen looked positively angry, and

Jeremy frowned. He tried to fight against the pull, take a step in any direction, but even thinking about trying to fight it left him shivering with pain.

"I suppose you're wondering why you're here." The doors to the balcony swung open, and a man swept out.

The man stank with evil, so much so that even Gruen bent backwards. Straps ran over his shoulders and around his torso, affixing a large pendant to his chest. Under the straps was a deep green set of robes that almost seemed to shimmer in the moonlight. A similarly colored cloak hung off his shoulders, falling down to the ground like a cape.

Above his attire was his face, dark and twisted. His eyes were solid black, and appeared at a glance to simply be black holes. His nose was long and pointed, and set just above a thin-lined mouth. Not an ounce of hair clung to his face, though a neatly-cropped set of hair sat on top of his head.

"It's crossed our minds." Jeremy spat. "Who are…"

"None of that." The man's voice was soft and piercing. "Are there not more of you? Only four?"

"Turning people into vampires isn't exactly easy." Gruen muttered. "I'm doing the best I can."

"I suppose you are." The man swept up to Jeremy. "You… You're a perfect example of his handiwork. You're barely vampire at all. In fact, I smell far more human on you than I do demon."

"I'm glad I passed the sniff test." Jeremy held his head high, trying to avoid the pain triggers. "Who are you? The vampire almighty?"

"Hardly." The man smiled. "Quite the opposite, actually. Do you know what created you, Gruen? You were the first, am I right?"

"You are." Gruen gasped. "I just woke up."

"You were carrying a shard in your hand when you awoke." The man swept closer to Gruen, pressing up next to him. "You discarded it like trash."

"I just thought…"

"No, you didn't." the man snapped. For the first time, his voice rose ever so slightly, and Jeremy's eardrums nearly burst. The man quieted down after a moment, and continued. "You never think. You haven't your entire life, otherwise you wouldn't have been in the position that allowed you to be turned into a vampire. Let me explain the situation for you."

He took a deep breath, and Jeremy prepared himself for a monologue. "That shard is part of an ancient tablet possessing nearly unlimited power. I'm trying to assemble the tablet to possess that power. Do your pathetic minds comprehend this statement?"

"Very much so." Jeremy nodded. "You want us to find this shard for you?"

"Hardly." The man held out his hand. Inside was a small shard of stone. It looked like it could have been a chip off nearly any building, except for the fact that it was glowing quite intensely.

"Then…" Jeremy paused. "What are we needed for?"

"When a shard activates, it must progress through a series of tasks." The man swept back and forth. "Think of it as a computer program. It has an end goal that it must progress towards before it can power down. I cannot use it and forge it with the others until it is powered down. Thus, I need you to start accelerating the progression of events."

Jeremy shook his head, despite the flash of pain that rapidly followed. "What do you mean? If this shard is as powerful as you say, we should already be unable to resist doing what it wants."

"*Should* is the operative word in that statement." The man growled, sending shivers up and down Jeremy's spine. "It appears that the vessel it chose to carry its mission wasn't up to the task, and none of the since-spawned vessels have had the gumption to continue."

Jeremy glared at the man. "What do you want us to do?"

The man chuckled softly. "That's simple, really. All you have to do is start expanding your numbers. Expand as rapidly as you can. Once you hit a certain point, I believe around two thousand, the shard will power down, and you never have to see me again."

Jeremy frowned. "You're going to kill us after all of this, aren't you?"

"I would have no need nor desire to." The man shook his head. "Once the shard is down, your current status as vampires will be uninterrupted. A small community of vampires still lives in seclusion, leftovers from the last time the shard did this. I myself have already come into contact with a zombie that survived a previous event earlier this year."

Jeremy nodded. "So… You drew us here, away from what we were doing, to tell us to turn more people into vampires? Which I'm fairly sure we were already doing?"

"I'm telling you to step up production." The man shrugged. "If you don't… Well, let this speak for my powers."

Pain blossomed in Jeremy's head, and he screamed. Dimly, he was aware that the rest of the vampires were also screaming, but he simply didn't care. After a moment, it went away, and the man smiled.

"I'm glad we understand each other. Naturally, you all feel a desire to feed. In addition to this, you will now also feel a physical pain the longer you go without turning someone. If you feed on them but either don't allow them to turn or you kill them, the pain will get worse. I rather doubt you will be able to resist it, not for long. Do I make myself clear?"

Jeremy nodded. "Perfectly."

"Good." The man slid between Gruen and Jeremy to look at the two newcomers. "You two haven't said much. Cat got your tongue?"

There were only low growls in answer. The man took a step back, glancing in confusion at Gruen. "What did you do to these people?"

"I think I sucked a bit too much blood out of them." Gruen shrugged. "They're pretty much just animals at this point."

"You are the most incompetent vampire I have *ever* met!" The man's voice began to rise yet again, making Jeremy's bones hurt. "Oh, well. The pain should be a teacher enough. If you continue to fail, you'll be in a good amount of it, indeed." He paused, then chuckled darkly.

"Ahh, it looks like the flash worked. We have visitors, and quite a few if I don't miss my guess. Your first new victims, I'd say."

"I'd rather die than help you." Jeremy spat. "I'll fight this."

"I think the pain will wear you down soon enough." The man chuckled. "Now, run free."

In an instant, Gruen and the two girls turned, transformed into bats, and flashed off into the night. Jeremy tried to leave, but found the pain bearing down on him yet again. The man stalked up to him slowly. The pendant on his chest gleamed, and Jeremy felt a stab of fear.

"You aren't like the others." The man growled. "You... You operate on an entirely different system."

"I don't want this curse." Jeremy gasped. "I hate it. I hate what I do to people."

"I was the same way, once." The man chuckled. "Ahh... To be free of that bondage. Nothing feels quite the same afterwards, though I suppose you wouldn't know that yet. Just you wait. I think you'll be pleased."

"And I think you're insane." Jeremy looked down at his hands. "There are so many benefits to this body, and yet so many weaknesses. I hate it."

"Yes, I suppose you do." The man took a deep breath. "Since you *are* different, I suppose I would be remiss if I didn't answer a few questions. I sense them burning in your mind. Go ahead. Ask."

Jeremy growled low in his throat. "Who are you?"

"The name is Incacheck." The man smiled. "Doctor Incacheck."

Jeremy raised an eyebrow. "The guy who took over a country in South America?"

"The one and only." Incacheck smiled. "And here I thought word of my exploits were fairly localized."

"I'd say that pretty much everyone in the United States knows who you are." Jeremy shrugged. "When you took over the country, they sent in troops to help liberate the area. All the troops were slaughtered, no one made it out alive. It was all over the news a few years back, the White House announced that your country had declared war on our own. When no counterstrike came, they assumed that you were too afraid to attack us, and we moved on. I think there still *is* an official declaration of war in effect, though."

"Interesting." Incacheck mused. "I remember those troops. To be honest, I thought it was a small scouting party. I destroyed them quite for fun, you see. The United States is so terrified of my country that they won't invade despite a declaration of war. How quaint."

Jeremy raised an eyebrow. "You're telling me you didn't know?"

"World politics bore me." Incacheck waved his hand. "Truth be told, I took over the country so I would have easier access to the official records of that country. I needed the information about the tablet, and-"

"Taking over a country was easier than breaking into a building." Jeremy raised an eyebrow. "Really?"

"It was a heavily fortified building, and at the time my powers were much weaker than they are now." Incacheck hissed. "It was easier to get the rebels to rise up against the government than to convince them to help me stage a break-in."

Jeremy rolled his eyes. "Okay. Well, as interesting as this is, I somehow doubt that you're up here just feeding me everything I want to know." He frowned as he realized that there was something inside him, probing his body. "Hey!"

"I needed you distracted for this to work." Incacheck shrugged. "Everyone knows that villains love to monologue. It was easy enough to get you to play along." He sneered. "Besides, I tire of minions who refuse to talk to me. Sometimes, I just need a good conversation, regardless of whether or not I'm telling the truth."

Jeremy tried to pull away, but found himself fixed securely in place. "You're sick, you know that?"

"It's been brought up a time or two." Incacheck waved his hand, sending a flash of pain through Jeremy's body. "There. All done."

Jeremy fell to the wood floor as something lanced through him. "What did you do to me?"

"Nothing major." Incacheck grinned. "I simply altered a bit of your physiology. You see, your body will now subconsciously measure any individual you are feeding on, stopping you from drinking the moment that the proper amount of blood has been removed. You'll create a vampire every time you feed."

"Why not do that to Gruen?" Jeremy gasped. "Why me?"

"I rather want to see him suffer." Incacheck shrugged. "He's... Well, he's funny. Now, if you don't mind, I have work to do. Have fun feeding."

"I refuse to-"

Jeremy stopped talking as Incacheck vanished into the house. The doors slammed behind him, propelled by whatever magic Incacheck used. He took a deep breath as something began to well up inside him. Hunger. Images of necks began to float through his mind, and something inside him growled.

Desperately, he grabbed onto the wood planks of the floor, the pillars, anything he could reach. He would *not* be undone by this!

With a final snap, his body transformed into a bat on its own accord. He had only a moment left to fight it before he was winged away, towards the fight… Towards his food.

CHAPTER 18

Garmund hit the ground running, tearing across the gravel driveway as fast as he could. Something zinged over his head, and he heard one of the soldiers scream. Idly, he hoped that the soldier was comforted by the fact that no one would care that he was dying.

Gunfire began to echo, and Garmund simply ran for the house as fast as he could. He was almost to the porch when he seemed to run into an invisible force field. After pressing against the field for several seconds, a small black object flashed out of the home and struck him in the chest, launching him back onto the driveway. He landed with a whump, scrambled to his feet, and raced for the trees.

Lights flashed through the air, and a new set of headlights swung into the drive. Unfortunately, he was given little chance to see who the new arrivals were as a female vampire landed in front of him, fangs bared. Desperately, he tore backwards, moving deep into the cover of the woods.

The vampire stayed on him, growling loudly. Garmund glanced back and forth, trying to find *something* he could use for a weapon. There were plenty of tree branches, but he sincerely doubted that he possessed the strength to rip a branch from its host tree. There were also plenty of branches littering the ground, but he was quite certain that many of them were far too rotten to be of use.

Hands latched down on his shoulders, and he felt something soft and wet grace his skin. Desperately, he swung to the side, battering it against a nearby tree. The vampire was thrown from his back, but he knew that it would only be a short time before it returned.

What had Jasper always been saying? There were always ways to fight back, always weapons available. He just had to find them. Besides, he didn't really have any other option. When it came down to it, it was much the same as hacking a computer, except that rather than finding a new way to break a firewall, he had to find a way to break skin.

After glancing at the ground for a few moments, he picked up two small sticks. They weren't much, but maybe they were enough. He held the both out in front of him, ready to defend himself against the darkness.

When the vampire hit him, it completely ignored the quite impressive show of force, and simply leapt over his defenses and slammed him in the chest. He crumpled backwards, stunned, and fell to the forest floor. The vampire straddled his chest, smiled, and bent down to begin kissing his neck.

Garmund quickly brought up his two sticks and began jabbing at her with as much force as he could. The twigs did little damage, though, and he sighed. At least he had tried before getting eaten.

A thought struck him just as teeth began to puncture his skin. What if... He had always heard that a cross was effective. Would a homemade cross work just as well? With no time for a test run, he put both sticks between himself and the vampire and crossed them as perfectly as he could.

The results were, in a word, spectacular. Light burst from the cross, and the vampire was propelled high into the air, slamming into the bottom side of a rather thick branch. Something in her body snapped, and she fell back to the ground. Garmund scrambled to his feet as the vampire flailed around in the leaves, her legs seemingly useless.

Before she could get the drop on him, Garmund kicked her in the face, flopping her over onto her back. He then planted a foot in her chest and crossed the branches above her. Light pulsed from the homemade cross yet again, and she screamed in pain. It was as if a physical force was pressing down on top of her, crushing her into nothingness. A few moments passed, and she turned into dust with a mild poof. Garmund smiled, nodded, and turned back towards the fight.

As he started stumbling back through the woods, he could only hear roars and gunfire from in front of him. With nothing else to do, he simply crossed his sticks and marched onward. It was time to end this. It was time to survive.

CHAPTER 19

Harold took a deep breath as the van roared into the mansion's driveway. He had almost thought that Aaron was going to call him out on not sleeping, but fortunately, the man had been too tired himself to be bothered with thinking things through. Small miracles.

With a screech, the van drew to a stop. Jasper awoke with a start, followed by Aaron. Aaron held up his hands and started snapping.

"Vampirekiller, now."

Jasper handed him a rifle that had been modified to shoot wooden chunks. "Here. Knock yourself out."

"Hopefully I'll be knocking vampires." Aaron muttered. "Alright. Kill any vamps you see, minus the one that seems to be trying to help. Save any civilians, and eliminate any members of the ARF that cross your path."

Harold frowned. "You're just joking, right?"

"Absolutely." Aaron nodded quite unconvincingly. "Let's roll."

He stepped out of the vehicle, took two steps, and was immediately slammed back into the side of the van by something large and black. Harold glanced at Jasper.

"I should probably go help him out."

"Probably." Jasper tossed a wooden sword to Bertha. "Have some fun."

Harold slid the door aside, stepped out, and found a vampire trying to chew Aaron's head off. It was a young female, probably a college freshman that had been turned. It still hadn't managed to land a bite on Aaron's neck, probably due to Aaron's excessive arm flapping.

Before it had a chance to do in their leader, Harold walked up, grabbed the vampire's neck, and snapped it as hard as he could. The creature collapsed on the ground, but didn't dissolve into dust. It's mouth snapped open and shut, trying to get at an unreachable prey.

Aaron shrugged and fired a round into its chest. The creature kept thrashing, and Aaron readjusted his aim. The next shot hit the heart, and he chuckled.

"That's a much smaller target than the movies lead you to believe."

"Yeah." Harold muttered. "Go kick some butt. Don't waste ammo, you only have a few dozen wooden rounds."

"Got it." Aaron nodded and ran off into the darkness. Harold shook his head and turned back to Jasper.

"You think we're ready for this?"

"I'm quite certain that we aren't." Jasper shrugged. "This guy is probably one of the most powerful alchemists on the planet. I struggle to turn drinking water into nitroglycerin. This guy can probably do pretty much anything his mind comes up with."

"Well, good thing we had time to prepare." Harold reached past Jasper and picked up a gas-fed plasma weapon. "I've been waiting for a chance to try this thing out."

"Honestly, I'm just ready to see if that thing works." Jasper grinned. "It's quite a weapon you created."

"My baby." Harold grinned. "Shall we?"

"We shall." Jasper muttered as he slammed the door shut, holding up a large machine gun. "Granted, it helps that you can't die."

"I'm already dead. There's nothing to say that I can't die again."

"That's true." Jasper shrugged, and they stepped out into the driveway, striding towards the house. "Still doesn't hurt anything."

As they walked, Harold began muttering under his breath, stirring up the air particles, trying to send out a sonic wave. It had worked well enough in the tunnels, maybe it would work now. Instantly, he was able to get a decent picture of the inside of the house, but it was too blurred to know exactly what was going on inside.

"I think he's in the back room." Harold frowned in concentration. "Either that, or he's in the upstairs kitchen. It's a fifty-fifty shot."

Jasper spun to the side, where a vampire ARF soldier charged at him. He unloaded a few rounds into its chest, transforming it into nothing but dust. "How'd you manage that?"

Harold spun to the side, firing a burst of plasma into another vampire soldier charging at his position. The man's head vanished in a ball of fire, and the body collapsed. If it wasn't dead, it wasn't going anywhere for quite awhile.

"It's an echoing technique. I learned it from your family's alchemy books."

"Good to know." Jasper started shooting towards the house at two vampires that were busy charging out of the front doors. Both of them transformed into bats and flashed past his bullets, vanishing into the night. "I have to read more."

"You just lack knowledge of anything not weaponry-based." Harold shrugged. "I was actually reading about a new technique last night. Want to see?"

"We're in the middle of a war zone."

"A war zone that isn't touching us." Harold held up his hands. "The vamps are all staying away."

"Probably scared of us." Jasper chuckled. "Okay, all our friends could be watching. You want them to know you're an alchemist?"

"Not particularly." Harold shrugged. "Good point."

The duo reached the front doors with no further issues. Harold paused just in front of the door, sensing an enormous amount of energy pulsing through the wood. Jasper reached for the handle, and Harold put his arm out.

"Wait." He held his hand just above the wood, sensing the ebb and pulse of the energy. "There's a trap here. Step back."

Jasper shrugged but did so. The moment he was out of harm's way, Harold put his hand on the doorknob, activating the trap. Instantly, the air around him began to heat up. Fire blazed from the knob, trying to consume everything it touched. Harold simply shook his head as the fire ate away the top layer of skin, only to be halted as his body healed itself faster than the fire could burn. It *did* manage to burn away the rest of the door.

As soon as the fire died down, Harold gestured at the now-gaping hole where the door used to be. Jasper shook his head and pointed at Harold. Harold just laughed as he stepped into the mansion.

He had only taken a few short steps before he felt something approach. Without hesitation, he brought up his plasma gun and began firing bursts of superheated gas into the woodworks. Walls, ceilings, doors, it all gave way before the weapon. A moment later, the plasma started to hit a black hole near the kitchen door that simply absorbed all the energy.

Jasper saw the phenomenon at the same time, and both of them unloaded their weapons into the void. There was no discernible effect, and as Harold's weapon began to click empty, a presence materialized out of the darkness.

"So. We meet again." The man that they had met at the pyramid stepped through the doorway, looking as if he hadn't changed a bit since that day. "You've gotten more cautious, I can tell. You thought that weapons would help defeat me."

"Actually, we just wanted to test our new prototypes." Harold shrugged. "Honestly, I wasn't sure that gun would last so long. I'm pretty sure that-"

"Silence." The man's word sealed Harold's jaw. He frowned, trying to figure out what had just happened. It took him a moment, but he quickly realized that the man had created some sort of salt in the muscle tissue, tightening the muscles in place. An interesting trick.

It took Harold a few moments to dissolve the salt and expel it from his dead sweat glands, and his jaw let up.

"Ahh, that feels better. You don't have to be *quite* so dramatic, you know."

The man laughed out loud, a booming torrent that tore through Harold's ears like a physical object. Now *that* was a technique he didn't know how to do.

"Just who do you think you are, boy? I've gone against the best that the alchemists' council has to offer."

Harold glanced at Jasper. "The alchemists have a council? This is news to me."

"They would probably throw you in their prison." The man shrugged. "You're a bit too unconventional for them. You're a bit too boring for me."

Harold felt the ground underneath him begin to change, and he thrust his hands downward. The liquifying floor solidified, and he grinned. "Who's boring now?"

The man stalked forward. "You will not-"

Harold pulled a pencil out of his pocket. He had been hoping for this chance. Without a word, he blew on the eraser end of the utensil. With a roar, the pencil transformed into a three-foot long spear made from pure electricity. It was strange, holding physical electricity. Alchemy was *so* weird.

The man's eyes went wide, and Harold let go of the object. Energy flowed across the room, slamming into the man's chest. He was thrown backwards, crashing through a wall and into a separate room. Knowing that he would only have a few moments, Harold ran over to Jasper's side, placed his hand on Jasper's jaw, and released all the salts blocking his movement.

"Thanks." Jasper gasped. "How'd you do all that?"

"Fight more, talk later." Harold turned back to the hole in the wall, which was beginning to stir with activity. In a rush, dozens of spears rushed out of the hole, towards their position.

Harold held up his hands, causing the air in front of them to solidify. It was no use, as in an instant, they were blown back outside, crashing into the gravel in the front driveway.

"You really think you can stop me?" The man roared as he swept out of the house. Defying gravity, he rose up into the air, fire glowing in his hands. "You really think you can take what's rightfully mine?"

Harold raised his hand, only to have it flattened back against the ground. Desperately, he tried to fight against the strain. He didn't want to go out like this. If he was going to die, he was going to die fighting.

CHAPTER 20

Jeremy flashed from the balcony, angling down through the air. A soldier leapt out of a military vehicle, pulsing with blood. So much blood…

Jeremy's human form reasserted itself, and he dropped out of the sky, slamming into the man's shoulders and driving him into the ground. Even as his mind fought, trying desperately to move away, his body arced forward, biting deep into his victim. Blood began to course over his tongue, and for a long moment, he lost himself in the flow. It was like drinking the best wine on the planet, like enjoying the finest of all dining.

With a rush, he was torn out of the pleasure. His stomach revolted, and he stood up, repulsed by the nearly dead body. Had he just done that? A wave rolled through him, and he bent over, vomiting up everything he had just eaten.

Gunfire sounded next to him, and he felt bullets tear through his body. Anger pulsed in his mind, and he leapt upward, knocking the gun away. In that instant, the soldier was simply standing there, a walking buffet. His stomach growled, and the taste of blood ran through his mouth. The soldier turned to run, and he leapt forward, slamming his teeth deep into the man's jugular.

After he had finished feeding on that soldier, he let the body drop with a thud. Slowly, he turned to face the battlefield. A new group of soldiers had just arrived, more fresh meat. Smiling, he stalked across the gravel towards the newcomers.

With a snap, the door opened, and a flash of recognition pulsed in Jeremy's mind. It was the man he had talked to when confronting Gruen! The one fighting the vampires! If he saw him here, blood dripping down his chin…

Without another thought, Jeremy ducked out of sight behind a nearby van. As soon as he was out of sight, no one left to feed on, a feeling of revulsion rolled through his body. He had just killed two more people! Would he ever stop?

Desperately, he started to run, charging into the woods. He had only gone a few feet when a noise started ringing in the back of his mind. A fraction of a second passed, and it blossomed into full-blown pain. He screamed and fell to the ground.

"I just fed!" He screamed up at the sky. "Have you no mercy?"

There was no answer, only the pulsing of gunfire in the distance. The pain began to grow, and he stood up. It lessened, but only for a moment. Slowly, he began to stalk back towards the area. Apparently he had been modified to want to feed whenever there was food available, not just after it had been quite some time.

He drug his feet as much as possible, trying to slow his arrival back at the area. He didn't want to kill anyone else. He hadn't even wanted to kill those two soldiers! Vanessa's face rose in his mind, and he knew she was gone. There was no way he would be able to look her in the eyes in two weeks and tell her that he hadn't fed on anyone. He hadn't even made it an hour after he promised her.

Misery began to overcome the pain, and he desperately tried to rationalize it. No. No, he hadn't eaten those people. Incacheck had forced him to eat those people. They were still on his conscience, but he hadn't wanted to do it. Incacheck had ruined his life, and now Incacheck was going to pay.

As he walked up to the clearing in front of the mansion, he saw the wizard floating out above the driveway, getting ready to kill two of the soldiers. Time to end that.

Without another thought, doing everything he could to ignore the pain brimming in the back of his skull, he launched himself at the evil mastermind. He wanted Jeremy to feed? Then feed was exactly what he would do.

CHAPTER 21

Aaron spun and shot a vampire soldier through the chest. The man stumbled backwards, but didn't die. Growling in frustration, Aaron put three more wooden bullets through the man before he finally dissolved. He smiled, gripped his weapon a little tighter, and started looking for more targets.

A blast shook the area, and he spun to see Harold and Jasper thrown from the house. Something whirled through the air, and a man floated out of the ruins of the building to hover in the air over the two soldiers. Aaron raised his gun, ready to start shooting.

Before he could pull the trigger, a black blur exploded out of the night, slamming into the man's neck. The man fell to the ground, slapping at a vampire that clung to him like a tick.

The man flicked his hand, the vampire screamed in pain and let go, and he stood back up. Blood dripped down onto his robes, and he raised his hands. When he spoke, the pure power shattered Aaron's skull.

"You all don't get it! I'm in charge here! I-"

Aaron fired a shot into the man's upper chest, just above a large pendant that hung from several straps. The bullet bounced off, doing no damage, and he growled.

"Fine! I take my leave of you. Just know that next time…" He chuckled. "Next time I won't be so forgiving."

With a blast of light, he vanished. The area fell quiet, apart from a few distant screams. Aaron ran out to Jasper and Harold, both of whom were starting to sit up.

"What happened in there?" Aaron gasped. "Who was that?"

"Your guess is as good as mine." Harold muttered. "What got him? Right before he was about to kill us. I'd like to shake its hand."

Aaron turned to see a dark mound on the ground. He walked over, already certain of what he would see. He bent down and flipped the body over, nodding at the sight of the helpful vampire. The boy appeared unconscious, and shuddered in pain. Aaron glanced at Harold, nodded, and took the boy's arms. Together, he and Harold lifted the boy up and started walking to their van.

"That's for Garmund!" Bertha came charging out of the forest, wooden sword in hand. She flicked the sword with ease, fighting off three ARF vampires at once. The first one missed a step, and she drove the sword straight through its heart. Without missing a beat, she stepped through the dissolving dust cloud, spun, and faced the next one.

The vamp had only a moment to look surprised before Bertha lobbed off its arms and drove the sword through it, transforming it into little more than a pile of debris. The third vampire turned to run, and Bertha threw the sword, pinning the vampire to a nearby tree. She stalked up to it, picked up a large stick from the ground, and began stabbing the monster over and over.

"Sometimes, I think we underestimate her." Jasper shrugged as they neared the van. "You ever consider giving her more responsibility?"

"She's in charge of cleaning." Aaron shrugged as he did his best to hold onto the vampire boy while kicking open the rear doors of the van. The moment they hefted him inside, he shook his head. Several seconds later, Bertha finally showed up. "Speaking of which, this van is filthy!"

"We stopped for chicken earlier tonight." Bertha shrugged. "Haven't really been near a trash can since then."

Aaron held up his arms. "Get on it as soon as we get home." After a moment, he glanced at his watch. "Or once we wake up in the morning. Just make sure to get it done."

"Yes, sir." Bertha hesitated for a moment. "Any particular reason we're bringing a *vampire* with us?"

"He's already helped us against others of his kind." Aaron shrugged. "He's the only reason Jasper and Harold are still alive."

"Well, good for him." Bertha climbed into the driver's seat. "Everybody in or I'm leaving you behind."

Aaron nodded and climbed into the passenger seat. The moment they were all inside, Bertha hit the gas and roared off in a cloud of dust. Aaron took a single glance back at the mansion, glad he would never have to look at it again. The fight was over. It was time to recuperate.

CHAPTER 22

Garmund trudged back through the forest, a feeling of power in his chest. He had discovered a simple and convenient way to defeat vampires! What were the odds?

As he stumbled back onto the gravel driveway, a lone soldier looked up at him, fear in his eyes. He snapped up a pistol, and Garmund raised his hands.

"Whoa! I'm still human!"

"Prove it." The soldier sounded weary.

Garmund crossed the branches in front of him. Nothing happened, and he shrugged. "See? Not a vampire."

"You expect me to believe that-"

A vampire materialized out of the woods, and Garmund spun, bringing up his sticks. Energy pulsed from the cross, and the vampire was thrown backwards and into a tree. There was a sickening crunch, and the vampire died as it was impaled on a branch. Garmund turned back to the soldier and crossed his arms.

"Satisfied?"

"Enough." The soldier nodded. "You're the last one left. I say we head back."

Garmund sucked in a breath. "I'm the last one?"

"According to the sensors in this van, there were only two more motion signatures in the woods after that last group clear out." The soldier sighed. "You were one of them. The other just died. I'd say we're good." After a moment, he shrugged. "Now, there's a solid chance that more vampires just flew away, but I'd rather not think about that at the moment."

Garmund sighed, walked to the other side of the van, popped the door open, and crawled inside. "Let's head back."

As they took off down the mountainside, Garmund sighed deeply. "Well, that was a nightmare."

"You're telling me." The soldier shook his head. "Everyone else in the squad, killed. We're going to have to requisition more troops from headquarters."

Garmund cocked an eyebrow. "You have no qualms about simply throwing more and more resources at an issue, even when it isn't working, don't you?"

"We killed the vampires, didn't we?" The soldier shrugged. After a few moments, he shook his head. "Less talk. I'm done thinking."

Garmund nodded and shut up as the van rocketed back down the hill.

When they finally pulled up to the frat house, Garmund cast a longing glance at his team's home. The windows were all dark, and he sighed deeply. He just wanted to be with his friends, not around the maniacal death squad that he was paired with at that moment.

As he stumbled up to the front door, it swung wide open. Rodger stepped out, a frown on his face.

"Where's everyone else?"

"Dead." Garmund muttered. "Each and every one of them."

"Great." Rodger shook his head. "Did we get the enemy, at least?"

"That much we did manage to accomplish." Garmund nodded. "Not a vamp left in this town." Even as he said it, he crossed his fingers. "I hope."

"Good." Rodger shrugged. "So…"

"Can it, you two." The soldier stumbled between them. "You know we're not allowed to talk in casual conversation outside of the battlefield."

"Tell me that again, and I'll put you in a coma." Garmund let his head fall. "I don't know how, but I'll find a way."

Rodger chuckled as the soldier vanished into the house. "Rough night?"

"You don't know the half of it." Garmund let out a long breath, walked through the door, and slumped into a chair in the living room. "It was a slaughterhouse. They would kill people, they would come back, we'd have to kill them all over again."

"How'd you manage to make it through?" Rodger slid into a chair opposite Garmund. "Hack them down like targets? Stake to the heart? Hide in the woods?"

Garmund chuckled and held his two index fingers up in a cross symbol. "Turns out that any cross, homemade or not, works just fine. I got creative."

"Now *that* is some next-level creativity." Rodger chuckled. "Where'd you learn that?"

Garmund paused for a moment. "There's a guy on my old team. Jasper. The guy can build a weapon out of anything. I just started thinking about what he would do."

"So you made a cross to drive them away."

"Actually, I just grabbed two sticks and tried to stake it." Garmund chuckled. "The cross was kind of an accident."

"Well, it worked out wonderfully." Rodger shook his head. "Well, now that you all are back, I'm heading to bed. I'm going to enjoy my room before they fill it with more walking meatbags with a deathwish."

Garmund laughed darkly. "What's with that, anyway? I feel like these people *want* to die."

"Any of them would give their lives in exchange for the survival of the human race." General Birch walked into the room, a scowl on his face. "If soldiers are emotionally attached to their comrades, they're more willing to grieve on the battlefield when one of them dies. If these soldiers aren't at the top of their game, they'll simply not be able to protect us when it is needed."

Garmund held up a hand. "You have one soldier left. Sure, you can just order more, but what would happen if there was an incident *right now*?"

"We would find a way to deal with it and make it work." Birch growled. "Now get to your quarters, both of you. Curfew has long since passed."

"Curfew?" Garmund shook his head as he forced himself out of his chair. "You're going to try to pull curfew after we just took out an entire nest of vampires?"

"Yes, soldier, I am." Birch's voice was hard. "Now get to it!"

Garmund shook his head and walked out of the living room. Rodger followed him for a short distance, until they reached the entrance to Rodger's bedroom.

"Well, I guess this is goodnight." Rodger shrugged. "See you in the morning. If, of course, there's still a morning to wake up to. The vampires could break in and kill us long before then. Of course, since vampires are just a fact of life now, it's also possible that we wake up with alien mind-control collars on our necks."

"You're telling me." Garmund shook his head. The whole situation just felt weird. "We took out all the vampires, but… I don't know. Something seems off. Like we missed something."

"Well, I'm sure we'll figure it out." Rodger grinned. "Probably right as its trying to kill us, but I'm sure we'll figure it out."

"You're just full of warm, comforting thoughts." Garmund muttered. "See you in the morning."

With that. Garmund turned and stalked down the hallway to the dorm room that he had been assigned to. Slowly, he pushed the door open. There was definitely something off, he just couldn't quite put his finger on it.

After a moment, as he flipped the light on, it hit him. The soldier that had came back with him was passed out on one of the cots in the room. Garmund was quite certain that the soldier was *not* one of the men who was assigned to that particular room, which sent dozens of questions up Garmund's spine. For soldiers who wouldn't disobey any form of a direct order, this one was pretty quick on the trigger.

Garmund took a deep breath, shrugged, and walked over to his bed. It was probably nothing at all, the man was certainly quite tired after all, and probably just happened to wander into the wrong room. That said…

It could never hurt to be careful. Idly, Garmund grabbed two pencils off a nearby table. He then found an old, abandoned pair of military boots and unstrung the shoelaces. A quick moment later, he was the proud owner of a pencil-cross. Without further ado, he walked over to his bed, tucked the cross under his pillow, and flopped onto the bed. The cross should have a large enough radius to protect his neck, at least for a short time while he woke up.

The moment his head touched the pillow, his vision swam. It had been a *long* night. He offered no protests, and soon swam off into sleep.

It felt like a moment had passed before a pulsing light brought him back to the land of the living. His eyes snapped open to see the soldier being thrown across the room, fangs bared. Garmund reached under his pillow for the cross, but the soldier was too fast. Without another word, the man threw open the door and vanished into the rest of the frat.

Garmund sighed. He knew that he should be going after the monster, but all he wanted to do was sleep. Pounding echoed on the upstairs floors, and he forced himself out of bed. Better to save the General and face the firing squad for being up past curfew than to go back to sleep and face the firing squad for letting the General die.

As he stepped out into the hallway, he saw the vampire banging on Rodger's door. Groggily, Garmund held up the cross and walked forward. It began to pulse with light, and the vampire turned. It hissed loudly, then spun and vanished around a corner. Garmund followed it chasing it through the house until it flashed out the front door.

Garmund nodded in satisfaction, turned, and took a step backwards as General Birch stormed down the stairs from the upper level.

"What do you think you're doing?"

"My brain is too far gone to worry about thinking." Garmund muttered. "That soldier we brought back was a vamp. Tried to eat me in my sleep, but I chased him off."

"You chased off a vampire?" Birch laughed. "Just how…"

"The same way I chased them off back in the forest." Garmund shook his head. He held up the homemade cross, and Birch just laughed.

"You expect me to believe…"

Something inside Garmund snapped. "Yes, sir, I do!"

Birch's face became more serious. "What are you doing, soldier?"

"You brought me onto this team for a reason!" Garmund roared. "Maybe you were just jealous, maybe you just wanted to poke at Herford, but I think there was more to it. You wanted me, and now that I'm here, all you want to do is sideline me. If I'm going to be on this team, you *have* to listen to what I have to say. Is that clear?"

Birch nodded tightly. "Please believe me when I say that I understand every word coming from your mouth. Do *you* understand what kind of treason you're spouting?"

"I understand perfectly." Garmund wasn't slowing down, not in the slightest. "All you want is a squad of perfect killing machines. Well, guess what? You've got humans. *Humans!* They have names, they have families, and they have individual interests and souls. Maybe it's less efficient if one of them falls, but I also know how the squad I used to work on functioned. One of them got injured or placed in harm's way, and the rest of them would fight through hell to rescue them. You've got your priorities all wrong, and unless you decide you're going to fix them, I'm walking out the front door no matter what the consequences might be."

Birch crossed his arms. "That's really how you feel?"

"It is." Garmund took a deep breath. "Now, if you'll excuse me, the world is starting to spin. I'm going to go get some rest. Think about what I said, okay?"

Birch nodded, and Garmund spun and stalked back to his room. For all he knew, he had just signed a one-way ticket out of the army. Oh, well. If he was executed, at least it would be in the knowledge that he wasn't responsible for so many deaths.

Without another thought, he collapsed on his bed. He hadn't even pulled up the think blankets before he spiraled out of the world, and on into his dreams.

CHAPTER 23

Jeremy's eyes fluttered open, taking in the sight. He was lying in a small room, on a bed that filled nearly the entire floor space. A small window sparkled with sunlight, but someone had been kind enough to draw the shades across, preventing him from burning to a crisp.

Slowly, he took a deep breath and tried to sit up. Surprisingly, he could do so with almost no effort at all. The pain, the crushing, overwhelming pain that he had felt earlier, was... Gone.

"Hey, you're awake." A head appeared in the doorway, a sandy-haired guy somewhere around his own age. "Sorry for the shock, I'm sure. You saved our butts last night, and Aaron said you were a good guy, so we figured we would try and stitch you back up."

Jeremy nodded. "Thank you." He flexed his wrists. "Thank you so much. Tell me, what exactly did you do to me?"

"A bit of this and a bit of that." The boy shrugged. "It's complicated medical stuff that I really don't understand. Want a bite to eat?"

"A bite to eat might be a bite too far." Jeremy chuckled. The boy frowned in confusion, then laughed.

"Maybe so. In any event, can I do anything for you? My name's Harold."

"Harold." Jeremy repeated. "My name's Jeremy. Honestly, I really don't think there is anything you can do. Well, if you had any raincoats or something to keep the sun away, that would be nice."

Harold frowned. "You're leaving? Already?"

Jeremy's stomach growled, and he nodded. "I can tell that I'm getting hungry again. Whatever sway Incachech had on me is gone, but that doesn't mean I should be around anyone."

"I heard someone say a bad word. Did someone say Incacheck?" Another head appeared in the doorway. "Ahh, you're awake!"

"Yes, I am." Jeremy nodded. "Thank you for your hospitality."

"You saved us." The man nodded. "We'll be there for you anytime you need us. Just say the word. Oh, name's Aaron. I'm the leader of this group."

"Yes, I recognize you." Jeremy nodded. "You were facing off against Gruen a few nights ago."

"Last night, actually." Aaron muttered.

Jeremy frowned. "That *was* last night, wasn't it? Wow, time's all disoriented for me."

"Us, too." Harold chuckled. "Not your average night, eh?"

"You're telling me." Jeremy took a deep breath. "Anyway, you asked about Incacheck. That was the guy in charge there. The guy who floated up into the air, looked like he was about ready to kill you all."

Aaron's face blanched. "That was Incacheck? The evil one?"

"I didn't know there were two." Jeremy held up his hands. "I'd never seen him before last night, but let me tell you, the guy can pack a punch. I'm not going to be forgetting him anytime soon."

"Me, either." Aaron shook his head. "I've always heard the guy was powerful, but... Wow, that kind of *power* is almost unfathomable. I just wish I knew what the source of his powers were."

Jeremy frowned. "Shards."

"Shards?" Aaron held up his hands. "What do you mean?"

"I mean he uses these stone shards to generate his powers." Jeremy nodded. "That's why he's here. He wants to use the shard that created the vampires, but it won't help him until its run its course. It has to make so many vampires before it goes inert again."

"I'll pretend I followed any of that." Aaron held up his hand. "What I'm hearing is that Incacheck wants lots of vampires. How many vampires do you think escaped last night?"

"Impossible to know for sure." Jeremy frowned in thought. He had attacked Incacheck long before the battle ended. "Several, for sure."

"Great." Aaron rubbed his jaw, then turned to Harold. "Be ready to move out tonight. I want everyone sleeping during the day and active at night. That's when the vampires are going to be the most active, so that's when we need to be moving." He paused for a moment. "If we can prevent the vampires from being created, we can stop Incacheck without ever actually having to fight him directly."

"Not a bad plan." Jeremy nodded. "At least until he gets sick of our meddling and decides to crush us. We might want to try and figure out where he is if we want to prevent that. I doubt he'll still be in the mansion, not after last night."

"I'll put Frank on it." Aaron nodded. After a moment, he sighed. "What will you be doing, and how can we help?"

Jeremy frowned and scratched his head. For the first time since becoming a vampire… He had a purpose. Incacheck was terrifying, and his plan was even more so. It was even more terrifying than his own condition, and that, in a way, was a comfort.

"I'll help stop them." Jeremy nodded. "There are vampires on the loose, and they'll need taken care of. Maybe I can sway some more of them to come to our side and stop rampantly making more vampires. Or, if I can capture some of them, you can do your magic to save them from Incacheck's sway."

"We're glad to have you." Aaron held out his hand, which Jeremy gladly shook. "Welcome to the Apocolyps Squad."

"Thanks." Jeremy flashed a small smile. His stomach gave a small rumble, and he frowned. "I should be going."

"You're leaving?" Aaron crossed his arms. "You're barely rested, after what you did for us, we can't let you just leave!"

"Whatever you guys did, I feel incredible." Jeremy smiled as he noticed their necks but didn't feel any pull from Incacheck to force him to feed. A definite hunger was there, but no pain. "That said, I'm getting really, really hungry. When I hit a certain point, I literally lose control of my body, so I doubt you want me around when that happens."

Aaron swept his arm out. "Let me walk you to the door."

Jeremy laughed as they swept through the house. As he reached the door, Harold walked up with a large raincoat.

"It's not perfect, but it should be enough to help you find shelter elsewhere until the sun sets."

"Thanks." Jeremy nodded. "I mean it."

"You saved us." Aaron shrugged. "I figure we owe you." He paused, and looked Jeremy in the eye. "Is there anything at all that we can do for you?"

Jeremy frowned in thought. "Maybe. It's morning, right?"

Harold nodded. "About nine o'clock. Why?"

"I know it's a lot to ask, but would anyone be willing to drive me up to Washington D.C.?" Jeremy frowned. "I think it's around a three-hour drive. If we hurry, we could be back by nightfall."

Aaron nodded slowly. "Of course. What do you need to go to D.C. for?"

Jeremy shrugged. Professor Inkwood's words still hung in his mind, ever-present. "Just a hunch. I was given the name of someone at the Smithsonian that might have some information about another vampire event that happened some time ago. I don't know for certain that he could help us, but it might be worth checking out."

Bertha materialized out of the dark hallway. "I'll take you."

Aaron raised an eyebrow. "Bertha?"

"I need to get out of here." She sighed and stuffed her hands in her pockets. "Too much of Garmund. If I don't blow off some steam, I'm going to go rip Birch's head off and-"

"I get the picture." Aaron nodded and gestured at Jeremy. "Go."

Bertha smirked and walked past him, taking Jeremy's arm and pulling him through the door. As they crossed the porch, Jeremy frantically pulled on the raincoat. The moment he stepped out past its protective covering, it was like stepping into the heart of a nuclear reactor. The sun beat down through the protective fabric like a hammer, sending pain sprinkling up and down his entire body. He fixed his eyes on the ground, as the entire sky above burned with an unmatched ferocity.

Bertha unlocked the van, and Jeremy slid inside, grateful for the partial cover. As she backed the vehicle out of the driveway, Jeremy caught a glimpse of the large, gothic house directly across the street. It was the same house that he had hidden inside when he first became a vampire! Who'd have thought?

With that, Bertha put the pedal to the metal, and they roared off down the street. Jeremy sighed and closed his eyes. He didn't know what he was going to face at the end of the ride... He could only desperately hope that he got his answers.

CHAPTER 24

Aaron sighed and walked into the garage, where Garmund's computers took up a large bulk of the space. An old, rusty scooter leaned against one of the monitors, while the chair in front of them was nothing more than a wicker lawn chair.

As he settled into the piece of old furniture, it gave a weary squeak under his weight. He ran his hands through his hair and took a deep breath, trying not to think about anything that had been happening. They had a lead on the vampires, and… Well, it wasn't nearly the lead he wanted.

"You okay?" Frank's grizzled voice drifted through the speakers. "Your image is all fuzzy, but I can still see enough to know you look like dirt."

Aaron sighed and looked up, his eyes drifting to the webcam that sat atop one of the monitors. A large pile of bird poop sat squarely on its top, where some of it had dripped down onto the lens. "Must just be a bad connection."

"Aaron." Frank's voice grew stern. One of the monitors, which had been displaying a lovely flower garden, switched to an image of the old security guard. "You had said you needed my advice. How does now sound?"

Aaron leaned back in the chair. He didn't want to talk. Well, he did. He wanted to want to talk, but at that moment, he didn't feel like moving at all.

"Why don't you start by telling me what's going on?" Frank's voice was soft. "I know the world is crazy these days. Just start be recapping it."

"You already know everything I could tell you." Aaron sighed. "You've seen it just like me. The elder Incacheck is here, we have a vampire on our team-"

"The elder Incacheck is there?" Frank's eyebrows show up into his hairline. "Come again?"

Belatedly, Aaron realized that Frank actually *hadn't* heard the latest news. He quickly filled him in on the conversation with Jeremy, then crossed his arms. "I just don't know what to do."

Frank frowned. "Seems to me that it's obvious. You have to fight the vampires and save lives."

"I get that, but…" Aaron held up his hands. All the equipment in front of him, it reminded him of one thing and one thing alone. The fact that Garmund wasn't there. "He's gone. Birch took Garmund. If he managed to take our best hacker, who's to say who he'll get next? We know nothing about Bertha. What if he manages to get her? Or Jasper? Or Harold?" Aaron's breath started to come faster. "Or you? Or-"

"Aaron." Frank held up a hand. "I know this is hard, but…" He sighed. "We'll get him back."

"But what if we can't?" Aaron shuddered. "The reason we had a job was because of Herford. Now, he's gone. He isn't here, beating down the door. We don't know where he is, but if Birch *did* do something to him, we're on our own."

Frank swallowed visibly. "Herford is okay." His voice trembled. "He'll be back."

So even Frank was terrified. "And if he isn't?"

"Then we'll do it on our own." Frank's voice solidified. "We have the vampires to take care of now. Focus on that, and *then* we'll get Garmund back."

Aaron nodded firmly, then sighed again, slowly letting himself slump forward. He risked a glance at the doorway, but saw no one. "Can I tell you something?"

Frank nodded. "Anything, you know that."

Aaron nodded and did his best to look at the camera. A tear slipped out of his eye and slid down his cheek. "Do you remember when we were down in Lambspoint? And I only cared about getting us out alive, I didn't care about actually saving the town?"

Frank frowned. "I don't remember it quite that way."

"Bertha screamed at me for it." Aaron could barely even whisper. Even now, it physically hurt him to speak the words. "I think I'm there again."

Frank leaned forward and tapped the computer screen. "What do you mean?"

"I mean, I don't care about these people." Aaron shrugged. "When it comes down to it, the only reason I want to save people is because that's the opposite of what

Birch wants to do. I want to rub it in his face that we won, I want to smash his ugly face into…" Aaron took a moment to compose himself. "I just want the team back. I want life to be good for us again. All these other people…" he shrugged. "I don't know them. I don't have any connection to them."

"It's like a movie." Frank nodded in understanding. "The heroes are concerned about saving the day, but as a viewer, you only care about the heroes. If a few people die in a fiery explosion, it's just a really cool set of special effects."

"Exactly." Aaron nodded. His chest ached as he said it, but… That's what the problem was. He just didn't care. "These are people's lives that we're playing with. I could be one of those students. You could. Any of us could. And I can't bring myself to care as long as we all get out alive."

Frank paused and scratched his beard for a few seconds. "Do you remember the Jim Paulo animated television series?"

Aaron smirked and nodded. It had been a classic staple of his childhood. "I loved that show when I was growing up. I would rewatch it for hours on end."

Frank chuckled. "There's just something about seeing vampire priests fighting Mayan mummies that gets the blood pumping." After a few moments, he sighed. "Anyway, do you remember the season five finale?"

Aaron did his best to remember the episode. It came to him after only a few moments, as it was one of the classic scenes of the franchise. A sun-worshipping death cult had kidnapped Jim Paulo's wife and were in the process of dragging her through the forest to a volcano. At the same time, the cult was descending on a small village to kill everyone in a mass sacrifice. With only minutes before the cult lay waste to the villagers, Jim Paulo was forced to make the hardest choice of his life.

"Yeah." Aaron nodded. "I don't think I had ever cried harder."

"Even adults watching the show cried." Frank sighed in memory. "Do you remember his speech, right before he saved the village?"

Aaron closed his eyes. "Not exactly."

"Then let me read it to you." Frank's voice drifted through Aaron's mind as he kept his eyes closed. "*Blood of my blood, breath of my breath, I am helpless as you are drawn away from me. Your voice calls to me in all that I see. The dew under my feet screams your name, the mockingbird sings a melody second only to your glorious whisper. If I go but a day without you, my lungs grow mold, and I descend into the dirt to rot.*

"*And yet, your voice is one out of a thousand that calls to me. Below, the valley will fill with blood if I spare you from the fire. These people are insects to me, the sting of a mosquito will burn worse than their deaths on my conscious. They have cast me aside, they have told me they desire not my help, until their hour of need. Now, I am worshiped as their savior, if only I will spare their lives.*

"*My love for you fades not with time, nor will it fail to flower even upon your death. These people, though they are swine to me, are still worthy of the same life granted to us by our creator. Godliness itself is not passion, chasing after something that you so desperately desire. Nay, Godliness is acting even in the absence of passion, making yourself take the action that you so readily despise.*

"*And so, I say farewell. One day, I will see you again. Until then, I will be content listening to your voice, soaking in your song as the sun rises every morning, and falling asleep to your lips as the stars sparkle down on the Earth. Goodbye, my love.*

Goodbye."

Aaron felt moisture dripping down his face, plopping onto the floor. "You know, he actually said that in real life." Aaron took a deep breath. "I couldn't even imagine."

"And yet, here you are." Frank sighed. "I know it isn't the same, but I think it's worthwhile. You don't feel anything for these people. Maybe you never will." The wizened man leaned forward. "That doesn't mean you shouldn't fight for them. I won't tell you to picture yourself as one of them to try and evoke cheap sympathy. You are a soldier, you are the head of the Apocolyps Squad. Our task is to stand on the edge of the world and hold back the monsters, even though we've never seen the lands that we fight to keep them from."

Aaron smirked quietly. The quote about standing on the edge of the world came from another adaptation of Jim Paulo's life, one of the most memorable comic book runs of all time. "I'll do my best."

"Aaron." Frank stroked his beard for a few slow seconds. "It isn't about doing your best. Saying that you'll do your best implies that you don't think you'll succeed. It's a cop-out answer."

Aaron nodded and took a deep breath. "Then I'm going to succeed."

"Do that." Frank nodded firmly, then leaned back. "I have to check some of the drones again. I'll turn off the camera to give you some privacy. Think about what I said. You don't have to care. You just have to do the right thing."

With that, Frank's image vanished. A little red light, half-obscured by bird poop, went dark, and Aaron leaned back in the chair again.

The talk with Frank… It hadn't been what he had expected. After it all, he still felt miserable. But then, maybe that was part of it. Maybe he *wouldn't* get to feeling better right off the bat. Maybe he was just going to have to suffer for a short time.

Maybe, all he could do was put one foot in front of the other. Slowly, he forced himself to his feet. He wanted to remain hidden, but he couldn't. Jeremy and Bertha were out and about. The least he could do was report to the Dean and see if he could get any more information.

It wasn't much, but it was something. And at that moment, that's all he had.

CHAPTER 25

"So, you need to go to the Smithsonian?" Bertha raised an eyebrow as the van skittered down the highway around Washington D.C.. "Can you give me any hints?"

Jeremy winced as the van zipped out of traffic and onto the shoulder to avoid a car that, in Bertha's words, *wasn't obeying the common-law traffic speed.* From his observations, very few people tended to obey her self-imposed speed limits.

"I already told you. There's a guy who knows something about the shards."

"Yeah, but what's the *real* story?" Bertha turned and looked at him, her eyes not at all focused on the road.

"That is the real story!" Jeremy gestured in front of them as they barreled up behind a semi. "Look out!"

Bertha didn't bother to look forward, but sent the van skittering back towards the center lane, narrowly dodging around the vehicle. "Why are you so jumpy? You're immortal!"

"Not really!" Jeremy protested. "The sun is out. If you wreck, I'll get exposed to the sun when I try to climb out of here."

"And here I thought meeting a vampire would be more exciting." Bertha sighed, then swung the steering wheel to the side, zipping across multiple lanes of traffic before barreling down an off-ramp. "At least you're actually letting me drive like this. Aaron always yells at me."

"What do you think *I'm* doing?" Jeremy tried to brace himself a bit more securely in the passenger seat as they screeched to a stop at a red light. "How much longer until we get there?"

"No long enough." Bertha muttered. "I'm about sick of all your negativity."

"My negativity?" Jeremy glanced at her. "Vampires are supposed to be the scary ones. Zombies. Incacheck. Literally any one of a thousand things that *isn't* driving down the highway."

"You people just don't do it right." Bertha sighed. "And only a few minutes. Coming up shortly."

Jeremy frowned. "I thought we were still a ways away."

"I know a shortcut." Bertha shrugged. "Hang on. You thought what you've already seen was crazy?"

Jeremy winced and grabbed ahold of the seat, doing everything in his power to hold on. As such, he was more than prepared when Bertha coasted around the intersection and began lazily tooling down a residential side street.

"This?" Jeremy sat back up and glanced out at the houses. "This is what you define as insane?"

"Anyone who would speed through a residential neighborhood is a terrible person." Bertha shrugged. "You could hit a child. I'd never do that."

"Uh, huh." Jeremy sighed and nodded. "Good to know that you have limits."

"Shut your mouth." Bertha grinned at him, then shrugged. "This road runs within a block of the Smithsonian. I'll have to drop you off while I go park, but I assume you'd rather be alone anyway."

Jeremy shrugged. "I'll share whatever I learn with the group."

Bertha glanced at him, then sighed. "Do what you have to do. Just…" She shrugged. "Be careful. You're a vampire, and that makes you different. If you find any secrets, don't be too willing to give them away. You might need them later."

Jeremy frowned in thought. "What do you mean?"

Bertha shrugged. "Oh, I don't know. Say you find out that there's a ritual you can perform to kill all vampires within a certain distance. I don't know if that's possible or not, but bear with me."

Jeremy nodded, not at all understanding where she was going with it. "Okay?"

"So you bring that information back to the squad, and you use it to help them kill the vampires. The day is saved, Incacheck doesn't get his shard, and life goes on. Right?"

Jeremy continued to nod. "Right. I'm still not following."

"You will." Bertha glanced to the sides as she coasted through an intersection. "Now, after this is all said and done, the government wants to know how everyone drove the vampires back, and the squad tells them about the ritual. The government will balk at the prospect at first, but with Herford backing us, they'll believe it eventually. With that, there's now a whole new door that's been opened. The possibility of combat rituals, used to slay America's enemies from afar. The only problem is that for that possibility to work, they need to test it out. And guess who happens to be the only vampire that they know?"

Jeremy nodded slowly. "Me."

"Exactly." Bertha nodded. "If you find something like that, you keep it close to your chest. Use it, by all means, but only show it to someone you *absolutely* trust."

Jeremy slowly crossed his arms. Vanessa was the only person that he knew he could trust, but at that moment, *she* didn't think she could trust *him*. And could she? He fought it as hard as he could, but he had already bitten so many people since his talk with her. Was he really any better than the monster she believed him to be?

He was spared from any further contemplation as Bertha reached a T-intersection. On the far side, a massive white building rose high into the sky. Bertha glanced at the car radio and shrugged.

"It's high noon. Better hurry. This place is big, you want to find him before closing."

Jeremy nodded and stepped out of the vehicle. Bertha roared away, and he slowly turned to face the enormous building. After a few moments of deliberation, he began walking down the sidewalk, looking for an entrance. He still had hours before closing, right? There was no need to rush.

His optimism soon began to wane as he realized just how truly enormous the Smithsonian was. Despite living so close, he had never actually been to it before, and was a bit surprised by the sheer scope of it. Dozens of buildings scattered across nearly half a mile of ground made for a *massive* haystack.

In the end, it took him three solid hours of searching before he finally found his way to Lark's office. The only reason he found it so quickly, in fact, was sheer luck after one of the security guards had been able to take him to a manager's office where he was able to browse the ten thousand-entry log of scientists and historians that worked at the location.

Finally, after far too long, he reached the small door towards the rear of the Museum of Supernatural History. The metal plate, screwed to the wood, simply read *Lark*, without a first name or a title. He could hear shouting coming from within, a man and a woman's voice, though he couldn't make anything out. Jeremy took a deep breath as he stepped up to the door and knocked several times.

The door burst open after a split second, and a frazzled-looking man with sandy hair tumbled out. He glanced up at Jeremy and flashed a withered smile.

"Ahh, welcome! Come in, please, we were just finishing up."

"No, we weren't!" A woman was on her knees in front of his desk, tears running down her cheeks. She wore clothes that could only be described as belonging to an archeologist, as if she had just come back from a dig site. "Please, don't do this!"

"I keep telling you, I don't have a choice." Lark crossed his arms and walked back behind the desk. "The board suspended your license, and until they decide to renew it, I can't procure any more items from you. It would discredit the entire museum."

The woman shook her head. "They shouldn't be able to take away my license!"

"You opened a sarcophagus without first ensuring that the contents inside would remain unharmed." Lark shrugged. "Rule number one. Never open *anything* before you've moved it to a secure setting."

"I was possessed!"

"Yes, I'm sure." Lark shrugged. "Please, I'm certain that this gentleman has important business with me. You may leave."

The woman shook her head. "I'm not leaving this office until you say I can keep working for you."

"Well, that's not happening." Lark puffed out his cheeks, then sighed. "Alright, here's the deal. There's an artifact that was stolen from the archives several years ago. A small pyramid rumored to belong to Queen Hatshepsut. If you can find it and bring it back to me, I'll make it worth your while."

"Thank you." The woman leapt to her feet. "Do you know where it is?"

"If I did, I would have it back by now." Lark sighed. "Look, I'll email you the details, okay? Same contact information as always?"

The woman nodded rapidly. "You won't regret this!"

With that, she turned and ran out the door. It fell shur behind her, and Lark groaned. "I already do." He crossed his arms and turned to Jeremy. "Now, what can I do for you, my oddly-dressed friend?"

Jeremy glanced down, realizing that wearing a vampire cape underneath a thick raincoat on a sunny day probably *did* appear a bit suspect.

"I need some information." Jeremy sat down in a chair just opposite of Lark's desk. The curator sat down at well, a curious look on his face. "A Professor Inkwood referred me to you. Do you know him?"

"Doctor Inkwood, yes." Lark nodded. "I haven't spoken to him in several years, but we had quite a long series of interactions when he was writing his dissertation. You're here about Jim Paulo, then?"

Jeremy nodded. "I need anything you could tell me about him. Anything that the comics don't show." He paused for a moment. "Anything about shards."

Lark raised an eyebrow. "You've seen another?"

Jeremy frowned. "Another?"

Lark nodded and leaned forward. "I myself was in possession of one of the shards last year. That... Didn't work out so well." He sighed. "I'm going to wager a guess from the outfit that you're a vampire?"

Jeremy snorted. "Most people would be surprised."

"Most people didn't live through a zombie invasion." Lark tapped his desk several times. "So, you've found a shard. Tell me what you know, and I'll do my best to fill in the gaps."

Jeremy nodded and did his best to recap the event, touching on the fact that the shard couldn't be used until it powered down. When he finished, Lark nodded slowly.

"That matches up with what I know." He sighed. "Do you want the short version of the story or the long version?"

"I think I need the long version." Jeremy shrugged. "I don't understand any of this."

"You'll understand even less by the time I'm done." Lark frowned. "Now, Jim Paulo is popular enough in culture these days. Comics, television shows, movies, you name it. The problem is that they just depict him as a monster hunter that *might* have been based off an actual missionary who did something or another hundreds of years ago."

Jeremy nodded. "Okay?"

Lark shrugged. "What the comics leave out is the fact that there was more to the story. When Jim Paulo's body was found, it was lying next to a mostly-completed tablet that shattered into dozens of pieces as soon as it was touched. This kicked off a series of supernatural events throughout the known world, in the mid seventeen-hundreds. At the time, though, the events were so isolated that no one really put the pieces together, and now that it's so far in the past, only a few people are willing to actually believe it."

Lark leaned forward. "The fact of the matter is that these shards are key to the legend of Jim Paulo. Most Paulo scholars believe that he brought a sizable portion of the tablet with him when he came to America during the Spanish Conquest. It seems that he was trying to complete it, though no one knows for certain *why* he would have been doing that. All the supernatural events, all the monsters he fought, they were shards activating and deactivating, progressing through their motions while he tried to claim them all."

Jeremy nodded slowly. "So, theoretically, if someone was to assemble the tablet, what would happen?"

"No one really knows for sure." Lark shrugged. "Paulo wasn't able to complete it before his death, and as I said, it shattered upon contact with another human. I suspect that whatever magic formed the tablet in the first place was designed to make it incredibly difficult to reassemble, likely to prevent whatever horror could be unleashed on the world. It doesn't make me hopeful, that's for sure."

Jeremy nodded slowly. "So… What about the vampires? Are there any reports of him battling the vampires?"

"As a matter of fact, yes." Lark nodded. "It's one of the more well-documented events, actually. The comic books did a remarkably faithful portrayal in The Unstoppable Jim Paulo Numbers 51-74. Of course, that entry didn't include the shards, but…" At Jeremy's impatient look, Lark plowed forward. "Apologies. The fact of the matter is that the shard was in the hands of a vampire lord when Paulo came across the event. In an attempt to prevent the shard from deactivating and the vampire lord gaining control over it, Paulo attempted to simply limit the number of vampires available. If there were never enough of them to allow the shard to deactivate, the lord could never win."

Jeremy frowned. There was something about the way Lark said it… "What's the catch?"

Lark sighed and glanced down at the table. "It was one of Paulo's largest regrets. If he had simply allowed the vampires to reproduce, only a few hundred people would have died. Instead, thousands perished as the vampires continuously sought to expand their ranks to fulfil the hunger of the shard. In addition, two of Paulo's closest friends died in the fruitless battles." Lark grimaced. "I know that's not what you wanted to hear, but that's the truth."

Jeremy glanced at the ground. It made him feel sick. "There's no other way?"

"Several hundred years later, vampires appeared in eastern Europe. They engulfed a small town, and that was the last anyone heard of them." Lark shrugged. "For all we know, they're still out there somewhere."

"Great." Jeremy sighed. He just needed *answers*. "Can't you tell me *anything* else?"

Lark shook his head. "I've spent my entire life piecing together the true story of Jim Paulo. You aren't going to be able to just figure it out in five minutes because you're impatient."

Jeremy climbed to his feet. Had the trip really been for nothing? "If he's so well-known, why is it *so* hard to learn anything?"

Lark sighed and scratched his head. "You have to understand the situation at the time. It was a new world, with untold implications. Every religion with more than ten members was ready to send missionaries to the Americas in a desperate attempt to become the new ruling power. Though it can't be substantiated, there were rumors that the pope at the time, Clement the Eighth, saw the new world as an opportunity to gather new believers in a bid to stay ahead of the aggressive Protestantism that was overtaking Europe."

Jeremy shrugged. "So what?"

"So, with the political and religious landscape being as tumultuous as it was, things got a bit hazy." Lark shrugged. "Jim Paulo was part of an early Catholic expedition to the new world. When he took a party of natives, as well as several other priests and nuns, and vanished shortly after their arrival, the Bishop that he served under began fabricating reports to the Vatican to make it appear that all was well. When reports of Hell on Earth began surfacing, the remaining Catholic missionaries quickly split into factions over whether or not they should even stay in the new world, or if it was cursed. On top of *that*, other missionaries began to arrive to witness the chaos. Lutheran missionaries saw it as a way to further break up the Catholic Church, while a particularly hopeful Orthodox priest saw the situation as a way to heal the schism between the Catholic church and his own beliefs. All of this led to hundreds of conflicting reports being sent overseas to dozens of different individuals. For many years, the only people who truly knew the reality of the situation were those individuals unlucky enough to be at Jim Paulo's side."

Jeremy nodded slowly. "And since then there hasn't been much progress."

Lark rapped his knuckles on the desk. "Bingo! After the discovery of the body, the Vatican declassified the reports that they had received. The Orthodox church did the same, while the various collectors that had gathered other reports released their own. More reports were fabricated in an attempt for scam artists to make money, and whatever truth that may once have been uncovered was squelched. Then, in the modern era, people began adapting his story, and since then, you'd be more likely to find a kernel of truth in a pop-up ad."

Jeremy nodded slowly. "Well… Thank you for your time."

He turned to leave, only to hear Lark jump to his feet.

"Wait."

Jeremy slowly turned back around. "Yes?"

Lark sighed and kicked at the ground for a few moments. Finally, he nodded and straightened up. "The only known source of truth is from Jim Paulo's journal itself. Of course, the modern version that you can buy in a bookstore is so muddled that it may as well be fiction. Here at the Smithsonian, we have the original on display. But…" Lark grimaced, obviously torn in an internal battle. "The journal that we have on display is only part of Paulo's journal."

Jeremy felt his breath freeze. "There's more?"

Lark nodded and met his eyes. "I don't know what they contain. Experts who have studied Paulo's journal for years have suspected that it isn't the whole story, as it often seems to reference passages that aren't present. As a member of the Smithsonian, I can confirm that when we received it from the descendants of the archaeologist who found the body, we were told that it was only a fraction of the total text. The rest of the journal was split into pieces and scattered among the family, and now rests in dozens of different safes and private collections across the world."

For the first time, Jeremy felt a flicker of hope. "And you think those might contain more information?"

Lark grimaced once more. "The journal that we have functions more as an index, a summary of his adventures. It never once mentions the shards or the tablet, only the supernatural forces that he faced. All that information is hidden. And, despite all my research and study, I have yet to uncover a single page of those secluded documents."

Jeremy forced himself to nod. "That's… That's still something."

"The only reason I'm telling you at all is because… Well, you're a vampire standing here in my office." Lark shrugged. "The world is progressing through another series of gauntlets, and I'd rather not get caught in the crossfire. If you can stop it, please, do."

"I'll do everything in my power." Jeremy nodded.

The two of them continued to stare at each other for a few awkward moments. Jeremy muttered out a goodbye, and stepped out into the hallway. Somehow, he was a bit unsurprised to find Bertha standing there, leaning against a wall like nothing had happened.

"Find what you were looking for?" Bertha raised an eyebrow questioningly.

Jeremy scratched his head. He was even more confused than before, but he *did* have a lead. The hidden diaries of Jim Paulo, wherever those happened to be. The words of Bertha drifted back to him, warnings of hidden agendas and protection. Those hidden journals…

Those hidden journals could easily have been the key to saving the world. On the other hand, Lark had told him that vampires had risen again in the seventeen hundreds, and all had turned out well. Those journals could, quite easily, wind up being the death of himself and countless others.

"No." Jeremy shook his head and forced himself to meet Bertha's eyes. "All I found were rumors."

CHAPTER 26

A blaring alarm brought Harold out of his concentration, from where he stooped over Jasper's weapon bench. In front of him, an assault rifle lay in a state of dismemberment, as he attempted to increase the fire rate by removing some of the key parts.

"Time to roll." Jasper stuck his head through the door. "Sundown City."

"Or just sundown." Harold turned away from the bench and picked up a large crossbow. While the compressed air had worked for a time, the crossbow that they had picked up from a sporting goods store worked far better, a fact that had rather bummed out Jasper. "You ready?"

"More ready than you, looks like." Jasper nodded at the gun. "Are you still working on that?"

"I've been a bit more focused on things that kill vampires." Harold chuckled and slung the crossbow over his shoulder before picking up a small cross to hang around his neck, a large stake that also happened to be cross-shaped, and series of pressed wooden daggers. "All we need is some garlic and we'll be set."

"The store was sold out when I went." Jasper shrugged. "I can see if I can get some in the next few days, but if we keep seeing the same number of vampires that we've *been* seeing..."

Jasper let the thought trail off, and Harold nodded. It had been nearly a week since the attack on the mansion, and since then, they hadn't seen a thing. Students were still going missing, and even the larger newspapers in the area were beginning to pick up stories about the vampire hunters seen walking around the campus, though neither the Squad nor the ARF had been able to bring in a single one of the creatures.

"What's the rotation for tonight?" Harold slid through the door, changing positions with Jasper, so he could pick up his own weaponry for the night.

"Aaron is patrolling with Bertha, I'm on my own, and you're with Jeremy." Jasper shrugged. "All by my lonesome, just trying to survive in a cold, cruel world."

Harold crossed his arms. "Why are you the one by yourself? Wouldn't it make more sense for me to be alone?"

"It would. In fact, it makes a great deal of sense for the two people who are *already* undead to take the dangerous jobs instead of us who still bother to do things like breathing." Jasper snorted. "Unless you'd like to explain that to Aaron, though, it *does* makes more sense for the more experienced fighter to be on his own."

"I suppose." Harold shrugged and readjusted the weapons on his shoulders. "Hurry up."

"Hey, give me some time" Jasper started slipping bullets into a large belt. "Preparation for a massive war is something that you don't just *rush*. It's like a fine meal. You *savor* it."

Aaron chose that moment to come walking up. "Well, your massive war is about to start without you." He glanced at Harold and Jasper. "Jeremy just made contact with one of our drones. Frank says that he's reporting major vampire activity across the campus. They're all coming out of hiding."

"We'll be there." Jasper flashed a grin. "Just give us a minute!"

Aaron nodded and turned to leave. The moment he was gone, Jasper turned and popped open a small compartment on the table. "Here, take a few of these."

Harold frowned as Jasper handed him several syringes filled with a reddish liquid. "And these are?"

"An expedited version of the stuff I used to cure Jeremy." Jasper shrugged. "Can't hurt to have one or two more on our side. Just in case you happen to corner one and can stab it easier than killing it."

"I'll do what I can." Harold slid the syringes into his pocket, attempting not to stick himself with them. He wasn't worried about the pain, but chemicals that could affect undead beings *did* give him a bit of pause.

With that, the two of them walked out of the room, through the tiny home, and out onto the porch. Overhead, the stars were just beginning to sparkle as the sun finished setting. Aaron and Bertha were already there, armed with stakes, crosses, and guns with wooden bullets.

"Alright, let's move." Aaron nodded. "Harold, Jeremy will meet you at the dorms. Bertha and I will cover the eastern side of the college, Jasper will cover the west. Use the headsets if you need help. Got it?"

"Got it." Harold nodded.

The rest of the squad nodded their affirmatives, and the group quickly set out. Harold wound his way through the residential neighborhood, feeling increasingly conspicuous as the streetlights flickered into existence above him. The dean had assured them that the police knew of their existence… And yet, Harold imagined that if a police car drove past at that moment, it would wind up being an uncomfortable conversation.

By the time he reached the dorms, it was pitch black out. Idly, he couldn't help but wish that zombies were granted the same night vision that Jeremy claimed to have. He began to wish this even harder as Jeremy simply dropped out of the sky and landed next to him with a loud thunk.

"There you are." Harold put a hand on his chest. "You almost gave me a heart attack."

"Sometimes, I wish that was still a possibility for me." Jeremy sighed and shrugged. "Ahh, well. Shall we begin?"

"Lead the way." Harold swept out his hand, and the two of them began wandering across the campus. Harold hadn't spent much time at all with the vampire since they had healed him, only a single conversation here and there. Jeremy shifted awkwardly under his cape, and Harold coughed.

"So… How are things going?"

"About as well as you'd expect." Jeremy shrugged. "I hide out during the day and look for vampires in the sewers, then come up at night and look for vampires in the sky. Not the most romantic life."

"True." Harold chuckled. "Of course, living with a bunch of guys and one random girl isn't exactly the most *romantic* thing either."

"I'd happily trade you." Jeremy took a deep breath, forcing air through dead lungs. "Did… Did you ever have a girlfriend?"

Harold shook his head. "Nothing serious. There were a couple girls I thought were attractive, but it never went anywhere." He frowned. "Why?"

"Oh, just…" Jeremy held up his hands. "It's hard to explain."

Harold glanced back at the dorms. The fact that Jeremy had been dating a girl before he was turned was one of the few things that Harold *did* know about him. "Have you talked to her recently?"

Jeremy shook his head. "Not since the night at the mansion. I just…" He balled his fists. "I love her. I know how it sounds, a freshman in college being in love, but I do." He turned to Harold, a pained look on his face. "I made a promise to her, and I broke it after a matter of hours. I can't face her again. I don't know what to do. I don't want to just let her go, but…" He held up his hands. "Look at me. What about *this* would she want?"

Harold grimaced. He wasn't exactly the best individual to ask about relationship advice. "If she truly loves you, she'll be able to see past the monster and see *you*."

Jeremy shook his head. "But what if I'm not really me? What if even my personality has changed? What if I really *am* the monster?"

Harold took a deep breath, forcing air through his own decaying lungs. Slowly, he reached up and clicked off his earpiece. "Trust me. You're undead, but that doesn't change *who* you are."

"Really?" Jeremy held up his hands. "How do you know that? *How?*"

Harold opened his mouth to reply, but was cut off by the sharp snap of a camera. The light momentarily blinded him, and he took a step back. A college student with a massive journaling kit stepped out of the shadows, a grin on his greasy face.

"Just keep moving." The boy spoke quickly. "You're the vampire hunters, aren't you? The whole campus has been talking about you people, but I'm the first to actually get a picture!" He glanced at the back of the camera, then frowned. "Uh, dude? You with the cape. You didn't show up on the picture."

Harold chuckled. Vampires didn't cast reflections in mirrors, so it made sense that pictures couldn't be taken of them, either.

"Sorry." Jeremy shrugged. "It's a medical condition."

"What kind of medical condition is *that?*" The reporter slid closer. "I'd love to do an interview. Oh, the journals that I could talk to. A disease that makes you not show up on-"

The reporter's voice was cut off as a shadow appeared out of the dark behind him. A cloaked student slammed into his back, driving him to the ground. Needlelike teeth sank into the reporter's neck long before Harold or Jeremy could so much as blink.

"Get away!" Harold jumped forward and held up a cross. Light blazed from the object, blasting the vampire off the reporter and sending him tumbling into the night. Jeremy ran after him, drawing two stakes from his belt. As the two vampires faded off into the distance, Harold flipped the now-unconscious reporter onto his back.

Even as he watched, the man's skin began to grow pale. Harold swore, then grabbed in his pocket for one of the vials that Jasper had given him. He didn't know if it would work, but if there was a chance, he had to try.

Harold stabbed the syringe into the reporter's neck, just next to the bite marks, and emptied the entire vial. Almost instantly, the man began to spasm, and Harold stood back up. There was nothing else he could do, nothing but wait.

Jeremy returned several long minutes later, a smirk on his face.

"Got him." He crossed his arms. "Took me a bit, but I got him." He finally glanced down at the corpse. "Is he turned?"

Harold shrugged. "It's hard to tell for certain, but I think the vampire was able to suck enough. We should know in a few minutes, at least."

Harold bent down next to the reporter, listening for any signs of life. Or un-life, whatever the case was. While he sat there, a flutter echoed through the air overhead, and he glanced up to see the stars blinking back and forth in rapid succession.

"There are bats flying overhead." Jeremy's voice was tight. "A lot of them."

"They're starting to make their move." Harold grimaced. "Alright, new plan. You stay with him, at least for a few more minutes. If he wakes up as a vampire, make sure that he's on our side. I gave him a dose of the stuff I gave you, so it *should* work." He stood up and started to jog in the direction that the vampires were flying. "I'll take these guys!"

Harold took off across the campus, sprinting as fast as he could run. Given that he didn't need to breathe, it was quite a clip. He reached up and turned his earpiece back on and began shouting at the squad.

"Vampires!" He glanced at the various landmarks. "Heading west! Jasper! Get ready!"

He quickly tore around the corner of a campus building to find exactly what the vampires were after. A massive cluster of tents covered an open area between a number of the buildings, a camp-out of some sort. Vampires were changing back from bat form and dropping down into the tents, attacking their prey.

"I'm here." Jasper's voice came back, tense and winded. "Other side. I can't tell who's living and who's dead."

Harold nodded as students streamed from their tents. Some of them sported bite marks, and soon fell to the ground as vampirism took hold. Others simply screamed and ran for their lives. Gunshots rang through the night air, followed by the screams of the injured.

"What do we do?" Harold snapped at his earpiece. "Aaron? I need answers!"

Only static came through the line, and Harold swore under his breath. "Jasper? Ideas?"

Silence once more. Harold shook his head and charged into the fray. He had to do *something*, even if it wasn't necessarily going to work out perfectly.

He grabbed at his pocket, pulling out several vials of the serum. A vampire flashed down out of the air, transforming and landing directly in front of him. He slammed the syringe into the side of the girl's neck, grimacing as she screamed. She collapsed in a heap, and Harold moved forward.

More vampires materialized out of the darkness. Two males and one more female. Harold slammed a syringe into the neck of the first male as he charged forward, then ducked under the blow of the second. He jabbed the syringe up into its ribcage, and dropped back as both of them fell to the ground spasming. He pulled out his last vial of serum and took a stance.

The female vampire leapt at him. He thrust out the syringe, but she transformed into a bat, causing him to miss and overstep. She transformed back, just behind him, and slammed a fist into his back. His spine snapped rather gruesomely, and his face smashed into the grass. The serum shattered onto the soil, its precious liquid leaking out into the wilderness.

"Well, now." The female vampire flipped him over onto his back and straddled him, a seductive smile on her face. "Look what I caught."

"Please don't bother trying to scare me." Harold didn't particularly want a repeat of the situation with Gruen. "It's not going to work."

"Oh, I wouldn't think of it." The girl, probably a freshman, bent down and flashed her fangs at Harold. Harold's back chose that exact moment to snap back into place with a loud *shlurp*, eliciting a soft gasp from the vampire. "My, aren't you excited?"

Harold sighed and flexed his hands. The girl's knees were quite firmly holding his wrists down, preventing him from making a move. She bent over, placing her lips only inches from his own. Harold groaned and slammed his forehead into hers, grimacing as pain flared up and down his body.

The vampire was knocked off-balance, and Harold rolled out from under her. He grabbed at a small pistol on his belt loaded with wooden bullets, and snapped it up to point in her direction. She raised her hands in mock surrender, a sultry smile on her face. As she turned to dust, the smile seemed to hang in the air, and Harold sighed.

"Will you stop making out with the vampires?" Jasper came rushing up, crossbow in hand. He snapped the weapon up and shot a vampire that was charging up behind Harold. The arrow struck the vampire in the arm, doing no permanent damage. As the creature reached Harold, he sidestepped it, broke off the arrow at the point of the wound, and stabbed the vampire through the heart.

"I wouldn't exactly say we were getting to know each other." Harold pulled several wooden daggers off his belt. "Any ideas?"

All around, it seemed that pure pandemonium raged. Vampires swept back and forth in their long, dark cloaks. Students screamed and tried to evade them. Even as Harold watched, a boy burst from his tent, only to fall within moments as a vampire latched onto his neck like a leech.

"No idea." Jasper shook his head. "There are so many. We can't just kill them all because we could be killing live students, but on the flip side-"

A young freshman girl ran past Harold, fear filling her eyes. A vampire dropped out of the sky, landing on her and driving her to the ground. Harold leapt forward and kicked it in the head, knocking it away from her. The vampire, a rather burly male, slowly climbed back to his feet.

"This is my meal." He snarled. "You'll pay for that."

The girl climbed to her feet, only to be slammed back to the ground by the vampire's massive foot. He growled, and Harold threw one of his wooden daggers. The vampire simply leaned to the side, avoiding the first projectile. In frustration, Harold threw the second dagger, only for the vampire to slap it out of the air.

Growing frustrated, Harold jumped forward, punching the vampire in the chest. The monster's eyes opened wide as he fell backward, striking the ground with a powerful thud. Harold stomped on the creature's chest, trying to keep the man down.

The vampire didn't hesitate, and simply reached up and grabbed Harold's leg. He had a brief moment to regret the decision before the vampire simply slammed him into a nearby tent, crushing the flimsy supports and flattening the structure entirely. Harold scrambled back to his feet, only to have a ham-sized fist connect with his chest, smashing him back into the ground.

"Here!" A samurai sword landed neck to Harold, gleaming in the night. Harold grabbed the weapon and slashed upward, taking off the vampire's head in one smooth motion. The body collapsed with a thud, and Harold kicked the head away as fast as he could. As he climbed to his feet, an older college girl ran up to him.

"Thought you might be able to use that." She helped the first girl to her feet as Jasper walked over. "Maybe now people will stop telling me that it's weird."

"Trust me when I say that it's totally awesome." Jasper flashed a grin, then sobered. "Get to safety, both of you. Now."

The two girls nodded, and Harold handed the sword back to the older girl. Both of them turned to walk away, jogging through the destruction.

Without warning, a burst of gunfire echoed through the campsite. Tents became ribbons as bullets sliced through the area, cutting down anything and everything. The two girls fell in pieces, riddled by the deadly projectiles. Harold threw himself in front of Jasper as armored troops charged in from the sides.

"No!" Harold screamed. "Stop this!"

Three living college students raced for the ARF troops. In the single moment that they were there, Harold saw their faces. The fear, etched in their eyes, the terror of fleeing the vampire threat. The hope, rising on their faces, as they saw their saviors rushing towards them. The confused agony as the ARF shot them down without so much as an afterthought.

Harold crouched down as bullets blew through his own body. He was protecting Jasper, but oh, he hoped that no one would notice that he was undead just like the vampires.

The ARF seemed not to care, and rushed past Harold and Jasper in an instant. Harold stood back up and caught one of them by the shoulder, spinning him around.

"What the hell do you think you're doing?" Harold screamed. "These people aren't all infected!"

"Some of them are." The soldier snapped back. "Birch's orders: Anyone dies who stands in our way." The man growled in his throat. "You're looking pretty suspicious in that matter."

Jasper climbed to his feet and slammed a fist into the side of the soldier's head. The man's eyes went hazy, and he collapsed in a heap. Jasper touched a few dials on his watch and nodded.

"High-frequency wave burst. Knocks people out for a few seconds."

"As long as it works." Harold turned and charged at the line of soldiers. "Come on!"

He didn't know what he was going to do. He didn't know how he was going to do it, but he was going to stop the ARF from killing anyone else in that camp. Behind him, Jasper kept pace, ready as well. In that moment, Harold didn't care about winning. The faces of the students that the ARF had so heartlessly gunned down rode in his mind, driving him forward.

The vampires were beasts, but the ARF were human. And he was going to make them *pay* for trying to blur that line.

CHAPTER 27

Jeremy sighed as he trudged back through the streets. By the time he had been able to reach the site of the massacre, it had already ended. Harold had urged them to leave before the ARF caught them, and both vampires had been happy to oblige. Beside him, the reporter swept along, skin as pale as paper and sporting a long cloak.

"What was that?" The boy, Riley, finally asked.

"For a reporter, you're slow to ask questions." Jeremy sighed and ran a hand through his hair. "That was the ARF. Long story short, they're bad news."

"Great." Riley grimaced. "So… What are we going to do about it?"

"Right now, hide." Jeremy sighed. "Once things have calmed down, we're going to head back out. Harold managed to stick a bunch of the vampires with the same serum that he used on you and me, which should mean that there are more of us out there who can fight Incachech's control."

"I'm okay with that." Riley scratched behind his head. "I know my old life is over, but I *do* still have contacts that I can use to help track down the freed vampires. It might come in handy."

"Do that." Jeremy nodded, a bit surprised at how easily Riley was handling the transition. "If we get very many, we can move back into the tunnels underneath the college. I'd just like to avoid it for now, until the ARF calms down a bit."

"I'm with you there." Riley nodded slowly. "Can't say as I want to be shot at anymore."

Jeremy could only nod in agreement. Slowly, the two of them wandered through the dark suburbs that surrounded the college. Ahead, the lights from the Squad's headquarters flickered in the distance. Jeremy flashed a small smile as they crossed over to the opposite side of the street and wandered to the ancient, peeling house that stood just across from the Squad's home.

Riley frowned in disgust at the massive structure. "This is where we're staying?"

"It's abandoned." Jeremy shrugged and walked through the front door. "Come on. We'll only be here a short while, anyway."

As the door fell shut behind them, the squeaking of several rodents interrupted Jeremy's thought processes. Several rats scampered across the floor, squeaking loudly before vanishing under a couch.

"It's not much." Jeremy walked over and plopped down on the couch, sending up a cloud of dust and sending the rats scurrying away once more. "But it's a good enough place to stay. And it'll keep us safe once the sun rises."

"I'm not sure I'm really liking this whole 'vampire' thing." Riley dropped down onto the couch next to Jeremy. "Can I get a refund?"

Jeremy snorted. He was preparing a witty response when a low whimpering noise drifted through the air. Both Jeremy and Riley jumped to their feet and glanced at each other.

"You heard that, right?" Riley's eyes narrowed.

"Yes, I did." Jeremy frowned and tried to listen harder. It sounded like the sound was coming from upstairs. Slowly, he began to move towards the staircase, and began to creep upwards.

The two vampires crept onto the upper landing and began winding through the hallways of the home, trying to find the source of the noise. It grew steadily louder, a pathetic whining that could have come from a sick puppy, until they reached a door to one of the upper bedrooms. Carefully, fearing what he might find inside, Jeremy twisted the knob and threw the door open.

Inside, Gruen lay on the floor, twisted into the fetal position. He gasped in agony as Jeremy stepped inside, and slowly looked up, sweat beaded on his brow.

"It hurts." Gruen whimpered, his eyes unfocused on anything in the room. "Oh, it hurts. How are you not dead?"

"I guess some of us are better at our jobs." Jeremy stomped over to Gruen and knelt down next to him. He gave the man a sharp flick, sending him spasming in agony.

"Care to explain?" Riley leaned up against the doorframe.

Jeremy sighed. "Incacheck did something to the vampires so that if they don't feed on schedule, they start experiencing pain. If they don't produce a vampire when feeding, they experience pain. And Gruen here is the worst vampire I've ever seen."

Riley frowned. "Should we help him?"

Jeremy slowly climbed to his feet. The Squad's house was right across the street, he could haul Gruen over there, throw him at their feet, and let them cure him. On the other hand, Gruen had killed dozens of people and had basically been personally responsible for all the deaths that had happened since the whole event started.

"No." Jeremy took a deep breath. "We're going to leave him there." He stalked past Riley before turning and barring his fangs at the writhing man. "We've got more important vampires to deal with."

CHAPTER 28

"Can I please shoot him?" Harold ground his teeth together as he and Jasper stalked across the campus. "One bullet. We have diplomatic immunity, right?"

"We have the exact opposite of diplomatic immunity." Jasper sighed and ran his fingers through his hair. "Just don't look at him."

Harold sighed and closed his eyes. Just in front of them, in full combat gear, an ARF soldier stomped down the concrete pathways as the sun began to set. It had been less than twenty-four hours since the ARF had killed an estimated hundred and fifty college students, and they were out patrolling like nothing had happened.

When he reopened his eyes, the soldier hadn't vanished. Harold swore under his breath and turned to the side, walking down a sidewalk that wound up the side of a sweeping hill dotted with glass sculptures. "Come on."

Jeremy frowned, but followed. "We're supposed to go to the Dean's office."

"We'll get there." Harold sighed. "I just can't stand the sight of him. I don't want to be associated with him."

Jasper nodded at the rifle that Harold was carrying. "You probably shouldn't be toting a weapon, then."

Harold just shook his head. He just didn't understand it. He didn't understand why the ARF was so willing to just kill people. As they walked, Harold saw students running for buildings and peeking out from behind curtains. The entire campus was terrified. And Harold frankly couldn't blame them.

"We are failing here." Harold finally spoke up again as they reached the peak of the hill. Devoid of trees, the landscape fell away in front of him, speckled only by white limestone structures and statues. "You realize that, right?"

"Yeah." Jasper sighed as they started down the other side. "Yeah, I know."

"We need to be out looking for these vampires." Harold tightened his grip on the rifle. "We need to be hunting them down and slaughtering them."

"We have the drones out."

"I know!" Harold turned and almost screamed into his friend's face. Jasper took a step back, and Harold sighed. "Sorry."

"What is it?" Jasper took a step forward. "You just seem-"

"Upset?" Harold raised an eyebrow. "Think back. It wasn't even a year ago that I was a normal human. I was a high school student, living out my life in Lambspoint.

Then, over the course of one single night, everything changed."

Jeremy sighed and nodded. "Yeah, I know."

"I don't think you do." Harold fell a well of frustration building up inside himself. "Those people who died last night? That was me." He shook his head. "These people here? They're terrified. They don't understand what's happening, all they know is that something out there is trying to kill them, and the only people who are available to help are causing even more damage to them."

Jasper frowned. "I'm not sure that's *exactly* what-"

"That's sure what it looked like to me." Harold held up a hand. "When I found out who you people really were, it almost crushed me. There were survivors last night, and I can't tell you how thankful I am for that, but those survivors are going to be painting a story of guns and terror and death. We're supposed to be the good guys. We're supposed to protect people. And now, all we're doing is going to meet with the dean to try and explain why those deaths were necessary."

Jasper held up a finger. "That's not-"

"That's exactly what we're doing." Harold sighed. "Don't even pretend that it's not."

Jasper held Harold's gaze, then sighed and nodded. "You're right." After a moment, he shrugged. "So what do we do?"

Harold was cut off by the sound of a nearby door opening. He turned to see a professor in a dapper suit and jacket slowly stepping out of what appeared to be a small lecture hall.

"Hello!" The man held up a hand. "Could I have a word with you?"

Harold sighed. Jasper gave a short shake of his head, and Harold slowly walked over to the professor. The man never took more than a single step from the door, and seemed ready to bolt at any moment. As Harold came to a stop, the distinguished individual sighed.

"Could you answer a question for me?"

"Maybe." Harold glanced at Jasper. "I can't answer everything, but there are a few things I can talk about."

"Word on the street is that there are vampires afoot." The professor flashed a small grin. "That's preposterous, right?"

Jasper coughed, which Harold roundly ignored. "No. It's not preposterous. There are vampires here. And we're not sure exactly how to stop them."

The professor nodded slowly. "Truly? I thought my associate was insane when he mentioned the possibility. He's more than a bit fascinated with the creatures, their lore and mythos."

Harold grimaced. "Tell him to stay away from them. They're not to be trusted."

"I would, except I haven't seen him for several days." The professor sighed. "Thus brings me to my second question. Have you, by any chance, managed to keep a record of who has been turned into a vampire and who has been killed as one?"

Jasper spoke up before Harold had a chance. "We're trying, but I'm afraid that's a tricky process."

"I understand." The professor nodded slowly. "Well, if you do happen to come across a Professor Inkwood, tell him that he's always welcome back in my classroom, undead or not. I greatly miss him."

Harold nodded slowly. "Of course we will."

The professor simply gave a short nod, turned, and stepped back inside. As the door fell shut, Jasper sighed.

"What was that about?"

"Giving people hope." Harold turned to walk away, down the sidewalk. "That's what we're supposed to do, right?"

"Well, yes, but-"

"Then that's what I'm going to do." Harold turned around and met Jasper's gaze. "Now are you with me? Or not?"

CHAPTER 29

The crash of a banging door echoed through the limestone frat house. Garmund did his best to ignore the clatter of armored boots as new ARF members stomped in to find their barracks while other members went out on patrol.

"I can't listen to this." Garmund pushed himself away from the computer as laughter drifted up through the air. "I just can't."

Rodger, relaxing on a bean bag near the rear of the room, sighed and nodded. "It makes me sick, that's for sure."

"They murdered kids!" Garmund slammed a fist onto the computer table. "Young adults. Whatever you want to call them. They cut them down in cold blood!"

"Yep." Rodger's voice was soft. "Yeah, they did."

Without warning, the door blew open, revealing Birch standing there. His arms were crossed behind his back, his eyebrows raised.

"Garmund. From what I gather, you really don't approve of our tactics."

"You killed innocent people." Garmund hissed, slowly climbing to his feet. "Did you see the numbers?"

Birch nodded curtly. "They were higher than I would have liked, but-"

"One hundred sixty-four." Garmund's voice shook. "One hundred sixty-four bodies. One hundred sixty-four lives. Three hundred twenty-eight parents that lost children. Who knows how many siblings. Some may even have lost parents."

Garmund paused for a breath, and Birch raised an eyebrow. "Are you finished?"

Garmund began to see twinges of red surrounding his vision. "Does that mean *nothing* to you?"

"Of course it means something." Birch crossed his arms. "It means that there are one hundred sixty-four fewer vampires to deal with."

Garmund swore. "Are these just numbers to you?"

"Of course not!" Birch barked. "But they certainly seem to just be numbers to you!"

Garmund slammed a fist into the wall, smashing the drywall. "How dare you-"

"Let's run the numbers, shall we?" Birch held up a finger. "Since we're both apparently tied to them. Your old squad has drones out and about, scanning almost constantly. As I'm sure you're aware, the ARF has drones as well. As it happens, when the tents began to rise, we directed fifteen of our drones to watch the area. After all, such a densely-populated region at night is likely to attract vampires, don't you think?"

Garmund nodded slowly. "Yes."

"I thought so. Which is why we had an eye on it. When the vampires came, no more than thirty of the creatures dropped in. Would you like to know how many emerged?"

Garmund ground his teeth together. "How many?"

"Two hundred seventy-three." Birch crossed his arms. "In case you're not feeling up to the math, that means that each and every one of the original vampires would have had to bite and turn at least eight people in the five minutes during which the confrontation took place. While I realize that this was a special case, based on those statistics, those two hundred seventy-three vampires could grow into two thousand, one hundred and eighty vampires in the course of a single night. If those extra one hundred and sixty-four students had survived, the potential would rise to nearly four thousand vampires. We killed people, but we saved nearly two thousand people in the process."

"You don't know that." Garmund ground out. "You don't have any proof."

"No, I don't." Birch shrugged. "Fine, then. Let's look without the numbers. I can fairly conclusively say that if we hadn't shown up, all the people that we killed would have been turned. Maybe one or two escape. Fine. They're dead, no matter which way you look at it. Now, which is better? For a parent to be given the body of their dead child to bury and grieve over? Or to be told that their child is now a soulless monster that kills without remorse and feeds off blood?"

Garmund closed his eyes. "It's still wrong."

"If you want to debate morality, go talk to the priests on campus." Birch shrugged. "I save lives. Sometimes that means taking them."

"Why did you come here?" Garmund crossed his arms.

"To ask for your help." Birch reached into his pocket and pulled out a small flashdrive. "Environmental data gathered from the night at the mansion. It comes from three weather stations in the area, five satellites, and several sensors right here. I had the techs back in Washington look at it, but they say that the data was scrambled by that big pink flash that night. I want you to unscramble it."

Birch tossed the flashdrive to Garmund. Garmund caught it, then frowned.

"You're giving me a job?"

"I didn't steal you just to let you mope." Birch turned to leave. "You want a better solution? You have until things go south to give it to me."

CHAPTER 30

"Any luck?" Aaron dropped onto the couch, twisting his fingers back and forth. "Surely you've got *something*."

"Not anything worthwhile." Frank's voice came through loud and clear. "I sent the drones through every alley, every building, and every sewer in the city. If anyone was hiding there, we would know."

Aaron sighed. "Thanks, Frank. Call it a day. Tomorrow, start sweeping sector twenty-nine. We'll pin this down eventually."

"I can just start sweeping now." Frank's voice was tight. "What Birch did… We have to find those vampires and put a stop to this before anyone else dies."

"Thanks." Aaron closed his eyes. "You know the drill. Let us know if there's anything out of the usual."

"Will do." Frank's voice ended with a click, and Aaron shut off his earpiece.

"Oh, this is just great." Aaron turned to face Jasper, the only other member of the Squad in the house. Everyone else had been out exploring since the massacre on campus two days earlier, the only reason that Jasper and Aaron were in the house at all was for a brief refresher before heading out once more. "You have no idea how much I wish Garmund was here right now."

"You and me both." Jasper sighed as he screwed a long spring onto the end of a rifle barrel. "I just want to put a bullet through Birch for good."

"I know." Aaron bounced his legs ever so slightly. By the time Aaron had arrived at the scene of the tents, the vampires had vanished, leaving only the ARF standing over the dead bodies of dozens of students that they had ruthlessly gunned down. Since that night, Birch had posted armed guards on his doorstep and had started sending his soldiers across the town in patrols that made the city feel like it was under martial law. "I don't even have words."

"I just wish we could find the vampires." Jasper turned to Aaron, a curious frown on his face. "They were *everywhere*, and then they just vanished. How could that have happened?"

"I don't have a clue." Aaron could only shake his head. "If you have any ideas, I'd be more than happy to listen to them. Anything that could help us find, well, anything?"

"Not a one." Jasper shook his head. "I design weapons, not plans."

Harold chose that moment to walk into the room, banging loudly through the front door. A scowl was etched across his face, the look of disappointment. He sat down on the floor in the middle of the room and crossed his arms.

"Nothing." He shrugged. "I just got done meeting with Jeremy, who spent the day patrolling the sewers. He's got nothing. Wherever these bloodsuckers went, they're hidden well."

"That's not what I want to hear." Aaron rubbed his forehead as he tried to think. "Alright, let's think about this. Where *haven't* we looked?"

Jasper shrugged. "We haven't checked outside the maximum possible flight radius based on Jeremy's maximum speed and total possible travel time."

"You know what I mean." Aaron groaned and leaned forward. "We've been checking empty houses, sewers, anywhere dark. Where *haven't* we looked? Even someplace that might not make sense?"

"The zoo?" Harold raised an eyebrow. "Could they be hiding there?"

Jasper shook his head. "Bertha went and checked out the zoo this morning. The zookeepers didn't report any strange activity, and none of the bat exhibits had more than they were supposed to have."

Jeremy sighed and held up his hands. "Are there any slaughterhouses in the area? Somewhere with blood that they could be living off of?"

Aaron nodded. The thought had occurred to Frank only earlier that day. They had sent dozens of drones, but nothing had turned up. There *were* still a few packing plants that they hadn't looked through yet, but the options were growing thinner.

"Still looking." Aaron sighed. "Nothing at the ones we've checked yet. Hospitals, blood clinics, plasma donation centers, there's nothing."

Harold frowned, then tapped the floor a few times. "Why don't we go back and check out the mansion?"

"What could possibly come from that?" Aaron raised an eyebrow. "That was the first place we checked. There was no residual sign of vampires, and nothing to indicate that Incacheck had been there for more than a short time. Just a house with a bunch of holes blown in it."

"I know." Harold paused. "I've just got a hunch. I think it would be worth it to send a drone back."

Aaron nodded. "Fair enough. I'll call Frank, let him know."

"I heard." Frank's voice came through the earpieces. "I'm one it. Redirecting one of the drones as we talk."

"Perfect." Aaron nodded, a bit annoyed that Frank had still been listening in even after he deactivated the earpiece. "Any reason behind your hunch?"

Harold shrugged. "Just the way he fought us. Something about his magical powers makes me think he might have left something behind. In any event, I think it would be worth a more thorough examination."

"If you want, once it gets there, you can use the terminal in the garage to examine it for yourself." Aaron gestured towards the system. "See if you can pick up something the rest of us didn't."

"Thanks." Harold nodded. "I'll do that."

He stood up and wandered out of the room, and Aaron let his head fall back.

"Do you think we could get Garmund back if we stormed the place?" Aaron mused. "We could kill Birch. Blame it on the vamps." He sat up suddenly. "Could you do that? Make me a weapon that leaves marks like a vampire?"

"Yeah." Jasper chuckled. "It's called releasing a cobra into his house. Except that it's less reliable than a typical weapon."

"No, no, no." Aaron waved his hand. "I want an actual gun. Maybe build me a mechanical cobra? Or a cane that has a snake head but actual venom in the fangs?"

"You'd get caught quicker than a rabbit in a snare." Jasper shook his head as he started attaching an oblong device to the front of the rifle. "Birch is annoying, but he's also *very* high-ranked."

"Which means that if we get him out of the way, we end the threat." Aaron muttered. "I just want Garmund back."

"We all do." Jasper set down his weapon. "We just have to face the fact that we might not get him for awhile. General Herford is going to have to pull some major strings, it's not something that we'll just be able to do."

"I know." Aaron muttered. "I just wish we could."

"Hey, guys?" Harold's voice called out from the garage. "I think you might want to come look at this."

"What's wrong now?" Aaron chuckled as he forced himself to his feet. "Something diabolical, no doubt."

"You could say that." Harold's voice grew louder as Aaron walked into the room. "It's not Incacheck, but…"

Aaron walked into the area, frowning at the monitors. They all showed the same image, a view from a drone camera hovering just above the level of the trees.

The mansion, just visible through several trunks, had been completely changed from the previous day. Boards replaced the gaping holes, and blinds were drawn securely over the windows. It looked as if there wasn't an ounce of life in the building, but Aaron was quite certain that *something* had done the remodeling for a very good reason.

"You think this is what we were looking for?" Harold turned and smirked.

"You know, I'd wager a bet that you're right." Aaron reached up and clicked his earpiece back on. "Bertha? You there?"

"Always." Bertha's voice came back through, crisp and at attention. "What's up?"

"I need you to take a message to Jeremy." Aaron leaned over the displays. "I think we have an issue. Tell him that something has been setting up shop on the mountain."

"Will do." Bertha's voice snapped back off. Aaron sighed, then nodded. "Frank? Is there any way we can tell if that's Incacheck or the vampires?"

Frank hummed softly. "Not with any of the scanning technology on these drones. What I *can* say is that if Incacheck rebuilt that mansion, I would think he would do it in style."

Aaron nodded. Excitement began to swell in his chest. They had found the vampires! "We need to know how many vampires are in there. They got a bunch of students, but we don't know how many." He frowned for an instant. "Frank? Any way you can run the numbers? Maybe look at the number of student bodies that they found versus the number of vanishings?"

"Working on it now." Frank's voice was focused. "Pulling up a list of noted murders versus vanishings, and we have... Damn."

"Do I even want to know?" Aaron wrung his hands. "What are we up against?"

"It looks like there's a major military training camp not far from here." Frank paused. "They had one of the worst disasters in recorded military history about two days ago. An armory exploded, killing dozens. Hundreds more were poisoned by some sort of toxic fumes released, and have been slowly dropping since then. Assuming that a vamp did this, you're talking almost five hundred vampires, all of which are heavily trained in military tactics."

"Great." Jasper took a deep breath. "There's no way we could take on that many. Assuming they were all lined up, and it only took us two shots to kill each one, we would have bullets for about half of them."

Aaron turned and mock-glared at the weapons expert. "What have you two been doing for the last two days?"

"Trying to create better ways of killing these things." Jasper shrugged. "Incidentally, I did manage to get a wooden cover for the RPG you stole from the ARF. Should do a bit of..."

Jasper trailed off, a curious look rising on his face. Aaron leaned forward, feeling a glimmer of hope. "You're having an idea."

"I think I know how we can kill them all." Jasper frowned. "It'll take some preparation, though. Somehow, I doubt that the cover of night is going to be a super great idea in this case."

Aaron nodded and glanced out the window of the garage. It was the middle of the day, high noon.

"Get that drone out of there, we don't want them seeing it when they come pouring out." Aaron ordered Frank. "Harold, Jasper, move. I don't know what your plan is, but..." He took a deep breath. "I want it done by tonight. If there are actually five hundred vampires in that house, they could wipe out the entire city in a single night."

Jasper nodded at Harold. "Time to shine, young apprentice!"

Harold and Jasper ran from the room, and Aaron grinned. Sure, there was a solid chance that they would die that night in a hail of bullets and vampires, but at least something was happening. It felt good to be in motion again, and he didn't plan on stopping until the problem was taken care of.

CHAPTER 31

"Sir, the scouts report someone approaching."
Riley appeared out of the darkness of the tunnels and swept
up to Jeremy. "A woman. I think it's the girl from your
friends' squad."

Jeremy nodded and puffed out his cheeks. Maybe
the Squad had finally found something? "I'll go meet her.
Oh, by the way, what's the status on the raiding party?"

"They haven't returned yet." Riley shook his head.
"I hope they get here soon, though. We're all getting
hungry, and you know…"

"I'm well aware of what happens." Jeremy
grimaced. "Been there a time or two."

Riley nodded, and Jeremy turned a swept away. He
made his way through the tunnel system under the campus,
feeling an odd sense of irony. Gruen had used the same
tunnel system to start the vampires, but it had been

abandoned after it was instantly discovered. Now that
Jeremy was building his own vampire army, he had gone
straight back to the tunnels.

He soon reached a manhole, popped it open, and
scrambled out into the shadow of the chemistry building.
The edges of the shadow burned with an unquenchable fire,
and even in the shade, Jeremy knew that he wouldn't be
able to stay outside for long. Thankfully, he didn't have to,
as Bertha stepped around the corner of the building and
slid up next to him.

"Got sent as messenger again?" Jeremy cocked an
eyebrow.

"Yep." She crossed her arms. "It's what I do best."

Jeremy cocked an eyebrow. "I've seen you in action
before. You're a better fighter than any two of them put
together."

"Okay." Bertha sighed. "It's what I *want* to do best.
Doing all that fighting takes effort."

"This is why the human race is doomed." Jeremy
looked up at the sky and chuckled before turning back to
Bertha. "What can I do for you? What's the message?"

Bertha shrugged. "We sent a drone back to the
mansion. They found it all boarded up, Aaron thinks that
the other vampires might be hiding out there."

"Interesting." Jeremy frowned. "I suppose it would
make sense, especially if Incacheck is still actively exerting
his power over them."

"Our thoughts exactly." Bertha nodded. "The
Squad is planning to attack tonight. I don't know the
specifics yet, Jasper and Harold are working all of that out,
but be ready to move."

Jeremy nodded. "Will do. I'll alert my troops."

"You have twenty vampires. Those don't count as troops." Bertha crossed her arms and smirked.

"Still more people than you have." Jeremy snorted. "Just let me know what to do, and we'll be there."

"If you can get Garmund out of Birch's clutches, do it." Bertha nodded firmly. "That's a good starting point."

Jeremy grimaced. Most of the other Squad members had said more or less the same thing at different points. "He meant a lot to you guys, didn't he?"

"Yeah." Bertha's voice was tight. For the first time since he met her, he noticed a drop of liquid forming at the side of her eye. "Yeah. he really did."

Jeremy didn't quite know what to say. After a few awkward moments, Bertha shrugged and held up her hand. "I have an odd question."

"Ask away." Jeremy nodded.

"I'm just curious what you guys eat." She frowned. "There are twenty of you, and I know you're not feeding on students, so how do you keep from…"

"Going on homicidal rampages?" Jeremy chuckled. "It's simple, actually. There's an animal laboratory on campus that keeps sheep and cattle around that we've been feeding on. It's not fantastic, and they kind of taste like mud, but it keeps us alive."

Bertha shrugged. "At least it's edible."

"It works." Jeremy shrugged. "It would be like eating nothing but tortilla shells."

"Huh." Bertha shrugged. "You should ask Jasper and Harold if they can whip up something for you."

"What do you mean?" Jeremy frowned. "You think they could synthesize human blood?"

"I haven't a clue." Bertha held up her hands. "I just know that I majored in chemistry in college, and I can guarantee that they regularly create compounds that should be impossible to create. I mean, creating a deadly acid from dirt? Come on. They've got some sort of pseudoscience thing going on, I'm just not sure what."

Jeremy held up a hand. "And you haven't mentioned this to Aaron because…"

"Why?" Bertha shrugged. "It's the same thing I told you on our way to the Smithsonian. Secrets are secret for a reason. If they want to keep it a secret, I'm not going to pry. Now, on the flip side, if they want to keep it a secret, they should be doing a better job, which is why I don't feel bad sending you in their direction." After a few moments, she shrugged. "Besides, Aaron could see it if he really wanted to, he just tends to avoid those kinds of confrontations."

"Makes sense." Jeremy shrugged. "Well, I'll certainly have a talk with them. If they could do that for us, it would make life much, much easier."

"Good." Bertha grinned. "Good luck with… Well, whatever happens."

"Thanks." Jeremy sighed. "I get the feeling that we're going to need it."

As Bertha walked away, Jeremy put his arms above his head and stretched. Riley poked his head out of the tunnel system, a concerned look on his face.

"Everything okay?"

"That depends entirely on your definition of the word." Jeremy puffed out his cheeks. "Get everyone ready. Tonight is going to be wild."

CHAPTER 32

"Have you ever done something absolutely terrifying, where you had no idea if you would come out alive or dead?" Jasper frowned as the van pulled off to the side of the road. "Anything at all?"

"You mean like diving headfirst into a giant plant zombie on the off-chance that it's being powered by something I can easily rip out?" Harold frowned. "Yeah, I know the feeling."

"Point taken." Jasper chuckled. "Well, that's how I feel about this."

Harold popped the door open the moment the van was stopped. "Hey, it's midday, the vamps can't venture outside their hideout. I'd say we're fine."

"It's four in the afternoon, and if any of them bother to put on a trenchcoat or facepoint, we could still be in trouble." Jasper muttered as he shut the car off. "Well, let's load up. Lots of work to do."

Harold slid out of the van and looked up at the trees. The mansion was hidden somewhere in the expanse, behind who knew how many acres of woodland. The driveway to the location was just visible on the top of a nearby hill. Hopefully, they were far enough away that they wouldn't be noticed.

Without another thought, Harold walked around to the back of the van as Jasper popped the rear doors open. He grabbed a gas-powered drill, smiled, and started walking towards the forest.

"Let's move, old man."

"I'll 'old man' you in a minute." Jasper muttered. "Are you sure you want to carry the drill? I can…"

"I don't get tired anymore." Harold shrugged. "I figured that I'd be the better person to deal with it."

"Right." Jasper grabbed several bags that they had prepared the night before. "In that case, lead on. You know what to do."

Harold nodded, grinned, and walked up to the nearest tree. With a dull roar, he fired up the drill and plunged it into the hard wood. His muscles strained to push the rotating bit deeper and deeper into the tree. Once he was sure that it was deep enough, he pulled the machine back out, spun, and walked to the next tree.

Jasper followed, dropping in various ingredients that they had cooked up. Harold grinned at the thought of what would happen when the time was ready. Oh, it was going to be glorious, indeed.

Though his muscles refused to tire, he soon found himself growing bored with the process. Even knowing

what was to come, it was incredibly repetitive to simply
bore a hole, pull out, and move to the next tree. Even
Jasper seemed to grow weary of the work after only a short
time, and Harold sighed. At the rate of one tree every thirty
seconds, it would take them nearly four hours to use up all
the supplies they brought with them. Great.

"Hey!" A voice cut into his drilling. "Hey!"

He let the drill power down and turned to see what
the commotion was about. To his surprise, he saw an
incredibly pale man standing just behind him, dressed in the
most ridiculous cloak that Harold had ever seen. It seemed
to have been formed out of several old pieces of clothing, a
suncloak similar to what Jeremy used to go outside during
the day. So the vampires *were* getting creative. Jasper stood
just behind the man, a confused look on his face. Harold
crossed his arms and raised an eyebrow.

"Yes? What can I do for you?"

"What are you doing here?" The man's voice was
smooth and papery. "I believe you are trespassing."

"City ordinances, pal." Harold crossed his arms.
"We got a report that these trees were infected with
barkworm. Do you know what barkworm can do to a local
population if it gets a strong hold?"

"What?" The man frowned. "I…"

"Total decimation." Harold shrugged. "Out in
California, they had a barkworm problem break out, and
they lost millions of acres of trees before it got solved. One
of the city inspectors here noticed indicators of barkworms,
so we're going around running some tests."

"By boring holes into the trees?" The man's eyes
narrowed.

"We have to be able to place sensors in the trees."
Harold gestured at the bag that Jasper was holding. "See?
They're harmless. Within a few months, the trees will grow
back around it all and you'll never know the difference."

"I think I would like to contend this order." The
man smiled. "I want you off our property."

"You'll have to contend with the city." Harold
shrugged. "The commissioner is off today, though, so you'll
have to wait until tomorrow before you can schedule an
appointment. I can give you the phone number of the
receptionist, she'll know which sub-department to direct
you to so your request can be processed, at which point
you'll be contacted by the appropriate-"

"Whatever." The man hissed. "Fine. Do your
work. Then get off my property."

The man glided away, and Harold went back to
work drilling holes. Several hours later, when he finally
finished, he set down the piping hot drill and grinned.

"Not bad for just flying off the cuff."

"You're going to get us killed." Jasper chuckled as
he filled up the last hole. "You think he believed us?"

"I don't know why he wouldn't." Harold shrugged.
"I guess we find out this evening."

With that, Harold and Jasper began packing their
supplies back into the van. Harold hopped into the driver's
seat, and they took off, back towards their frat house.

They had only been driving a few moments before
Jasper fell asleep. Harold smiled at the sight. The rituals
required to create the materials had nearly wiped the man
out. Now that they were done, Jasper could use the rest,
especially since there was probably going to be very little
sleeping done that night.

Harold grinned as he speed back towards the frat house. Part of him was terrified for the upcoming confrontation. Another part of him, a deeper, more furious part, simply couldn't wait.

CHAPTER 33

Aaron took a deep breath as Bertha allowed the van to come to a stop near the driveway to the woodland mansion. When they had discovered the vampire hive only hours earlier, it hadn't quite clicked in his brain that the attack was happening *now*. It made sense to go ahead and make the assault, especially since the ARF didn't seem to be aware of the situation, but it was a bit jarring to have so many days of downtime and then an epic showdown without much warning. Slowly, he reached up and clicked his earpiece to *talk*.

"Alright, Jeremy. You ready to go?" Aaron paused as the van neared the entrance to the mansion's driveway. "Anything you can tell us?"

"Nothing you don't already know." Jeremy sounded disappointed. "We've still got a few minutes until sundown. My troops are standing ready as soon as we can fly without dying."

"Alright, then." Aaron nodded. "We'll go in first. After we've sprung our trap, you guys follow up. Sound good?"

"My army is yours to command." Jeremy sounded proud. "They all stand ready to fight for what they believe in."

Aaron chuckled. "Your army of twenty people? They're really willing to fight against such overwhelming odds?"

"It's still bigger than yours, if we're really comparing sizes." Jeremy chuckled. "And yes, they are. There's a guy out there who can manipulate us. Not many people really want that kind of leash attached to them."

"Makes sense." Aaron nodded. "Alright, we're going in. Be ready!"

Aaron clicked off his earpiece before hearing Jeremy's reply. Smiling, Aaron picked up the wood-bullet rifle that Jasper had crafted. If the weapons designer was right, this would pack quite the punch, indeed.

Bertha sent the van screeching into the mansion's driveway. Aaron threw the door open, stepped out, and raised his rifle. Behind him, he heard a small pop as Harold readied the RPG. With a roar, the missile fired away, arcing through the air, towards the front door.

With a dull blast, the wooden rocket detonated against the planks covering the entryway. A blast shook the area, and the front of the mansion was blown open yet again. Aaron rushed forward, gun at the ready. Beside him, Bertha charged forward with a wooden sword held high.

On his other side, Jasper and Harold came up strong, weapons at the ready.

As they drew near the front of the mansion, something flickered in the back of Aaron's mind. There simply wasn't anyone home. No vampires were rushing out to meet the charge, no one was coming in from the side to flank them. It was simply... Empty.

"Jeremy?" Aaron held his hand up to his ear. "Frank? Someone! This place is empty!"

"That doesn't make any sense." Jasper breathed. "There was someone here today, a vampire trying to get us off the property. Could all that really have been a fakeout?"

"Nope!" Jeremy's voice came back on, followed by a flurry of profanity. Aaron desperately tapped the earpiece.

"What's happening? Jeremy, what's going on?"

"They're coming through the tunnels!" Jeremy's voice was quick. "They must have burrowed from the mansion into the city's sewers so we wouldn't detect them."

"Well, that's fantastic." Aaron muttered. "Where is *here*, exactly?"

"The campus!" Jeremy gasped. "Look, I have to get going. The sun is setting, and there are hundreds of these things. It looks like most of the other army is trying to take the administration building, I'll take my troops and head there."

"We're on our way." Aaron nodded. He clicked the earpiece off and turned to Bertha. "Back to the college!"

Bertha nodded, the van did a one-eighty spin in the driveway, and they rocketed back out onto the open road. Aaron took a deep breath. A battle with that many students around couldn't go well in any sense of the word.

"Man, that's a bummer." Harold frowned. "We put a lot of work into our trap!"

"You may yet get to use it." Aaron shrugged. "You never know how these things go."

"That's true." Harold leaned forward and crossed his fingers. "Here's hoping."

"I'm just hoping more people don't die." Bertha shrugged. "You know how hard it's going to be to avoid civilian casualties?"

"No kidding." Aaron paused. "Frank? You there?"

"As ever." Frank's response was instantaneous. "What's up?"

"Do you still have the recon drones deployed near the college?"

Frank paused. "They're close. Do you want me to pull them off the search for Incacheck?"

"Yeah." Aaron nodded. "We need an accurate way to determine the difference between a living student and a vampire who's posing as a student."

"That's a tough one." Frank's voice sounded thoughtful. "Try wearing a low-cut shirt. If they bite your neck, they're probably a vampire."

"Not helping." Aaron shook his head. "I meant something like their heat signature or something. Maybe they're room temperature because they aren't alive?"

"I'll play with the extra settings on the drones, see what I can come up with."

"Good. Have something ready by the time we get there. And keep an eye on the ARF, they're not going to miss out on this one." Aaron clicked the device off. Idly, he noticed that Harold was shifting back and forth in his seat, like he was nervous.

"Antsy for the battle?" Aaron held up his hands. "You doing alright?"

"Yeah." Harold's response was quick. "I'm just a little antsy."

"Okay." Aaron shrugged slowly. He didn't really believe Harold at all, but whatever was bothering him, it was sure to go away once they hit the battle.

The engine of the van screamed as they tore around a corner, and they rocketed into the growing night.

CHAPTER 34

Jeremy ducked as a wooden stake slashed through the air above his head. He grabbed the arm of the vampire that was trying to kill him, twisted it behind the vamp's back, and wrenched the stake out of his hand. With a thrust, he drove it through the vamp's own heart, transforming him into little more than a pile of dust.

"We can't keep this up much longer." Riley threw a stake through the heart of another charging vampire. "There are only ten of us left."

Jeremy glanced at his few remaining vampires. They were in the hallway of the administration building, trying to hold the area. He could see enemy vampires clustered at both entrances, just waiting to come charging in. The only reason they weren't was because Jeremy and his team had managed to dust quite a few.

Jeremy paused as screaming echoed through the air. The swarm of vampires that had came swooping into the campus had to be at least five hundred strong. Based on Incacheck's rant, if indeed it was true, each vampire only had to bite three humans to complete the shard's programing. Great.

"You know what?" Riley edged up next to Jeremy. "I'm beginning to regret sneaking out that night to try and get the story."

"It wasn't one of your smarter moves." Jeremy chuckled. "People going missing. Soldiers patrolling through the streets. Reports of vampires. And you go out at *night* to try and get a new scoop."

"Hey, I just do what I can to advance free speech." Riley took a deep breath. "Even if it does wind up resulting in my death."

Jeremy shook his head. "If we don't make it through this, I'm going to miss you."

"And I you." Riley paused. "Now find us a way to get out of this alive. Or at least… Undead instead of truly dead."

Jeremy paused as another scream echoed through the air. Slowly, he took a deep breath, and his brain began to switch from survival to protection. "We have to protect the students."

"Protect the students?" Riley paused. "How do we do that? We're fighting for our own survival, here."

Jeremy tried to think. "We need… We need something that can broadcast a message to the entire college."

Riley spun towards the offices. "The dean's office."

Jeremy nodded and sprinted towards the door leading to the administration, mentally smacking himself. They had already been in the administration building for the better part of an hour, and the thought had never once crossed his mind. He tore into the hallway and raced for the office. A grin split his face as he reached for the door. This was how he won!

With a crack, the door exploded outward, driving him back against the opposite wall. He shoved the door away from him, only to see a group of vampires standing in the room. The glass window was shattered, and they looked up at him, surprised.

With a rush, he turned and ran back towards his group. He threw open the door leading back to the hall, only to find that the vampires were pushing through the entrance again.

"Trouble?" Riley took a deep breath. "That doesn't look like a good thing."

"They're coming through the windows that way." Jeremy gestured. "If we're going to save anyone on this campus, we have to retake that room. Without destroying anything."

"On it." Riley turned and pointed at the offices. "Retake that room!"

Jeremy's group of vampires turned en masse and rushed at the door. Jeremy led the charge, throwing open the doors in a rush. Five vamps in the hallway turned to look at him. They had a mere moment to look surprised before Jeremy drove a stake through the first one's heart, turning him into a pile of dust.

With that, the battle was on. One of Jeremy's men slid past him, fighting an enemy vamp that was trying to get

to Jeremy. As Jeremy watched, the enemy vamp drove a stake through Jeremy's soldier. Jeremy screamed and leapt forward.

As he jumped, he transformed into a bat, a much, much smaller target. The enemy's stake flashed through the air next to him, plenty of room to spare. As Jeremy passed the enemy's head, he transformed back into a human, wrapped his arms around the enemy's head, and twisted. The vamp's neck snapped, and he dropped to the floor. Jeremy was quite certain that the man would heal in a relatively short amount of time, but he was immobilized for the moment. With a rush, Jeremy drove a stake through his heart, ending his chances of healing.

Riley appeared next to Jeremy's side. "Go make the call. I'll cover you."

Jeremy nodded and backed through the office door while the battle raged in the hallway. Riley had a stake in each hand, ready to defend against anything. Jeremy leapt behind the desk, grabbed the phone, and started looking at the numbers. A piece of notebook paper taped to the side of the receiver had a list of operations, which Jeremy quickly glanced through. Without further ado, he pushed the *one* button, smiled, and started talking.

With a boom, his voice echoed through the speakers in the building, and, hopefully, the speakers across campus.

"Students! As you may have noticed, our campus is under attack. Make no mistake, these creatures are dangerous, and they will kill you. That said, they are beatable. Go to your dorm rooms, leave the doors open, but don't invite anyone inside. Humans will be able to enter the room, but none of the monsters will be able to harm you as long as you *don't invite them in.* If you are trapped outside, look for an open dorm room. It may make things uncomfortable, but all humans are going to have to bond together to stop this. I…"

With a rush, something hit Jeremy from behind. He was driven into the desk, and groaned as something slammed down onto his back. Desperately, he tried to force himself up, but the pressure only increased. From his rather uncomfortable position, he could see Riley spin and leap into action, onto to be knocked backwards. With a rush, the second-in-command dissolved into a pile of dust, and Jeremy screamed.

"No! You…"

Jeremy was flipped over, flat on his back, looking up at a vampire that looked far too evil for the part. He wore soldier attire, presumably one of the soldiers Jeremy had encountered at the mansion. Actually holding Jeremy down were two more vampires, both of whom looked like they had once been professional bouncers.

"You're making life *very* difficult for us." The vampire hissed. "Why would you want to do that?"

"You're helping a madman." Jeremy thrashed against the guards. "You follow his plan, and we're all doomed."

"You mean Incacheck." The soldier mused. "Ahh, yes. You know, I really don't think people give him the credit he deserves."

"He's insane." Jeremy hissed. "He'll kill on a whim, he'll torture anyone just for the sake of it. He tried to manipulate me into…"

"He does what he has to." The soldier grinned. "As do I. I've been instructed to bring you to him, actually."

Jeremy rolled his head to the side, trying to flick the earpiece on. "You want to take me to Incacheck?"

"Yes, we do." The soldier laughed. "If you think that radio you've got in your head is going to help you, you're sorely mistaken. We're jamming all transmissions made from campus."

"I made that broadcast well enough." Jeremy grinned.

"That phone is hardwired into the system." The soldier shrugged. "Unfortunate enough, but understandable given the ancient design of this place. Well, enough dilly-dally. Let's get you to the boss, shall we?" The soldier started to walk away. One of the guards reached into his pocket and pulled out a small wooden ball that appeared covered with small spikes. The second guard forced Jeremy's mouth open, and the first guard shoved it inside.

Jeremy gagged on the ball for a few moments. The spikes weren't sharp, but they weren't overly pleasant, either. Oh, well. Jeremy prepared himself to transform into a bat to escape, when something dawned on him.

If he transformed into a bat, the ball in his mouth would suddenly be larger than his entire head. He didn't know what kind of damage it would cause, but it certainly wouldn't be pretty, or likely survivable. With nothing else to do, Jeremy was lead from the office. He only hoped that his warning had done enough that some people would be able to survive.

CHAPTER 35

Alarms blared through the frat house. Garmund leapt off his bed and ran for the living room. Soldiers tore back and forth through the house, gathering gear and weapons. Garmund sighed at the sight. Another group, ready to go sacrifice themselves for the greater good.

"Hold, men." General Birch stepped into the living room and held up his hand as the men formed into ranks. "We're not doing it this way this time."

There was a ripple of confusion. Garmund frowned at the statement. Birch doing something different? That was a new one.

"What's the situation?" Rodger stepped into the room. "What are we up against?"

Birch frowned, then continued. "The campus has been overrun by vampires. Early estimates are close to one thousand of the creatures. Given such information, the only course of action I can see is to call in a ballistic strike against the campus. We wipe out the vampires once and for all, ending their potential to spread across the globe."

Garmund held up a hand. "Sir? There are civilians on that campus."

"There won't be for long." Birch shrugged. "In a matter of hours, all life on the campus will be undead. We may as well nip it in the bud before it really becomes an issue. We've talked about this."

There was a round of cheering from the soldiers, and Garmund held up a hand. "Have we figured out what caused the vampires yet?"

Birch cocked an eyebrow. "Caused? What do you mean?"

"I mean, something caused all these vampires to form in the first place." Garmund shrugged. "If you don't find the source, taking out the campus won't do a lick of good, since they'll just find a way to start back up again."

Birch groaned. "Do you have some way to find out what the source is?"

"I actually do." Garmund nodded. "Ever since you gave me the environmental data, I've been trying to sort through it."

"If you haven't succeeded by now, I don't think you will." Birch raised an eyebrow. "Now quit wasting my time."

"How long will it take you to order the missile strike?" Garmund held up his hands. "How long?"

Birch shrugged. "Thirty minutes."

"Then give me thirty minutes with the data. If I don't find anything, we let the matter drop."

Birch just shrugged once more. "I'm launching those missiles in thirty minutes whether you find something or not. But sure, feel free to look for something that will convince me."

Garmund grinned and ran back towards the computer room. Thirty minutes was almost nothing. Time to sort through layer upon layer of data. Time to save a campus.

CHAPTER 38

Tires screeched as the van slid up to the campus. Harold took a deep breath as the door kicked open. He was holding a small machine gun that had been modified to shoot wooden bullets, though it would still be easy enough to switch back to metal bullets once his wooden stash ran out.

The four of them jumped out, and for a moment, just stood there. Bats swooped through the air, so many of them that they blocked out the night sky in places. Harold could see vampires roaming back and forth across the campus, chasing students.

With a blast, the intercom system came on, warning students to stay inside. Harold grinned. That was Jeremy's voice, which meant that at least someone was on top of things. When the transmission cut off with a blast, Harold's jaw set.

"Alright, people." Aaron stood slightly in front of them, rifle at the ready. "Ready for the fight of your life?"

"I was born ready." Jasper grinned. "Any fancy orders?"

Aaron paused. "Kill vampires. Don't kill them if they're loyal to Jeremy. You should probably go guard the dorms."

Harold nodded. "I'll take the closest dorm."

"I'll head for the one across the way." Jasper gestured. Bertha followed him as he took off, and Aaron shrugged.

"I guess I'm with you."

Harold nodded, then turned and took off towards the building. Screams echoed from within, and he shivered. He couldn't imagine what that was like, being a college student when the university came under siege.

As he neared the front entrance to the nearest dorm building, several vampires turned to face him. He grinned and squeezed down on the trigger, sending dozens of wooden splinters through the air. The vamps had a mere moment to look surprised before they were cut down, and Harold let the gun wind down.

Without further ado, he walked through the front doors of the building. In the lobby, a group of students were on their knees, surrounded by vampires. One of them turned, and Harold cut loose. He was able to cut down all the vampires on one side of the building, while Aaron opened up on the group on the other side. It took mere moments before the room was cleared, and the students looked up at them in shock.

"Did you hear the broadcast?" Harold bent down next to them. "Get to an open room, and don't invite anyone inside. If they can enter the room, you're safe. If they can't, you're still safe."

There was a round of head-nods, and the shell-shocked students climbed to their feet and wandered into the hallways. More screams echoed from above, and Harold took a deep breath.

"We have to split up to cover more ground. You take odd floors, I'll take evens."

Aaron shook his head. "I thought I was the boss."

"You are. Good bosses know when to take suggestions from their employees."

"Got it." Aaron chuckled. "Alright, then. Let's move."

Harold nodded, turned, and raced up the stairs. He broke out onto the second floor to find a similar scenario. Students were being held in the middle of the room, surrounded by vampires that were starting to feed. A few rounds of machine gun fire, and the problem was solved.

When he was done with floor two, he moved up to floor four. There were only a handful of vampires there, which he easily dispatched. As the students streamed out into the hallways, a girl walked up to him.

"Thank you."

"It was my pleasure." Harold smiled. It was the first time a girl had smiled at him since he'd become a zombie! "I'd love to stay and talk, but… Well, there are still vamps in the building."

"I completely understand." She smiled. After a few moments' hesitation, she leaned in and gave him a peck on the cheek. Harold smiled, and she dashed into the hallway.

A smile on his face, Harold made his way up to the sixth floor. For some reason, he just couldn't get the grin to go away. A feeling of confidence in his veins, he pushed the door open.

Every ounce of confidence evaporated as he took in the sight. It was an entire room full of vampires. Glistening fangs, searching eyes. At least fifty, all packed into the same tiny space. Harold glanced down at his clip of wooden bullets. Even if he hit one vamp with every shot, there was no way he could kill them all.

"Silly human." One of the vamps stepped closer. "You should know that metal can't hurt us."

"It can hurt. It just can't kill." Harold ejected the wooden clip and snapped in a regular set of rounds. "Wood, on the other hand, is an entirely different story."

The nearest vampire raised its eyebrows. "You're going to tell us you have wooden bullets?"

Harold shrugged. "I guess we'll find out."

With nothing else to do, Harold took a deep breath and drummed his fingers on the side of the weapon. The vibrations ran through the device, making the bullets shudder even as he pulled the trigger. If he was doing it right…

As the first bullet rushed out of the gun barrel, he could *feel* the change. He could feel the crystalline form of the metal, the packed, immobile structure, begin to change. It shifted, transforming into polymers, into proteins, into *wood*.

The nearest vamp's eyes shot wide open as it dissolved into a pile of dust. With a roar, Harold opened up on the rest, watching the bullets transform as they rattled from the barrel. Not a single vampire made it out of the room. As the last one fell, he let the gun wind down.

Instantly, a flood of energy left him, and he sank back against the nearest wall.

Apparently Jasper had known what he was talking about when he said that changing metal into wood was a difficult task. Harold felt like he had just ran a full marathon, like he had just completed some sort of major game show challenge. Idly, he held up his hands, feeling them tremble.

His hands lifted into view, and Harold's jaw dropped. Skin hung loosely from the bones, a pale, almost translucent material. Desperately, Harold pulled up his sleeves, but it was the same story there. He looked like a skeleton with a small bit of skin hanging off him. He looked... Well, he looked quite dead. He sure didn't want to know what his face looked like.

The elevator gave a ding, and he shook his head. If Aaron saw him in that state, all was lost. There was no way the team would keep him on, Shoot, even Jasper occasionally looked uncomfortable at the fact that he was technically dead.

Carefully, Harold reached into his pocket and grabbed the shard of the Philosopher's Stone that he still carried with him. Instantly, raw power flooded from it, filling Harold's veins. His skin bulged out as muscle tissue filled his body again. The elevator opened, and Aaron stepped out, He frowned at Harold for a moment.

"Did you just... Are you okay?"

"Peachy." Harold climbed to his feet. "Why wouldn't I be?"

"Oh, I don't know." Aaron shrugged and walked over to the floor-to-ceiling windows that ran along the wall of the dorm lobby, allowing for a wonderful view of campus. "You just looked off there for a moment."

Harold let go of the shard. "I don't know. I mean, I felt a little weird there, but I think I'm fine now."

Aaron's eyes narrowed. "You're not a vampire, are you?"

"I most certainly am not." Harold chuckled. "That much you can count on."

"Good." Aaron nodded. "Well, ready for the next building?"

"I am at that." Harold grinned. "Let's show these vampires who's in charge."

CHAPTER 37

Garmund's fingers flew over the keyboard. Rodger floated into the room behind him, but Garmund didn't dare look up. He was down to less than ten minutes before the missiles launched, and he was nowhere closer to figuring anything out.

"Still drawing up blank?" Rodger sighed. "What's wrong?"

Garmund shook his head. "I don't have a clue. It's the same problem I've had ever since I first got the data. Everything's all jumbled. It's like the blast just scrambled all the sensors and the subsequent data."

"Scrambled the data?" Rodger leaned forward. "Like it encrypted it?"

"No, it…" Garmund paused. "It's encrypted!"

Rodger paused. "That's a good thing?"

"No." Garmund shook his head. "it means that someone in this place, probably Birch, really doesn't want me to find anything to mess up his operation. Well, buddy, it's time to see what I can do."

Garmund reached into his pocket and pulled out a small flashdrive. Rodger's eyes narrowed as Garmund clicked it into a small slot in the computer.

"What exactly are you doing?"

"Breaking nearly every single digital privacy law on the planet." Garmund grinned. "And maybe saving some lives in the process."

With a whir, the computer screen lit up. Garmund grinned and began shutting down the computer's natural defenses. In an instant, his decrypting software began to work its magic. The scrambled data began to shift, and he smiled.

"What are you doing?" Birch appeared in the doorway. "You're…"

"Finding a pattern." Garmund nodded at Richard. "Please keep him out of here for a few moments."

"You'll…"

"Look!" Garmund turned around and roared. "You gave me false data! You encrypted the sensor data, and you sent me on a wild goose chase just so you could blow up an entire college!"

"What the hell are you talking about?" Birch frowned. "I never sent you encrypted data. I got that straight from the satellites."

"Then *someone* in the government fed us encrypted data, because we've got a mess on our hands!"

For the first time, Garmund saw a flicker of doubt cross the general's face. "The missiles launch in seven minutes. I can't stop them. Give me another target."

"On it, boss." Garmund grinned. "Here we go."

Birch walked over and sat down on the desk next to the computer. "What's happening?"

"I've got the data." Garmund's fingers felt like they were on fire. "Removing environmental data, and… Bingo."

A series of jagged lines appeared on the screen. "These are atmospheric readings taken at the time of the blast. Excessive alpha radiation, it looks like."

"Alpha radiation?" Birch frowned. "That's really bad, isn't it?"

"Everyone thinks gamma radiation is the worst." Garmund nodded. "Gamma will go straight through you and you'll never know it. Alpha, on the other hand, is caused by atoms ejecting protons and neutrons. Those can rip straight through you and leave a mark. This, whatever it was, it emitted a *lot* of alpha radiation. Here's the interesting part, though. None of the radiation reached the ground. It was all absorbed by… Well, by *something*."

"What does that mean?"

Garmund frowned. "We need access to whatever surveillance satellites we have. I want any alpha radiation anomalies located in the last two weeks to be shown here."

Birch cleared his throat. "My password is-"

"Got it." Garmund shrugged as the data appeared on the screen. "Looks like there have been almost three dozens instances. All of them have been…" His voice trailed off as the implications of the data finally registered in his mind.

"What?" Birch frowned. "Where are they?"

Garmund turned and gestured across the street. "There's a frat house directly across the street from us. Looks like there's been a *ton* of radiation coming from the basement."

Birch nodded. "I'll give the order to clear out of this house. Send the missiles here."

"On it." Garmund sent his software in a different direction. "I… Shoot."

"What?" Birch paused. "The missiles launched, didn't they?"

"Five minutes ahead of time." Garmund paused. "Alright. I've got this."

"How?" Birch threw his hands up. "They've launched!"

"They launched from New York, which means we have about five more minutes before they get here." Garmund's fingers flew across the keypad. In an instant, he had hacked into the Apocalypse Squad's drones. "I'll have these drones meet them halfway. The missiles are powered by an on-board computer guidance system. I'm going to have the drones transmit laser pulses to give the computers a bit of new information."

"Will that work?" Birch frowned.

"Well, the drones are moving into position." Garmund pushed himself away from the computer. "If it works, the missiles will be here in about three minutes. I suggest we not be here when that happens."

Birch nodded. "Rodger? Get your vehicle fired up. I get the feeling we're going to want something fast."

"Yes, sir." Rodger vanished out the doorway. Birch ran out, screaming orders. Garmund paused, then grabbed a piece of paper. It was a desperate plan, but it was something.

A moment later, he had finished scribbling and tore out the door as quickly as he could. He knew that, given the ARF's track record for simply running out on things, it would probably be a long time before he saw his friends again. Hopefully… Hopefully this would help things at least somewhat.

CHAPTER 38

"And now, you can speak again." The vampire guard ripped the wooden ball out of Jeremy's mouth. Wooden splinters tore at Jeremy's cheeks, burning for several long moments. He wasn't sure why the guard was letting him go, but he wasn't planning on wasting any time.

Without hesitation, he transformed into a bat. Or rather… He *tried* to transform into a bat. His body refused to change, his muscles just didn't seem to work. With a rush, his legs took over for him, and he began to walk, not of his own accord, down the street. The soldier let go of him, laughed, and flapped away.

Idly, he noticed that he was walking through a rather familiar part of town. It… It was in the same location as the frat house where he had holed up in the initial phases of learning that he was a vampire. His eyes opened in surprise as he walked up the steps of the old frat house and through the front door.

Without stopping, he walked through the living room and to a small door set in the side of the area. Upon opening it, he found a small staircase that seemed to lead down into the very depths of hell. Of course, it probably only seemed like that due to the flickering torchlight and ominous groans echoing through the air, but it was still quite convincing.

With no way to resist, Jeremy simply walked down the stairs, down and down. It seemed like the stairs would never end, and Jeremy quickly came to the conclusion that this wasn't part of the original house. After an uncertain amount of time, he finally came to a large, wooden door. They opened on their own, revealing a large, open cave.

In the middle of the cave, surrounded by dozens of beakers, cauldrons, and smoking pipes, was Incacheck. He spun, his robe twirling, and he smiled.

"Jeremy! So good to see you."

"Go to hell." Jeremy muttered. Idly, he noticed that Incacheck had allowed him to speak. Small miracles.

Incacheck spread his hands. "Is this not the epitome of hell? You're here to be tortured for what will certainly feel like an eternity."

"Hell is having to listen to you prattle on and on." Jeremy shrugged. "What am I doing down here?"

"I want to know something." Incacheck stalked closer to Jeremy. "I want to know how you broke my power."

"You're weaker than you thought." Jeremy spat. "It just took some strong focus, and-"

Incacheck waved his hand, and Jeremy was lifted into the air and drawn across the cavern. He landed in front of a large cauldron filled with a greenish fluid.

"It's a potion designed to reflect your thoughts." Incacheck grinned. "At least that's what the ancients believed. In reality, it has a property that builds a series of temporary pathways identical to the pathways of the closest mind. In other words, it copies your brain, along with whatever you happen to be thinking. Fascinating, isn't it?"

Jeremy closed his eyes and tried to think about Vanessa. It wouldn't give Incacheck anything he wanted, and would help him stay focused.

"Oh, none of that." Incacheck's voice was low. "I want you to not think about how you escaped my power. Don't think for a moment about the moment that you didn't feel the pain in your body."

Jeremy grimaced as the image of Harold flashed through his mind. The inside of the room, the moment that he woke up in the Squad's house.

"The Apocalypse Squad." Incacheck mused. "It looks like the boy is a stronger alchemist than I gave him credit for. Granted, he's also a zombie, which probably helps, but it's still fascinating."

"What are you talking about?" Jeremy gasped. "Who's a zombie?"

"No one of consequence." Incacheck turned to leave. "I'll just have to deal with the problem on…"

A loud explosion shook the area, and Jeremy felt the paralysis vanish. He leapt to his feet to see Incacheck holding both of his hands towards the ceiling of the cave.

"If you're going to try and run, I would suggest against it." Incacheck laughed as another explosion, this one much louder, shook the area. "Looks like someone found us. Leave this area, and you'll be away from my protection."

A third blast sent cracks through the ceiling of the room, and Jeremy had a flash of insight. He might die, but at least Incacheck would be dead, too. Without a word, without a hint of intent, he launched himself at Incacheck. Knock down the pillar holding the room together, and all that could happen was collapse.

CHAPTER 39

Aaron ran towards the center of campus, rifle in hand. Two vampires swooped down behind him, and he spun, shooting them as they transformed back into humans. Harold raised his machine gun beside him, emptying a clip into a herd of vampires that was charging towards them. None of them died, but a number of loud screams echoed through the night air, and many of them fell to the ground with broken limbs.

Before Aaron could start shooting, Bertha appeared from the side, looking like a whirlwind of action. Her sword stabbed deep into the vampires, dusting them one at a time. Most of them were so badly wounded that they couldn't do a thing to fight back, and a moment later, she was standing alone in the expanse.

"I've never felt so alive." She grinned as she jogged up to them. "What next?"

"Where's Jasper?" Aaron frowned. "Is he-"

Flames belched from the opposite side of the area, and Aaron's eyes opened wide as a group of vampires was transformed into ash, not by the sunlight, but by a blazingly bright flamethrower. Jasper appeared a few seconds later, excitement written all over his face.

"We've dusted at least two hundred of them." He laughed. "Oh, I live for this."

"Good to know." Aaron muttered. "We've probably hit as many, but that still leaves quite a few."

Harold shook his head. "If we could just get them to the forest, we could get rid of the whole lot at one time."

"Well, that would be fantastic." Aaron shrugged. "Unfortunately, we can't do that. I'm also almost out of wooden ammo, I know that Harold is out, and my guess is that you two aren't doing much better."

"I can't run out of ammo." Bertha grinned. "Suck that, you vampire-"

"Maybe we can draw the vampires away." Jasper frowned. "Something drew them to that mansion in the first place."

"Yeah. The elder Incacheck." Aaron muttered. "Who we still haven't managed to locate."

"Right. But he did it somehow." Jasper took a deep breath. "Maybe we can replicate it."

"That would take research, something we don't have a ton of time to deal with." Aaron shook his head. "We need to find a way to gather them all up, and we need to do it *now*.""

"Blood." Bertha's head shot up. "They want blood. That's it, that's their trigger. Jeremy said that they had been eating pig blood, which means that all his troops are going to be itching for human blood. The other vamps are probably bloodthirsty, which means-"

"We need a way to fake human blood." Jasper frowned in thought. "I can do that."

"You can?" Aaron raised an eyebrow. "You can fake human blood?"

"I've done it before." Jasper nodded. "I needed to fake a death, so I mixed a few ingredients together. It's really not hard. Get me to a drug store and I can have it in a few minutes."

"On it." Aaron nodded. "What then? We create a vat of this stuff, then just paint it on a wall?"

"We make a vat of this stuff, load it into an rpg, and fire it into the air." Jasper nodded. "We create a feeding frenzy, then lead them once they're so crazed they can't see reason."

"They're sentient beings." Aaron shook his head. "You can't just drive them crazy."

"They're sentient beings." Jasper grinned. "They're easier than anything to drive into a frenzy. Trust me."

"Alright." Aaron shook his head. "If you're sure."

Jasper opened his mouth to reply, but was cut off by a massive explosion that shook the area. Aaron bent down, feeling the impact in his knees. It was followed by another explosion, followed by another. Fire belched into the air, appearing to have came from the direction of their frat house. The concussions continued as fire roared, powerful blasts that shattered windows in many of the surrounding buildings.

"Alright, plan." Aaron nodded. "Jasper and I go draw the vamps away from the campus. Harold, you and Bertha go check that out. Kill anything evil you find."

"On it." Harold grinned.

With that, Aaron turned and jogged towards the van, Jasper in tow. Something tingled in the back of his mind, something telling him that this was where it all drew together. They were going to win, or they were going to fail. There was no turning back.

CHAPTER 40

Harold and Bertha flew across the lawn, moving as fast as they could. Bertha soon began to heave, and Harold slowed down. He didn't have any need to move slowly, but he knew that simply leaving her alone to fend for herself wouldn't be a smart idea.

The moment that he matched pace with her, she started waving her hands. "No. Go."

"But…"

"I'll be fine." Bertha snapped. "I'm better at taking care of myself than anyone else on this team. You, for some reason unknown to me, don't have any need to sleep, rest, eat, or do anything else that most of us consider necessary for survival. I don't care what it is, but I'd rather appreciate it if you didn't hold back for the rest of us."

Harold nodded. "Thank you."

Without waiting for an answer, he put everything he had into running, and soon found himself tearing across the ground like it was nothing. He was running nearly as fast as an Olympic sprint, and yet he didn't feel an ounce of pain. He knew that he could get used to that feeling.

It took him mere moments to reach the edge of campus. As he had feared, several dozen blocks of the city had been leveled. Houses lay scattered and blackened, trees had been ripped from the ground. Only a single building still stood, the frat house that the ARF had lived in.

Even though it was still standing, the massive limestone building was hardly in a livable condition. Windows had been blown out, the doors had been blown in, and good deal of the limestone had been shattered. The Squad's house, on the other hand, was completely flat. Apparently stone was, indeed, a better building material than wood.

Across the street from the two homes, the third frat house was simply… Missing. Completely, utterly, gone. A large crater sat in its place, and Harold sighed. The last time he had dealt with a large crater, it hadn't gone so well.

With a rush, he ran up to the side of the crater and looked down inside. It looked like the explosion had exposed a large cave, though it was hard to tell much more than that. Debris covered the bottom of the cave, pieces of the ceiling and frat house that had collapsed in on itself.

A brief flicker of motion fluttered at the bottom of the area, and Harold frowned. There was a bit of green showing…

With a start, Harold realized that this was Incacheck's lair. Without hesitating, he leapt down into the crater, falling the nearly fifty feet to the cave floor. His feet shook the ground when he landed, and he smiled. Yet another benefit of not having to worry about dying.

The debris shifted even more, and Harold held his arms out in front of him. Before, he had only ever manipulated matter based on low vibrations and taps. There had been something at the back of his mind, though. Something that made him think that there was more that he was capable of.

"*Move.*" Harold whispered the word. "*Move!*"

With a rush, the stone debris exploded off the floor and rushed into the air. Incacheck scrambled to his feet, a confused look on his face. Harold gave him no chance to figure things out, and directed the stone towards the man. It slammed into his body, driving him into a nearby wall.

"*Melt.*" Harold hissed. "*Harden.*"

The stone hissed as it melted, formed a skintight cocoon around the doctor, and solidified again. Harold smiled. If Incacheck couldn't move, couldn't breathe, there was no way he could work any form of alchemy. It was…

The cocoon exploded with a massive blast. Harold was driven back by the force of it, and Incacheck stormed out, fire in his eyes. He raised his hands, drawing the stone into a large pike behind him. A blast shook the air, and the stone rushed across the expanse, drawing a line for Harold's heart.

"*Change.*" Harold crossed his arms. "*Protect.*"

The stone stopped an inch from his body, whirled around him, and formed a protective barrier. Harold grinned, but only for a moment. A mere second later, fire exploded through the barrier, melting the stone and sending Harold rolling. His skin healed instantly, but he actually felt a stab of pain in the flames. Desperate, he leapt to his feet as Incacheck approached.

"You're the first person in a *long* time who's managed to challenge me." Incacheck grinned. "You've even grown more powerful in the last few weeks. I'm impressed."

"You're still going to kill me." Harold snapped. "You're going to kill everyone."

"*Kill* everyone?" Incacheck crossed his arms and put a finger on his lips. "Are you truly dead? Clinically, yes. You wouldn't pass a physical examination, but you're more alive than ever before. I could give this to everyone."

"Really?" Harold hissed. "Are you trying to get me to join you?"

"I want you to consider the possibilities." Incacheck mused. "When I get all the pieces of the Stone, I can open a portal to hell itself. Everyone is going to die anyway. We may as well give them a chance to experience it on Earth. It might even elongate their time in this world."

"You're insane." Harold shook his head.

"I'm also good at distracting." Incacheck shrugged as something slammed through Harold's chest from behind. He glanced down to see a massive spike protruding from his body, and he frowned.

"That was rude."

"Most people would be dead." Incacheck shrugged. "I'd say that you were the rude one for not obliging me. Now, let's see about killing you. Maybe if we chop off an arm?"

Incacheck held up a finger and gave it a soft flick. A piece of stone slashed downward, chopping Harold's right arm from his body. He immediately began to shift, twisting around the spike, as his body's center of gravity shifted.

"Hmm." Incacheck shook his head. "This is no good. Maybe another arm?"

Harold's other arm dropped to the ground. Harold scowled, not enjoying the experience whatsoever. A moment later, he had lost both legs as well. A mere torso, he was helpless to respond as Incacheck stalked closer.

"I think it's time for you to go." He grinned. "What happens when you lose your head?"

Something moved behind Incacheck. Harold did his best to only watch the movement in the corners of his vision, not daring to look at it for fear that Incacheck would notice. If he was right, it looked like Jeremy had somehow managed to survive the blast.

Harold did his best to shrug. "Most people would say that jumping into a pit with the most notorious murderer in the last decade amounts to losing your head."

Incacheck only grinned. "Any last words?"

"Yeah, actually." Harold smiled. "*Enhance.*"

CHAPTER 41

"Alright, I'm ready!" Aaron called upwards. "What do I need to do now?"

"Get ready to drive!" Jasper called back. "Ready to move… Now!"

A flash of light signaled the launch of an RPG, and a loud explosion shook the vehicle. If Jasper did his job right, that meant that the human blood had been released into the air. Of course, it was anyone's guess whether or not the crazy scheme would actually work.

"Drive!" Jasper's voice was crazed. "Now!"

Aaron pressed down on the gas, and the van rocketed into the night. Idly, as he turned onto a highway, he glanced in his rearview mirror. Whatever he was looking for, he certainly wasn't expecting to see a massive hoard of bats flooding the road, filling every ounce of his vision.

Desperately, he shook his head and simply pressed his foot to the floorboard. The van rocketed down the freeway, eating up the asphalt. Aaron took a deep breath as he threw the vehicle through its corners. This wasn't going to be good for anyone if they wrecked.

"How's it going?" Jasper's head appeared between the seats. "Any major issues?"

"The cloud of bats following us is an issue." Aaron muttered. "I knew you said you were going to drive them insane, I didn't realize-"

"Just how effective it would be?" Jasper grinned. "It's better than catnip."

"Right now, I wouldn't be sad if it was less effective." Aaron muttered. "What's the plan when we get there?"

"Well, at this rate, I doubt we have enough time to get out of the vehicle and make it to the safe zone before they get us." Jasper grimaced. "We dug shallow graves that you could drop into right before it gets set off. Kind of provide some protection."

"Graves?"

"Well, that's what they look like." Jasper waved his hand. "Anyway, we're not going to make it. There's a small gap in the trees. You'll have to bounce through the ditch, but it's our best bet."

"Drive into the trees."

"Yeah." Jasper shrugged. "Just hit a narrow gap at seventy miles per hour, knowing that we'll die if you miss it."

"I think I liked the zombie apocalypse better." Aaron muttered. "Alright, we're getting closer. You'll have to tell me-"

"There!" Jasper gestured at the wall of trees that was steadily drawing closer. "There are two big oaks. Right between them!"

"That's barely big enough for the van!"

"It's *something*."

Aaron muttered his opinion of the gap under his breath, braced himself, and turned the steering wheel. With a massive lurch, he barreled through the ditch and tore between the trees. A loud screech echoed through the vehicle as the window was torn off, and he grinned. At least...

With a mighty whump, the vehicle came to a roaring stop as it slammed into another tree. Aaron felt his body driven back into the seat by the airbag, and he tasted blood in his mouth.

"Are we there?" He gasped. "Are we... Jasper?"

He turned his head, painfully, trying to find the man. It wasn't hard, Jasper was sprawled out in the center console, a large gash on his forehead. His eyes were open, and unfocused on anything in the vehicle.

Aaron reached for him, but found his right arm unable to move. Desperately, he grabbed with his left arm, clawing for his friend. A shadow materialized from the night, and the van began to shake as vampires transformed back into humans. Several landed on the hood and started pounding at the fractured glass.

"Jasper!" Aaron yelled. "Do it now!"

Jasper didn't respond, and Aaron glanced back and forth. Where was the detonator? Jasper had had it, but where had it gone after the wreck?

After spending entirely too much time thrashing back and forth, Aaron finally located it. The small, red box was underneath Jasper's left hand, resting on the passenger seat next to him. Aaron lunged for it, only to have himself held back by the seatbelts. Pain lanced through his body, and he screamed. His side erupted in flames, and spikes erupted through his back. He couldn't move, it…

The glass cracked as the vampires got closer to breaking through, and Aaron threw himself into the passenger seat. He threw his right arm up, ignoring the spears that seemed to be impaling it, the ribbons of flesh that seemed to be falling from the appendage every moment.

His hand closed over the detonator, and he squeezed as hard as he could. With a mighty roar, the forest outside transformed into the deadliest trap the vampires had ever seen. Each tree, carefully prepared with explosives, exploded, sending thousands of splinters flashing every direction. A vampire's heart was a small thing, but when millions of guns were firing at once, the targets had to be hit one way or another.

As the roar died down, Aaron did his best to sit up. Pain continually lanced through his side, but it was growing easier to ignore. Outside the splintered window, nearly three acres of forest had been decimated. Splintered wood lay across the entire expanse, nearly two feet of wood. Coating the wood was a wonderful, thick layer of dust. A smile split Aaron's face, and he sank back into the seat.

Sirens sounded in the distance, and he took a deep breath. Help would be there soon. They would be saved.

CHAPTER 42

Jeremy paused as he watched Incacheck dissect Harold. He had to wait until the alchemist was completely distracted, probably right before he killed the zombie. In any event, losing the limbs didn't seem to bother Harold in the slightest. In fact, he almost just looked bored.

Carefully, he crept forward. There was only one limb left… Nope, it was gone. Incacheck stepped up to Harold's head, and Jeremy moved forward. It was now or never.

Enhance.

The word echoed in Jeremy's mind, and he gasped. Light lanced up and down his body, filling him with a power unlike anything he had ever felt before. His muscles tightened, his bones hardened, and his teeth sharpened. His vision grew more acute, and he smiled.

Before Incacheck could realize what had happened, he stepped up and slammed a fist into the scientist's side. The man was *actually* tossed across the room and into a wall. He looked up, and Jeremy leapt forward.

With a rush, Jeremy simply *flew*. No bat form, the cape simply spread and carried him forward. His fist connected with Incacheck's chest, driving him back into the wall again. The man gasped, and Jeremy grabbed the pendant on Incacheck's chest.

"Oh, no, you don't." Incacheck roared. "Die!"

Jeremy glanced back and forth. Nothing had happened. With a shrug, he pulled the man away from the wall, spun, and launched him into the opposite wall. Incacheck groaned, and Jeremy flashed back over to him.

"You have something we want." Jeremy held out his hand. "The shard."

Incacheck laughed. "You really think that I'll give it to you?"

Jeremy didn't bother to answer, and instead simply slammed a fist down onto the pendant hanging on Incacheck's chest. At least… He tried to.

Incacheck's hand flashed up, catching the fist solidly. Jeremy winced upon impact, as it felt like hitting stone. The pendant began to glow, and Incacheck laughed. Electricity pulsed down the straps holding the object, flowing through the device like a liquid. After a moment, pure energy erupted outward from the device, spiking through Jeremy's chest and leaving him with a rather large hole in his body.

"You're good." Incacheck glanced over Jeremy's shoulder at Harold. "I'll give you that much."

Before Jeremy could react, Incacheck swept his legs out from under him and punched him in the face. A concussive wave erupted from the fist, slamming Jeremy back across the hole and into the far wall. Stone cracked under the impact, and Jeremy groaned.

Heal.

The word poured through Jeremy's body, fusing his dead flesh back together. Incacheck's eyes opened slightly, only to be blindsided by a torrent of fire coming from Harold's direction. Jeremy climbed back to his feet and flexed his hands. On the other side of the hole, Incacheck stood tall, hands outstretched, stopping the fire with some sort of ward spell.

After a few seconds, Incacheck slowly glanced up at the sky. He chuckled softly, then reached into his pocket, withdrawing the shard. It was glowing brilliantly, even brighter than Harold's fire.

"Looks like the process is nearly complete." Incacheck dipped his head. "You've done marvelous work. Thank-"

A loud crack echoed through the air as a baseball bat connected with the side of his head. He fell to the ground, revealing Bertha standing just behind him. A steel bat, now bent into a nearly ninety-degree angle, hung in her hands.

"I'm slow. Never said I wasn't strong."

On the ground, Incacheck groaned. The shard fell from his nerveless fingers, and he muttered a quick incantation under his breath. Light pulsed across his body, and he vanished in a blur of energy. Bertha tossed the baseball bat to the side, bent down, and picked the shard back up. After a few seconds, it began to dim, returning to a simple piece of stone.

"He's gone." Jeremy frowned as the mysterious power flowed back out of his body. "Why would he just leave?"

"Simple." Harold muttered from where he still hung on the spike of rock. "He could have beaten us after time, but why bother? There are still dozens of shards out in the world. If he goes and collects a few more, it'll be an easier battle."

"So he gets to level up a few more times." Jeremy sighed and shook his head. "Great."

Bertha crossed her arms. "Is no one going to be impressed that I just jumped down a fifty-foot hole and took out the guy you were both struggling to defeat?"

Jeremy shrugged. "You're talking to a zombie and a vampire."

Bertha sighed and kicked a small rock, launching it across the battlefield. "Fair enough." After a few seconds, she scowled. "Dang it. I should have revealed my powers sooner."

"Probably." Jeremy chuckled and rolled his eyes. After a few seconds, he turned to Harold. "On a different note, what in the world did you do to me?"

"A little trick I learned." Harold shook his head. "I could explain it, but… It's complicated. Now would you mind bringing my limbs back to me? I think they'll just reattach, but I'd rather like to be fixed before my Squad shows back up."

Jeremy shrugged, picked up a leg, and held it up to Harold's body. Sure enough, it reattached after a moment, healing like nothing had happened.

"I take it your team doesn't know?" Jeremy frowned as he reattached the other leg, then glanced at Bertha. "Do they know about either of you?"

"Jasper knows a little." Harold frowned. "He knows I'm a zombie and that I practice alchemy. I don't think he knows the extent of it."

Bertha shook her head. "Garmund has come close to picking up my secret a few times, but I've managed to talk him out of it every time."

"Could you hurry up and reattach my limbs?" Harold frowned at Jeremy, then glanced up at Bertha again. "And what *is* your secret?"

Bertha flashed a coy smile. "*If* I tell anyone, Gar is going to be the first. Besides…" She let out a long breath. "It's not going to be long before crap *really* hits the fan. You'll find out soon enough, I suspect."

"Well, both your secrets are safe with me." Jeremy paused as he reattached Harold's left arm. "Thanks for saving me."

"It was nothing." Harold shrugged. "I'm just glad we got the shard back. Incacheck has to take a *few* more steps to achieve world domination. Can I see it?"

Bertha shrugged and passed the shard over. Harold clutched it in his left hand while Jeremy picked up his right arm. Harold turned it over and over, frowning. As the zombie held it, the mysterious, glowing stone chip continued to dim. After a few seconds, it had ceased to emit any sort of light at all.

"Do you recognize this symbol?" Harold twisted it towards Jeremy, then Bertha. Jeremy frowned as he looked at the image. It looked like the letter P, except that there were two extra lines inside the bulge. It almost looked like someone had inscribed a letter K inside it.

"Never seen it before." Jeremy shook his head. "Either of you?"

Bertha snorted. "What do I look like, a computer?"

"No, I don't recognize it." Harold flexed his right arm as it sealed, then put his hands on the spike that was sticking through his chest, pulled, and popped himself off the stone. "It looks similar to something else, though."

Jeremy frowned as Harold reached into his pocket and pulled out a similar shard. It was inscribed with something that resembled a drawn bow, and Jeremy shook his head.

"You have one, too?"

"I think it's what turned me into a zombie." Harold let out a long breath. "Looks like this one powered down."

"Yeah." Jeremy shook his head. "The fiasco on campus must have created enough of the monsters to complete its programming."

"I guess." Harold shook his head. "Do… Do you mind if I take the shard?"

"Wouldn't it be better if they were separated?" Jeremy frowned. "That way Incacheck wouldn't be able to track it down?"

"He's already tracking them down." Harold flexed his limbs, as if testing them. "When I was given this shard, I was allowed to see each and every shard on the planet. Believe me, there's quite a few. Every one that Jasper and I tried to retrieve was already missing. Well, save the one that Incacheck took from me right after I found it. Somehow, he knows where they're hidden. Hiding it will only allow us to remain in the dark when he tracks it down again."

"He didn't realize that there was one on your body." Jeremy held up his hands. "That's something."

"That's true." Harold paused. "Up to you. Being an alchemist, I'm probably not super objective on this subject. If you think it's better to separate them, I'll send one with you and never look for it again."

Jeremy held up his hand. "What do you mean, alchemy? I'm still a little behind the ball."

Harold raised his eyebrows. "Ever hear of the Philosopher's Stone?"

"Yes, and I've now heard enough." Jeremy shook his head. "Take the shard. It'll probably be safer with a powerhouse like yourself protecting it." He glanced at Bertha, who was glaring at him. "Well, you and Bertha."

Harold nodded and slipped both shards into his pocket. "You know, we have an opening on our team. One of our members got kicked out, I'm sure they'd love to have you."

"No one can replace Garmund." Bertha growled.

"I don't want to replace anyone." Jeremy held up a hand. "And even if I did… Believe me, it sounds like a blast, but I'm afraid that I have some other things to accomplish."

"I understand." Harold nodded and held out a hand. "I hope we cross paths again."

"As do I." Jeremy shook the extended hand, then paused and shuddered. "I just said that to a *zombie*."

"There an issue with that?" Harold chuckled.

"Not per say." Jeremy laughed. "Call it inner instinct. There just seems to be something *wrong* with zombies and vampires interacting. Like upper class royalty interacting with peasants."

Harold laughed. "Well, this peasant is about to kick your sorry vampire ass."

"I'm on my way."

Jeremy launched himself up into the air, transforming into a bat, and shot into the night sky. With a rush, he blasted off into the night, free of battle, free of tyranny. Free to set things right.

CHAPTER 43

"That was a gutsy thing you did back there." Birch sighed as he sank into a chair next to Garmund. "You hacked military-grade hardware using illegal equipment, which you gained access to by hacking past my private security code using an incredibly illegal technique."

Garmund shrugged. "I just did what I had to do."

"You did it to save lives." Birch paused. "I've always done things one way. I've certainly had people tell me different, and I've had people rage at me. I've had people throw things, I've had people defy my orders. You, though… You were the first person I've ever had *stand up* to me."

Garmund raised an eyebrow. "Is this a compliment or a sentencing?"

"Both, depending on how you look at it." Birch clapped him on the shoulder. "Here's what I appreciate

about you. You do things unorthodoxly. You do it your
own way. But you do it *right*. You're quick, you're fast. The
rest of your team would rather sit around and wait until the
right time before they're willing to do anything. They're
sloppy, they just go out there and goof around."

Garmund raised his eyebrows. "I'm not sure what
you're saying."

"I want you as part of this squad." Birch nodded.
"I want you to stand up to me, tell me when we need to do
things differently. I want to see members of this squad start
to survive, learn, and fight battle after battle. I want this
squad to become the scourge of the underworld. I want you
to be my second-in-command."

Garmund's jaw dropped, and Birch laughed.
"Think it over. I don't expect an answer by tomorrow
morning. Well, unless the world starts ending tomorrow.
You have until the next major event to decide, however
long that is."

With that, Birch stood and stalked out of the room.
Garmund just sat there, stunned. Slowly, he forced himself
off his bunk, glanced around at the barracks he was
stationed in, and stalked from the room.

"What was that about?" Rodger jogged up to him
the moment he walked out into the cool evening air.
"Anything good?"

"That probably depends on your definition of the
word." Garmund shrugged. "I don't know. It was
something."

"Well, here's to hoping it was good." Rodger
chuckled. "Hey, want to come help me work on the jeep
I'm tricking out? I managed to requisition a pile of old

computers, radios, that sort of thing, but I'm honestly not quite sure what would be the best way to install them."

Garmund raised his eyebrows. "I've never done that to a jeep before. I'm in."

"Great!" Rodger grinned. He threw his arm around Garmund's shoulders and drug him towards the garage. "You can help me get something legitimate out of this place. You'd think we'd get some cool alien tech or *something.* I mean, come on. Area 51? This is the lamest secret base I've ever been in."

Garmund chuckled and glanced around. Beyond the large, metal fences, beyond the massive private airfield, there was only desert and dry mountains. It had remained hidden from the world for decades, and he had no doubt it would remain hidden for centuries to come.

"Sure." He laughed. "Let's go build something worthy of this base."

"To worth!" Rodger thrust his fist into the air. Garmund had no choice but to follow suit. He wasn't sure if he wanted to be there or not. He wasn't sure if he wanted to go back with his friends or if he wanted to stay as Birch's second-in-command.

As long as he was there, though, he supposed that he may as well make the most of it.

CHAPTER 44

Jeremy paused as he flashed up to Vanessa's room. He was terrified to do anything, but he knew he had to face her, at least one more time. Slowly, he approached the window. Rather than hanging from the top of the frame, he landed on the lower ledge, bowed his head, and scratched the glass with his wing.

A few moments later, the window swung open. He looked up to see Vanessa, an odd look on her face. She nodded, and he flew inside and transformed back into a human.

"I know it's been a while, but-"

"Oh, Jeremy." She flew into his arms. "I'm glad you survived."

Jeremy frowned and hugged her back. "Not the response I was expecting, but I'm certainly not complaining."

She sighed. "Look, I… I didn't give you a fair chance. You didn't know how to control your body, you-"

"I bit a *lot* more people." Jeremy took a deep breath. "I kind of made an army."

"You made it to fight evil." Vanessa shrugged. "It may have backfired, but you tried. And when you… You tried to save the university. You were on the front lines, defending us. When your voice came through that speaker system, it was the best feeling I've ever had."

Jeremy shrugged. "I had to do something."

"You did more than that." Vanessa shrugged. "I was outside when they came. One of the vampires guarded me from the others while I ran and hid in the church. He asked me who I was, and when I told him, he said that you never stopped talking about me. He said you felt awful about building the army because it went against what I had told you."

Jeremy felt tears spring to his eyes. "I love you, Vanessa."

"I love you, too." For several long moments they just stood there, staring at each other. Vanessa flashed a small smile, then raised her eyebrows. "So, what now?"

Jeremy took a deep breath. "Well, the danger is over. I know someone who can synthesize me blood, which means I don't need to bite humans anymore." After a few seconds, he frowned. "Admittedly, I don't know where he is right now, but from this point on, I'm not biting anyone else."

"Anyone else?" Vanessa slipped her collar down the side of her shoulder. "You wouldn't want to bite one more person?"

Jeremy felt the room grow warm. "What are you…"

"You're a hero." Vanessa raised an eyebrow. "You're the love of my life, and I would do anything to be with you. Forever."

A grin spread across Jeremy's face, and he stalked towards her. Now, they could be together forever. Now, he would never have to go lonely again.

CHAPTER 45

Aaron slowly rose to consciousness, blinking against the overwhelmingly bright lights that were apparently trying to blind him. Gasps sounded from around him, and he prepared to fight away all the vampires surrounding him.

"He's awake!" The vampire sounded annoyingly like Harold, and he frowned. That was no good.

"Hey, stop fighting!" Hands pressed down on his shoulders, and he yelled as loud as he could. With a rush, he sat up, and...

With a snap, he rushed fully back into reality, finding himself sitting up in a hospital bed. Harold, Bertha, and Jasper stood next to the bed, smiles all over their faces. Aaron frowned as he glanced back and forth across the group.

"I thought Jasper was the one knocked out."

"I was." Jasper chuckled. "Got a bit of a concussion, but nothing that a few months' rest won't cure. You broke half a dozen bones and had some major splinters deep in your body. You were in surgery for hours."

"Great." Aaron muttered. After a moment, a thought struck him. "Did I get any mechanical body parts?"

"Unfortunately, no." Harold shook his head. "You're just fine. You just need a bit more rest."

"I hate rest." He grimaced and sank back. "Well, unless it involves video games. Or comics. Or movies. Or books." He frowned as it dawned on him that he was rambling. "I'm assuming we won?"

"You killed all the vampires with the trap, and we sent the good doctor packing." Bertha grinned, then frowed. "Oh, right, you might not know about that. Turns out all those explosions came from Incacheck's lair. Harold and Jeremy took him down. Quite a show, really."

"Really?" Aaron frowned. "How'd they manage to do that?"

Harold opened his mouth to reply, but Bertha beat him to it. "I mean, Jeremy is a vampire. He's not like the rest of us."

"Good." Aaron nodded. "That's two Incachecks down. Any more to go?"

"None in this state." An old, grizzled voice sounded in the doorway, and Frank stepped into view. "At least not when I last checked the sensors."

"Frank!" Aaron smiled. "You came."

"I wasn't really given much choice in the matter." Frank grumbled, then smiled. "But yes, I came. Couldn't leave our leader in the hospital without a visit, could I?"

Aaron smiled back. "We missed you out there, you know that, Frank?"

"I know." Frank paused. "You know, after being out of the field for a mission, I've came to a decision."

"I'd love to hear it." Aaron grinned.

"I am never joining you in the field again." Frank nodded. "At home, I can do everything I could do in the field, and I can do it without fear of getting eaten, bitten, or-"

"We'll talk." Aaron shook his head. "Any word on the ARF?"

"We know it was their missiles that blew up the top of Incacheck's hideout." Jasper shrugged. "We checked out their frat house, though, and they had pulled out. We've been trying to contact them about getting Garmund back, but no word as of yet."

Aaron grimaced. "Great. We'll just have to keep trying, then. I know none of you can just hack the government like he could, but I want all eyes on the lookout for any trace of the ARF."

"Don't worry." Bertha soothed, then flashed a sad smile. "We *did* manage to find something." She fished around in her pocket and pulled out a small piece of paper. "It was on a desk in one of the rear rooms. We think Garmund left it for us."

"What is it?" Aaron frowned. "It looks like a website."

"It is." Harold nodded. "It's a private dropbox. We can leave messages there, and other people, namely Garmund, can look at it and see what we wrote. He can then write back. Best of all, there's no way to track who sent what, so as long as we don't sign the messages, they can't trace it back to us. As far as the government will know, *if* they ever find the box, is that it's a way old high school buddies can talk trash on each other without revealing themselves publicly."

"Brilliant." Aaron grinned. "Well, that's that, then. We just have to get Garmund back, and we'll be back in our headquarters like nothing ever happened."

The team all just started down at him. Bertha slowly reached up and wiped a tear away from her eyes, then turned away towards a nearby window. Jasper and Frank both glanced at each other, and Harold scratched his head awkwardly. Aaron frowned and leaned forward.

"What? What is it you guys aren't telling me?"

Frank sighed. "I think it'll be better coming from me."

"No arguments here." Bertha clapped him on the shoulder and glanced back at Aaron. "I'll go get the van ready. Just give me thirty seconds of warning."

"We're staying until they find us." Frank grumbled back. "Just… Go. Can't hurt to be prepared, anyway."

The other Squad members cleared out, and Aaron closed his eyes.

"Frank?" His voice trembled. "What's happening?"

Frank sighed. "Can you look out the window?"

Aaron opened his eyes again and glanced towards the window that Bertha had just been standing at. All he could see was blue sky, nothing more. Slowly, at Frank's urging, he swung his legs over the side of the bed, forced his aching muscles to pull him to his feet, and shuffled over to the window.

As he stared out, his eyes opened wide. The hospital, like most, was far taller than the buildings surrounding it. Which, naturally, allowed him to see a *long* way. Which allowed him to see the peak of the Washington Monument in the distance, just visible above the treeline.

"Frank?" Aaron tried to keep his voice steady. "Why are we in Washington D.C.? We were in Pennsylvania when I got knocked out."

"Yes." Frank nodded slowly. "We were. See…" He sighed. "While we *did* stop the vampires, there was something else going on. There was some sort of Alpha radiation that the government is blaming for the creation of the vampires. Turns out, it was coming from Incacheck's hideout. The same hideout that the ARF dropped a kiloton of explosives on top of."

Aaron closed his eyes for a moment. "Don't tell me. The ARF got all the credit."

"Lock, stock, and barrel." Frank ran his hand through his hair. "They're being hailed as heroes, and we're… We're being charged with the destruction of public and private property, trespassing, and more. Trust me, you don't want to see the list. It's long."

Aaron hung his head. "What's Birch doing with that? I bet he's through the roof."

Frank put a hand on Aaron's arm. "Actually, Birch isn't pressing charges against us. He isn't even trying to claim our base. That's where things get a bit interesting." Frank leaned up next to the window. "We got a message from him. A short one, perhaps, but an interesting one. He claims that someone in the government was restricting *his* access to data. It almost resulted in the destruction of the entire campus."

Aaron frowned. "I thought Birch had a monopoly on evil government stuff."

"As did I." Frank shrugged. "And, as it happens, things get even more interesting from there. Charges *are* being pressed against us, with federal warrants going out across the board. SWAT teams are already sweeping Kansas City, hence our hiding here. *Someone* in a position of power is riding our tails, and as of this moment, no one knows who."

Aaron crossed his arms. "Have we been able to contact my uncle?"

"General Herford." Frank sighed. "No. He went MIA in Egypt, right before this all went down. No one has seen or heard from him since."

"Great." Aaron closed his eyes again. "So, what do we do?"

Frank snorted. "I just give you advice. Our actual course of action is on you." He hesitated for a moment. "Leader."

Aaron opened his eyes as the world snapped into clarity. Outside, on nearby streets, he could see red and blue flashing lights. Police, coming straight for them. With force, he ripped the IV bags out of his veins, turned, and swept out of the room. Frank followed closely. Outside, Jasper and Harold jumped to their feet as he approached.

Aaron simply nodded at them and made his way through the hospital. None of the doctors bothered to stop him, none of the nurses so much as glanced his way. The quartet swept out into the parking lot, where Bertha had the van idling. She tore up to them, Aaron slid into the shotgun seat, everyone else piled in, and they were off. As they roared out of the parking lot, police cars pulled in, sirens wailing.

"Alright, now." Aaron clapped his hands and glanced back at the group. "We're on the run. Bertha, keep us ahead of the police and away from any form of security cameras. Get us out of the capitol and into a less dense part of the country."

"I'm three steps ahead of you." Bertha grinned and stomped down on the gas pedal.

In the back, Harold leaned forward and frowned. "Assuming we can get out of here alive, what then? What do we do next?"

Aaron scratched his head and nodded slowly. "We keep fighting. Correct me if I'm wrong, but I think it's a safe assumption that there are going to be more apocalypses happening. They might be in the United States, they might be elsewhere on the planet, but they'll be coming. We have to stop them."

"How exactly are we going to do that?" Bertha tore around a corner, nearly lifting the vehicle up onto two wheels. "We don't have any more resources. We can't keep tapping into security feeds, we don't have-"

"We have each other." Aaron glanced back at the group and flashed a thin smile. "And, until someone catches up with us, we're not letting anyone else come between that."

After a few seconds, he nodded. "Alright, then. We need to get a base, and soon. The SWAT teams will clear out of Kansas City fast enough, it's honestly as good a place to hide out as any. There's some old warehouses we can hide in, I'm sure of it. Once we find a place, Bertha, make sure the place is spotless. I also want you to get in contact with Inspector Birch, see if you can get him to gloat about anything interesting. Just make sure he can't find us. Frank,

I want you on the internet at all times. Get social media, watch the news sites, anything it takes. Tabloids, too. I want to know the *instant* that anything else rears its head.

"Jasper? Harold? Weapons. I want you researching mythology and coming up with counter-attacks against anything and everything the nether regions have to throw at us. If there's something with a weakness to ice, I want ice bullets. Understand?"

"We'll get right on it." Jasper nodded. "You won't be disappointed."

"No, I don't think I will be." Aaron smiled. "You have your tasks. Get to them. I want the undead to shudder in fear when they emerge. The Apocolyps Squad is on the job."

CHAPTER 48

Herford sighed as the truck rumbled to a stop. A sharp hiss announced the air brakes firing, the smell of diesel nearly caused him to choke. Slowly, he glanced out the passenger window, gazing at the small, country gas station.

"We're here." Stanley, a trucker that Herford had hired, picked up a sandwich and started munching on the snack. After a few seconds, he sighed, put it down, and cracked the door open. "I'll be inside. Once you're finished meeting with your guy, we should be on the road again."

Herford nodded silently, popped open the rusty door, and climbed down as well. The sweet odor of corn and fuel filled the night air as a warm breeze ruffled his stained t-shirt. Stanley lumbered past, his hulking form making its way to the tiny, dimly-lit building.

"Ahh, the mighty general, brought down a peg!" A cackling laugh filled the night air. Herford slowly turned as the mad scientist climbed out of a nearby ditch and wandered towards him.

Herford simply raised an eye at the mudstained lab coat and cracked glasses that the scientist now sported. "You're not doing too hot yourself."

"I'm doing as hot as anyone could be in this situation!" Incacheck bounced on the balls of his feet before sighing. "This sucks."

"Quite so." Herford held out his hand. "Would you like to step into my office? We can talk better inside."

Incacheck turned and glanced at the enormous semi trailer, complete with an advertisement for a frozen food company. He broke into a fit of laughter that Herford was certain would alert nearly anyone nearby to possible danger. At least it would, if there had been anyone else nearby.

Without another word, Herford made his way to the rear of the trailer, where he pressed a small button concealed in the mass of wires and lights suspended there. A small panel slid aside, a hole around three feet on each side, allowing them access inside. Herford was certain he looked quite undignified as he scrambled up into the trailer, but at that moment, he didn't see as he had any other options. Incacheck followed him, climbing up into the mobile office unit.

Inside the trailer was as much as Herford had been able to fit in. Computing units filled most of the front half of the vehicle, with several computer terminals wired in for access. A small satellite dish sat near the rear, with an assortment of weaponry taking up space in between.

Perhaps the most out-of-place thing, though, was the sarcophagus leaning up against the wall near the back.

"You really managed to get this put together, didn't you?" Incacheck was back to sounding relatively sane. "I'm impressed."

"As you should be." Herford sighed. "I can't access most of my government data I used to have at my fingertips, but I *am* wired into your detection system. I assume that's why you want to meet up?"

Incacheck nodded and reached into his pocket, fishing out a small piece of rather dirty paper. "The password. My sensor net is now global. If a shard activates anywhere on the planet, we'll know about it the moment it happens."

"Good." Herford nodded and sat down in a chair at one of the terminals. He motioned for Incacheck to do the same, though the scientist declined it. "Things are heating up."

"You're telling me!" Incacheck screamed. "Seven shards now! Seven! And where has your precious Squad been during all of it?"

"They were in Pennsylvania, and they managed to acquire that shard." Herford kept his voice level. "That's something."

"They have two shards. Two!" Incacheck stamped his foot angrily. "My father has the rest. And what's that stupid barf team doing?"

"The ARF." Herford corrected before sighing. "And they're making a mess of things, that's for sure."

"They've destroyed two cities!" Incacheck began punching the wall. "Two! They *handed* my father the shards!"

"I'm not arguing." Herford shrugged. "They're a problem."

"Then *deal* with them!" Incacheck crossed his arms. "Or do you want me to get rid of the problem?"

Herford sighed and closed his eyes. A year earlier, he would have balked at what Incacheck was suggesting. Now…

"Kill as few of them as possible. We *are* trying to save lives."

"As you wish!" Incacheck laughed for several seconds, then frowned. "Why aren't *you* on this? What happened to you?"

"I thought you'd never ask." It was a true enough statement, he truly hadn't thought Incacheck would care in the slightest. "Upon returning from Egypt, I found that my power in the government has been somewhat… Diminished. My rank stayed the same, but I was locked out of almost everything. I was being excluded from meetings, my clearance cards wouldn't work. Then, despite being in the United States for over a week, I found that my official status was still MIA after the Egypt incident."

Incacheck frowned. "What does that mean?"

"I don't know." Herford shrugged. "I honestly don't know. Maybe your father tapped into the United States system, but that doesn't explain why everyone else in the capitol was acting so cold towards me. I don't *think* Birch has the kind of power needed to do that, but… It's possible."

"Interesting." Incacheck crossed his arms. "I'm afraid I have more questions than answers."

"As do I." Herford sighed and climbed to his feet. "I tried to track down the answers, but when I started getting followed by men in black trench coats, I decided it wasn't worth it. And that pretty much brings us to this point now."

"I see." Incacheck frowned, in a more sober mood than Herford had ever seen him. "If *you're* on the run, that means that your squad isn't faring any better."

Herford sighed. "I'm trying to track them now. It's not easy."

"I imagine not." Incacheck raised his eyebrows and snorted. "What will you do now, then?"

"I'm going to stay on the move, try to stay ahead of whoever's trying to kill me." Herford shrugged. "Try to find my squad, keep an eye on the sensors, and… Go from there."

Incacheck turned and kicked a wall. "If my father gets all those shards, he'll literally be able to open a portal to Hell. He'll become the overlord of a new land that I *don't* think we want to live in."

"Believe me, I understand the stakes." Herford shrugged, then snorted. "For what it's worth, I *did* get one small victory from the Egypt trip. It's not much, but it's certainly something."

Incacheck turned to the sarcophagus and laughed. "I finally get to see what's inside?"

"That you do." Herford inclined his head, climbed to his feet, and walked over to the object. He gave a sharp rap on the cover and stood back as a series of clicks echoed from within.

"Herford?" Incacheck took a step back. "There's something inside there."

"We've already established that." Herford grinned as the lid swung open fully. A dusty gasp sounded from within, and a withered foot slowly stepped out of the casket. Incacheck turned white as the mummy, dressed in white grave clothes and body wraps, slowly took several short steps away from its home. The head slowly swiveled to face Herford, while the mouth worked uselessly under the rags.

"Is it trying to talk?" Incacheck frowned. "Should we remove-"

"Oh, no. Trust me, she's disgusting without those rags on." Herford glanced at his watch. Two in the morning. "She can talk just fine, just not *right* this second. Though she can't return the courtesy, I think it would be appropriate to introduce you." He held out his hand, which the mummy slowly reached up and took. "Incacheck, I'd like to introduce you to Queen Hatshepsut, wife of Thutmose II and mother of Thutmose III."

"How do you do, ma'am?" Incacheck's voice wavered.

"She does quite well." Herford took a deep breath. "And, believe it or not… She's going to help us take down your father once and for all."

Coming soon:

Apocolyps Squad III

Spring 2020

For more great content, check out
www.leadpyramidpublishing.com

The Eternal Quest

An orc, a dwarf, and an elf walk into a bar.
What happens next?

Volume 1: Shadows of the Wondrisil
Three adventurers find themselves meeting in a small, unassuming coastal town in Donisil. After finding a magical book, they are thrown into a mad hunt for a mysterious race of beings…

Volume 2: Beings of Light
The new team heads north, looking for answers. While none present themselves, they begin to realize that their actions were a bit more far-reaching than they had anticipated…

Volume 3: Creatures of Darkness
Caught in the crossfire of a war that has spanned countless realms, Elsinor becomes the battleground for the Angels of Light and Angels of Darkness. No matter which side wins, the realm of Calsin is likely to be the one to suffer the most…

New chapters release every single week! Only available through www.leadpyramidpublishing.com